ARTEMIS FOWL

aurum potestas est

A RTEMIS FOWL is a child prodigy from Ireland who has dedicated his brilliant mind to criminal activities. When Artemis discovers that there is a fairy civilization below ground, he sees it as a golden opportunity. Now there is a whole new species to exploit with his ingenious schemes. But Artemis doesn't know as much as he thinks about the fairy People. And what he doesn't know could hurt him . . .

NEVER HAS A CRIMINAL MASTERMIND
RECEIVED SUCH PRAISE

'A winning combination of humour, action and ingenuity'
— *Sunday Times*

'It grips like an electromagnet until the last word'
— *Independent*

'What every child will want for Christmas'
— *Guardian*

'*The Eternity Code* is poised for worldwide domination'
— *Funday Times*

'Eoin Colfer is such a fast and exciting writer that my
11-year-old raced through the book in a day and then passed it
around his class. In two weeks he amassed 34 packets of sweets
from lending out my advanced copy to friends who couldn't
wait for their own'
— *Daily Mail*

'Full of suspense, humour and Colfer's trademark cheeky
wit. *The Eternity Code* will not disappoint the
legions of Artemis fans'
— *Evening Standard*

'Hollywood-style action, comic henchmen and cunning plans'
— *Sunday Herald*

'Full of action, weaponry, farting dwarves and
Chandleresque one-liners'
— *Evening Standard*

EOIN COLFER

ARTEMIS FOWL

AND THE ETERNITY CODE

PUFFIN

PUFFIN BOOKS

UK | USA | Canada | Ireland | Australia
India | New Zealand | South Africa

Puffin Books is part of the Penguin Random House group of companies
whose addresses can be found at global.penguinrandomhouse.com.

www.penguin.co.uk   www.puffin.co.uk   www.ladybird.co.uk

First published by Puffin Books 2003
Published in paperback 2004
This edition published 2017
002

Text copyright © Eoin Colfer, 2003
Map illustrations by Kev Walker
All rights reserved

The moral right of the author has been asserted

Set in 13.5/16.3pt Perpetua

Printed in Great Britain by Clays Ltd, Elcograf S.p.A.
A CIP catalogue record for this book is available from the British Library

ISBN: 978–0–241–33561–1

All correspondence to:
Puffin Books, Penguin Random House Children's
80 Strand, London WC2R 0RL

To the Power family.
In-laws and outlaws.

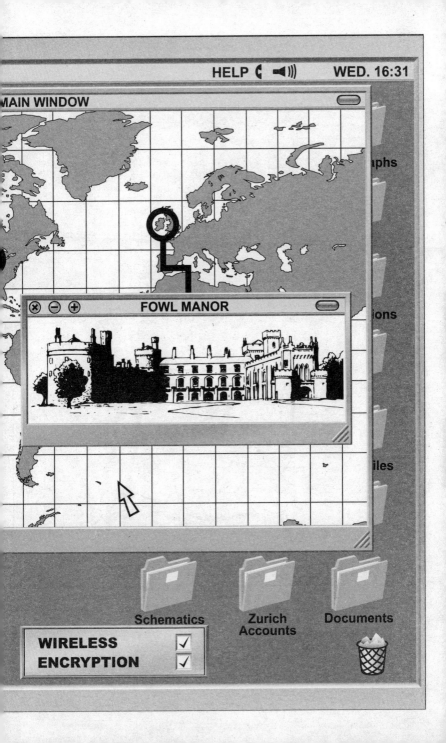

CONTENTS

PROLOGUE

Excerpt from Artemis Fowl's diary. Disk 2. Encrypted.

FOR the past two years my business enterprises have thrived without parental interference. In this time, I have sold the Pyramids to a Western businessman, forged and auctioned off the lost diaries of Leonardo da Vinci and separated the fairy People from a large portion of their precious gold. But my freedom to plot is almost at an end. As I write, my father lies in a hospital bed in Helsinki, where he recovers after a two-year imprisonment by the Russian Mafiya. He is still unconscious following his ordeal, but he will awaken soon and retake control of the Fowl finances.

With two parents resident in Fowl Manor, it will be impossible for me to conduct my various illegal ventures undetected. Previously this would not have been a problem as my father was a bigger crook than me, but Mother is determined that the Fowls are going straight.

However, there is time for one last job. Something that my mother would not approve of. I don't think the fairy folk would like it much either. So I shall not tell them.

PART I: **ATTACK**

CHAPTER 1: **THE CUBE**

En Fin, Knightsbridge, London

 ARTEMIS Fowl was almost content. His father would be discharged from Helsinki's University Hospital any day now. He himself was looking forward to a delicious late lunch at En Fin, a London seafood restaurant, and his business contact should arrive any moment. All according to plan.

His bodyguard, Butler, was not quite so relaxed. But then again he was never truly at ease – one did not become one of the world's deadliest men by dropping one's guard. The giant Eurasian flitted between tables in the Knightsbridge bistro, positioning the usual security items and clearing exit routes.

'Are you wearing the earplugs?' he asked his employer.

Artemis sighed deeply. 'Yes, Butler. Though I hardly

think we are in danger here. It's a perfectly legal business meeting in broad daylight, for heaven's sake.'

The earplugs were actually sonic filter sponges, cannibalized from fairy Lower Elements Police helmets. Butler had obtained the helmets, along with a treasure trove of fairy technology, over a year previously when one of Artemis's schemes pitted him against a fairy SWAT team. The sponges were grown in LEP labs, and had tiny porous membranes that sealed automatically when decibel levels surpassed safety standards.

'Maybe so, Artemis, but the thing about assassins is that they like to catch you unawares.'

'Perhaps,' replied Artemis, perusing the menu's entrée section. 'But who could possibly have a motive to kill us?'

Butler shot one of the half-dozen diners a fierce glare, just in case she was planning something. The woman must have been at least eighty.

'They might not be after *us*. Remember, Jon Spiro is a powerful man. He put a lot of companies out of business. We could be caught in a crossfire.'

Artemis nodded. As usual, Butler was right, which explained why they were both still alive. Jon Spiro, the American he was meeting, was just the kind of man to attract assassins' bullets. A successful IT billionaire, with a shady past and alleged mob connections. Rumour had it that his company, Fission Chips, had made it to the top on the back of stolen research. Of course, nothing was ever proved – not that Chicago's district attorney hadn't tried. Several times.

A waitress wandered over, giving them a dazzling smile.

'Hello there, young man. Would you like to see the children's menu?'

A vein pulsed in Artemis's temple.

'No, mademoiselle, I would not like to see the *children's menu*. I have no doubt the *children's menu* itself tastes better than the meals on it. I would like to order à la carte. Or don't you serve fish to minors?'

The waitress's smile shrank by a couple of molars. Artemis's vocabulary had that effect on most people.

Butler rolled his eyes. And Artemis wondered who would want to kill him. Most of the waiters and tailors in Europe, for a start.

'Yes, sir,' stammered the unfortunate waitress. 'Whatever you like.'

'What I would like is a medley of shark and swordfish, pan-seared, on a bed of vegetables and new potatoes.'

'And to drink?'

'Spring water. Irish, if you have it. And no ice, please, as your ice is no doubt made from tap water, which rather defeats the purpose of spring water.'

The waitress scurried to the kitchen, relieved to escape from the pale youth at table six. She'd seen a vampire movie once. The undead creature had the very same hypnotic stare. Maybe the kid spoke like a grown-up because he was actually five hundred years old.

Artemis smiled in anticipation of his meal, unaware of the consternation he'd caused.

'You're going to be a big hit at the school dances,' Butler commented.

'Pardon?'

'That poor girl was almost in tears. It wouldn't hurt you to be nice occasionally.'

Artemis was surprised. Butler rarely offered opinions on personal matters.

'I don't see myself at school dances, Butler.'

'Dancing isn't the point. It's all about communication.'

'Communication?' scoffed young Master Fowl. 'I doubt there is a teenager alive with a vocabulary equal to mine.'

Butler was about to point out the difference between talking and communicating when the restaurant door opened. A small tanned man entered, flanked by a veritable giant. Jon Spiro and his security.

Butler bent low to whisper in his charge's ear. 'Be careful, Artemis. I know the big one by reputation.'

Spiro wound through the tables, arms outstretched. He was a middle-aged American, thin as a javelin, and barely taller than Artemis himself. In the eighties, shipping had been his thing; in the nineties he made a killing in stocks and shares. Now, it was communications.

He wore his trademark white linen suit, and there was enough jewellery hanging from his wrists and fingers to gold leaf the Taj Mahal.

Artemis rose to greet his associate. 'Mister Spiro, welcome.'

'Hey, little Artemis Fowl. How the hell are you?'

Artemis shook the man's hand. His jewellery jangled like a rattlesnake's tail.

'I am well. Glad you could come.'

Spiro took a chair. 'Artemis Fowl calls with a proposition: I would've walked across broken glass to be here.'

The bodyguards appraised each other openly. Apart from their bulk, the two were polar opposites. Butler was the epitome of understated efficiency. Black suit, shaven head, as inconspicuous as it was possible to be at almost seven feet tall. The newcomer had bleached blond hair, a cut-off T-shirt and silver pirate rings in both ears. This was not a man who wanted to be forgotten, or ignored.

'Arno Blunt,' said Butler. 'I've heard about you.'

Blunt took up his position at Jon Spiro's shoulder.

'Butler. One of *the* Butlers,' he said, in a New Zealand drawl. 'I hear you guys are the best. That's what I hear. Let's hope we don't have to find out.'

Spiro laughed. It sounded like a box of crickets.

'Arno, please. We are among friends here. This is not a day for threats.'

10

Butler was not so sure. His soldier's sense was buzzing like a nest of hornets at the base of his skull. There was danger here.

'So, my friend. To business,' said Spiro, fixing Artemis with his close-set dark eyes. 'I've been salivating all the way across the Atlantic. What have you got for me?'

Artemis frowned. He'd hoped business could wait until after lunch.

'Wouldn't you like to see a menu?'

'No. I don't eat much any more. Pills and liquids mostly. Gut problems.'

'Very well,' said Artemis, laying an aluminium briefcase on the table. 'To business then.'

He flipped the case's lid, revealing a red cube the size of a minidisc player, nestling in blue foam.

Spiro cleaned his spectacles with the tail end of his tie.

'What am I seeing here, kid?'

Artemis placed the shining box on the table.

'The future, Mister Spiro. Ahead of schedule.'

Jon Spiro leaned in, taking a good look.

'Looks like a paperweight to me.'

Arno Blunt sniggered, his eyes taunting Butler.

'A demonstration then,' said Artemis, picking up the metal box. He pressed a button and the gadget purred into life. Sections slid back to reveal speakers and a screen.

'Cute,' muttered Spiro. 'I flew three thousand miles for a micro-TV?'

Artemis nodded. 'A micro-TV. But also a verbally controlled computer, a mobile phone, a diagnostic aid. This little box can read any information on absolutely any platform, electrical or organic. It can play videos, laserdiscs, DVDs; go online, retrieve e-mail, hack any computer. It can even scan your chest to see how fast your heart's beating. Its battery is good for two years and, of course, it's completely wireless.'

Artemis paused, to let it sink in.

Spiro's eyes seemed huge behind his spectacles.

'You mean, this box …?'

'Will render all other technology obsolete. Your computer plants will be worthless.'

The American took several deep breaths.

'But how … how?'

Artemis flipped the box over. An infrared sensor pulsed gently on the back.

'This is the secret. An omni-sensor. It can read anything you ask it to. And if the source is programmed in, it can piggyback any satellite you choose.'

Spiro wagged a finger. 'But that's illegal, isn't it?'

'No, no,' said Artemis, smiling. 'There are no laws against something like this. And there won't be for at least two years after it comes out. Look how long it took to shut down Napster.'

The American rested his face in his hands. It was too much.

'I don't understand. This is years, no, *decades* ahead of anything we have now. You're nothing but a thirteen-year-old kid. How did you do it?'

Artemis thought for a second. What was he going to say? Sixteen months ago Butler took on a Lower Elements Police Retrieval squad and confiscated their fairy technology? Then he, Artemis, had taken the components and built this wonderful box? Hardly.

'Let's just say I'm a very smart boy, Mister Spiro.'

Spiro's eyes narrowed. 'Maybe not as smart as you'd like us to think. I want a demonstration.'

'Fair enough.' Artemis nodded. 'Do you have a mobile phone?'

'Naturally.' Spiro placed his mobile phone on the table. It was the latest Fission Chips model.

'Secure, I take it?'

Spiro nodded arrogantly. 'Five hundred bit encryption. Best in its class. You're not getting into the Fission 400 without a code.'

'We shall see.'

Artemis pointed the sensor at the handset. The screen instantly displayed an image of the mobile phone's workings.

'Download?' enquired a metallic voice from the speaker.

'Confirm.'

In less than a second, the job was done. 'Download complete,' said the box, with a hint of smugness.

Spiro was aghast. 'I don't believe it. That system cost twenty million dollars.'

'Worthless,' said Artemis, showing him the screen. 'Would you like to call home? Or maybe move some funds around? You really shouldn't keep your bank account numbers on a sim card.'

The American thought for several moments.

'It's a trick,' he pronounced finally. 'You must've known about my phone. Somehow, don't ask me how, you got access to it earlier.'

'That is logical,' admitted Artemis. 'It's what I would suspect. Name your test.'

Spiro cast his eyes around the restaurant, fingers drumming the tabletop.

'Over there,' he said, pointing to a video shelf above the bar. 'Play one of those tapes.'

'That's it?'

'It'll do, for a start.'

Arno Blunt made a huge show of flicking through the tapes, eventually selecting one without a label. He slapped it down on the table, bouncing the engraved silver cutlery into the air.

Artemis resisted the urge to roll his eyes and placed the red box directly on to the tape's surface.

An image of the cassette's innards appeared on the tiny plasma screen.

'Download?' asked the box.

⊗▯•⸙⚹⚵⊗•∞⚵⸙⟩⚹⚬⸙•▯•⸙⚵⚶•

Artemis nodded. 'Download, compensate and play.'

Again, the operation was completed in under a second. An old episode of an English soap crackled into life.

'DVD quality,' commented Artemis. 'Regardless of the input, the C Cube will compensate.'

'The what?'

'C Cube,' repeated Artemis. 'The name I have given my little box. A tad obvious, I admit. But appropriate. The cube that sees everything.'

Spiro snatched the video cassette. 'Check it,' he ordered, tossing the tape to Arno Blunt.

The bleached-blond bodyguard activated the bar's TV, sliding the video into its slot. *Coronation Street* flickered across the screen. The same show. Nowhere near the same quality.

'Convinced?' asked Artemis.

The American tinkered with one of his many bracelets.

'Almost. One last test. I have a feeling that the government is monitoring me. Could you check it out?'

Artemis thought for a moment, then addressed the red box again.

'Cube, do you read any surveillance beams concentrated on this building?'

The machine whirred for a moment.

'The strongest ion beam is eighty kilometres due west, emanating from US satellite code number ST1132P. Registered to the Central Intelligence Agency. Estimated time of arrival, eight minutes. There are also several LEP probes connected to …'

Artemis hit the mute button before the Cube could continue. Obviously the computer's fairy components could pick up Lower Elements technology too. He would have to remedy that. In the wrong hands that information would be devastating to fairy security.

'What's the matter, kid? The box was still talking. Who are the LEP?'

Artemis shrugged. 'No pay, no play, as you Americans say. One example is enough. The CIA no less.'

'The CIA,' breathed Spiro. 'They suspect me of selling military secrets. They've pulled one of their birds out of orbit, just to track me.'

'Or perhaps me,' noted Artemis.

'Perhaps you,' agreed Spiro. 'You're looking more dangerous by the second.'

Arno Blunt chuckled derisively.

Butler ignored it. One of them had to be professional.

Spiro cracked his knuckles, a habit Artemis detested.

'We've got eight minutes, so let's get down to the nitty gritty, kid. How much for the box?'

Artemis was not paying attention, distracted by the LEP information that the Cube had almost revealed. In a careless moment, he had nearly exposed his subterranean friends to exactly the kind of man who would exploit them.

'I'm sorry, what did you say?'

'I said, how much for the box?'

'Firstly, it's a Cube,' corrected Artemis. 'And secondly, it's not for sale.'

Jon Spiro took a deep, shuddering breath. 'Not for sale? You brought me across the Atlantic to show me something you're not going to sell me? What's going on here?'

Butler wrapped his fingers around the handle of a pistol in his waistband. Arno Blunt's hand disappeared behind his back. The tension cranked up another notch.

Artemis steepled his fingers. 'Mister Spiro. Jon. I am not a complete idiot. I realize the value of my Cube. There is not enough money in the world to pay for this particular item. Whatever you could give me, it would be worth a thousand per cent more in a week.'

'So what's the deal, Fowl?' asked Spiro, through gritted teeth. 'What are you offering?'

'I'm offering you twelve months. For the right price, I'm prepared to keep my Cube off the market for a year.'

Jon Spiro toyed with his ID bracelet. A birthday present to himself.

'You'll suppress the technology for a year?'

'Correct. That should give you ample time to sell your stocks before they crash, and to use the profits to buy into Fowl Industries.'

'There is no Fowl Industries.'

Artemis smirked. 'There will be.'

Butler squeezed his employer's shoulder. It was not a good idea to bait a man like Jon Spiro.

But Spiro hadn't even noticed the jibe. He was too busy calculating, twisting his bracelet like a string of worry beads.

'Your price?' he asked eventually.

'Gold. One metric ton,' replied the heir to the Fowl estate.

'That's a lot of gold.'

Artemis shrugged. 'I like gold. It holds its value. And anyway, it's a pittance compared to what this deal will save you.'

Spiro thought about it. At his shoulder, Arno Blunt continued staring at Butler. The Fowl bodyguard blinked freely: in the event of confrontation, dry eyeballs would only lessen his advantage. Staring matches were for amateurs.

'Let's say I don't like your terms,' said Jon Spiro. 'Let's say I decide to take your little gadget with me right now.'

Arno Blunt's chest puffed out another centimetre.

'Even if you could take the Cube,' said Artemis, smiling, 'it would be of little use to you. The technology is beyond anything your engineers have ever seen.'

Spiro gave a thin, mirthless smile. 'Oh, I'm sure they could figure it out. Even if it took a couple of years, it won't matter to you. Not where you're going.'

'If I *go* anywhere, then the C Cube's secrets go with me. Its every function is coded to my voice patterns. It's quite a clever code.'

Butler bent his knees slightly, ready to spring.

'I bet we could break that code. I got one helluva team assembled in Fission Chips.'

'Pardon me if I am unimpressed by your "*one helluva team*",' said Artemis. 'Thus far you have been trailing several years behind Phonetix.'

Spiro jumped to his feet. He did not like the P word. Phonetix was the only communications company whose stock was higher than Fission Chips's.

'OK, kid, you've had your fun. Now it's my turn. I have to go now, before the satellite beam gets here. But I'm leaving Mister Blunt behind.' He patted his bodyguard on the shoulder. 'You know what you have to do.'

Blunt nodded. He knew. He was looking forward to it.

For the first time since the meeting began, Artemis forgot about his lunch and concentrated completely on the situation at hand. This was not going according to plan.

'Mister Spiro. You cannot be serious. We are in a public place, surrounded by civilians. Your man cannot hope to compete with Butler. If you persist with these ludicrous threats, I will be forced to withdraw my offer, and will release the C Cube immediately.'

Spiro placed his palms on the table. 'Listen, kid,' he whispered. 'I like you. In a couple of years, you could have

been just like me. But did you ever put a gun to
somebody's head and pull the trigger?'

Artemis didn't reply.

'No?' grunted Spiro. 'I didn't think so. Sometimes
that's all it takes. Guts. And you don't have them.'

Artemis was at a loss for words. Something that had
only happened twice since his fifth birthday. Butler
stepped in to fill the silence. Unveiled threats were more
his area.

'Mister Spiro. Don't try to bluff us. Blunt may be big,
but I can snap him like a twig. Then there's nobody
between me and you. And, take my word for it, you don't
want that.'

Spiro's smile spread across his nicotine-stained teeth
like a smear of treacle.

'Oh, I wouldn't say there's nobody between us.'

Butler got that sinking feeling. The one you get when
there are a dozen laser sights playing across your chest.
They had been set up. Somehow Spiro had
outmanoeuvred Artemis.

'Hey, Fowl?' said the American. 'I wonder how come
your lunch is taking so long.'

It was at that moment Artemis realized just how much
trouble they were in.

It all happened in a heartbeat. Spiro clicked his fingers and
every single customer in En Fin drew a weapon from

inside his or her coat. The eighty-year-old lady suddenly looked a lot more threatening with a revolver in her bony fist. Two armed waiters emerged from the kitchen wielding folding-stock machine guns. Butler never even had time to draw breath.

Spiro tipped over the salt cellar. 'Check and mate. My game, kid.'

Artemis tried to concentrate. There must be a way out. There was always a way out. But it wouldn't come. He had been hoodwinked. Perhaps fatally. No human had ever outsmarted Artemis Fowl. Then again, it only had to happen once.

'I'm going now,' continued Spiro, pocketing the C Cube, 'before that satellite beam shows up, and those other ones. The LEP, I've never heard of that particular agency. And as soon as I get this gizmo working they're going to wish they never heard of me. It's been fun doing business with you.'

On his way to the door, Spiro winked at his bodyguard.

'You got six minutes, Arno. A dream come true, eh? You get to be the guy who took out the great Butler.' He turned back to Artemis, unable to resist a final jibe.

'Oh, and by the way – Artemis, isn't that a girl's name?' And he was gone, into the multicultural throngs of tourists on the high street.

The old lady locked the door behind him. The click echoed around the restaurant.

Artemis decided to take the initiative. 'Now, ladies and gentlemen,' he said, trying to avoid staring down the black-eyed gun barrels. 'I'm sure we can come to an arrangement.'

'Quiet, Artemis!'

It took a moment for Artemis's brain to process the fact that Butler had *ordered* him to be silent. Most impertinently in fact.

'I beg your pardon ...'

Butler clamped a hand over his employer's mouth.

'Quiet, Artemis. These people are professionals, not to be bargained with.'

Blunt rotated his skull, cracking the tendons in his neck.

'You got that right, Butler. We're here to kill you. As soon as Mister Spiro got the call we started sending people in. I can't believe you fell for it, man. You must be getting old.'

Butler couldn't believe it either. There was a time when he would have staked out any rendezvous site for a week before giving it the thumbs-up. Maybe he *was* getting old, but there was an excellent chance he wouldn't be getting any older.

'OK, Blunt,' said Butler, stretching out his empty palms before him. 'You and me. One on one.'

'Very noble,' said Blunt. 'That's your Asian code of honour, I suppose. Me, I don't have a code. If you think I'm going to risk you somehow getting out of here, you're crazy. This is an uncomplicated deal. I shoot you. You die. No face-off, no duel.'

Blunt reached lazily into his waistband. Why hurry? One move from Butler and a dozen bullets would find their mark.

Artemis's brain seemed to have shut down. The usual stream of ideas had dried up. I'm going to die, he thought. I don't believe it.

Butler was saying something. Artemis decided he should listen.

'Richard of York gave battle in vain,' said the bodyguard, enunciating clearly.

Blunt was screwing a silencer on to the muzzle of his ceramic pistol.

'What are you saying? What kind of gibberish is that? Don't say the great Butler is cracking up! Wait till I tell the guys.'

But the old woman looked thoughtful.

'Richard of York ... I know that.'

Artemis knew it too. It was virtually the entire verbal detonation code for the fairy sonix grenade magnetized to the underside of the table. One of Butler's little security devices. All they needed was one more word and the grenade would explode, sending a solid wall of sound charging through the building, blowing out every window and eardrum. There would be no smoke or flames, but anyone within a ten-metre radius not wearing earplugs had about five seconds before severe pain set in. One more word.

The old lady scratched her head with the revolver's barrel.

'Richard of York? I remember now, the nuns taught us that in school. Richard of York gave battle in vain. It's one of those memory tricks. The colours of the rainbow.'

Rainbow. The final word. Artemis remembered – just in time – to slacken his jaw. If his teeth were clenched, the sonic waves would shatter them like sugar glass.

The grenade detonated in a blast of compressed sound, instantaneously hurling eleven people to the furthest extremities of the room, until they came into contact with various walls. The lucky ones hit partitions and went straight through. The unlucky ones collided with cavity block walls. Things broke. Not the blocks.

Artemis was safe in Butler's bear-hug. The bodyguard had anchored himself against a solid door frame, folding the flying boy into his arms. And they had several other advantages over Spiro's assassins: their teeth were intact, they did not suffer from any compound fractures and the sonic filter sponges had sealed, saving their eardrums from perforation.

Butler surveyed the room. The assassins were all down, clutching their ears. They wouldn't be uncrossing their eyes for several days. The manservant drew his Sig Sauer pistol from a shoulder holster.

'Stay here,' he commanded. 'I'm going to check the kitchen.'

Artemis settled back into his chair, drawing several shaky breaths. All around was a chaos of dust and moans. But once again, Butler had saved them. All was not lost. It was even possible that they could catch Spiro before he left the country. Butler had a contact in Heathrow Security: Sid Commons, an ex-Green Beret he'd served with on bodyguard duty in Monte Carlo.

A large figure came into view, blocking out the sunlight. It was Butler, returned from his reconnoitre. Artemis breathed deeply, feelingly uncharacteristically emotional.

'Butler,' he began. 'We really must talk regarding your salary ...'

But it wasn't Butler. It was Arno Blunt. He had something in each hand. On his left palm, two tiny cones of yellow foam.

'Ear plugs,' he spat through broken teeth. 'I always wear 'em before a fire fight. Good thing too, eh?'

In his right hand, Blunt held a silenced pistol.

'You first,' he said. 'Then the ape.'

Arno Blunt cocked the gun, took aim briefly and fired.

CHAPTER 2: **LOCKDOWN**

 THOUGH Artemis did not intend it, the Cube's scan for surveillance beams was to have far-reaching repercussions. The search parameters were so vague that the Cube sent probes into deep space and, of course, deep underground.

Below the surface, the Lower Elements Police were stretched to their limits following the recent goblin revolution. Three months after the attempted goblin takeover, most of the major players were in custody. But there were still isolated pockets of the B'wa Kell triad loping around Haven's tunnels with illegal Softnose lasers.

Every available LEP officer had been drafted in to help with Operation Mop-Up before the tourist season got started. The last thing the city Council wanted was tourists spending their leisure gold in Atlantis because

Haven's pedestrianized central plaza was not safe to wander through. Tourism, after all, accounted for eighteen per cent of the capital's revenue.

Captain Holly Short was on loan from the Reconnaissance squad. Generally, her job was to fly to the surface on the trail of fairies who had ventured above ground without a visa. If even one renegade fairy got himself captured by the Mud People, then Haven ceased to be a haven. So until every gang goblin was licking his eyeballs in Howler's Peak correctional facility, Holly's duties were the same as every other LEP officer: rapid response to any B'wa Kell alert.

Today she was escorting four rowdy goblin hoods to Police Plaza for processing. They had been found asleep in an insect delicatessen, stomachs distended after a night of gluttony. It was lucky for them that Holly had arrived when she did, because the deli's dwarf owner was on the point of lowering the scaly foursome into the deep-fat fryer.

Holly's ride-along for Operation Mop-Up was Corporal Grub Kelp, little brother to the famous Captain Trouble Kelp, one of the LEP's most decorated officers. Grub, however, did not share his brother's stoic personality.

'I got a hangnail cuffing that last goblin,' said the junior officer, chewing on his thumb.

'Painful,' said Holly, trying to sound interested.

They were driving along a magnastrip to Police Plaza, with the perpetrators manacled in the rear of their LEP wagon. It wasn't actually a regulation wagon. The B'wa Kell had managed to burn out so many police vehicles during their short-lived revolution that the LEP had been forced to commandeer anything with an engine and room in the back for a few prisoners. In reality, Holly was piloting a curry van with the LEP acorn symbol spray-painted on the side. The motor-pool gnomes had simply bolted the serving hatch and removed the ovens. A pity they couldn't remove the smell.

Grub studied his wounded thumb. 'Those cuffs have sharp edges. I should lodge a complaint.'

Holly concentrated on the road, though the magnastrip did the steering for her. If Grub did lodge a complaint, it wouldn't be his first, or even his twentieth. Trouble's little brother found fault with everything, except himself. In this instance he was completely wrong: there were no sharp edges on the perspex vacuum cuffs. If there had been, a goblin might think to poke a hole in the other mitt and allow oxygen to reach his hand, and nobody wanted goblins hurling fireballs in the back of their vehicles.

'I know it sounds petty to lodge a complaint over hangnails, but no one could accuse *me* of being petty.'

'You! Petty! Perish the thought.'

Grub puffed up his chest. 'After all, I am the only

member of LEPretrieval One to have faced down the human, Butler.'

Holly groaned loudly. This, she fervently hoped, would dissuade Grub from telling his Artemis Fowl war story yet again. It grew longer and more fantastical each time. In reality, Butler had let him go, as a fisherman would a minnow.

But Grub was not about to take a hint.

'I remember it well,' he began melodramatically. 'It was a dark night.'

And, as though his very words carried immeasurable magic, every light in the city went out.

Not only that, but the magnastrip's power failed, leaving them stranded in the middle lane of a frozen highway.

'I didn't do that, did I?' whispered Grub.

Holly didn't answer, already halfway out of the wagon door. Overhead, the sun strips that replicated surface light were fading to black. In the last moments of half-light Holly squinted towards the Northern Tunnel and, sure enough, the door was sliding down, emergency lights revolving along its lower edge. Sixty metres of solid steel separating Haven from the outside world. Similar doors were dropping at strategic arches all over the city. Lockdown. There were only three reasons why the Council would initiate a city-wide lockdown: flood, quarantine, or discovery by the humans.

Holly looked around her. Nobody was drowning; nobody was sick. So the Mud People were coming. Finally, every fairy's worst nightmare was coming true.

Emergency lights flickered on overhead, the sun strips' soft white glow replaced by an eerie orange. Official vehicles would receive a burst of power from the magnastrip, enough to get them to the nearest depot.

Ordinary citizens were not so lucky; they would have to walk. Hundreds stumbled from their automobiles, too scared to protest. That would come later.

'Captain Short! Holly!'

It was Grub. No doubt he would be lodging a complaint with someone.

'Corporal,' she said, turning back to the vehicle. 'This is no time for panic. We need to set an example ...'

The lecture petered out in her throat when she saw what was happening to the wagon. All LEP vehicles would have by now received the regulation ten-minute burst of power from the magnastrip to get them and their cargo to safety. This power would also keep the perspex cuffs vacuumed. Of course, as they weren't using an official LEP vehicle they hadn't been cleared for emergency power – something the goblins obviously realized, because they were trying to burn their way out of the wagon.

Grub stumbled from the cab, his helmet blackened by soot.

'The cuffs have popped open, so now they've started blasting the doors,' he panted, retreating to a safe distance.

Goblins. Evolution's little joke. Pick the dumbest creatures on the planet and give them the ability to conjure fire. If the goblins didn't stop blasting the wagon's reinforced interior they would soon be encased in molten metal. Not a nice way to go, even if you were fireproof.

Holly activated the amplifier in her LEP helmet.

'You there, in the wagon. Cease fire. The vehicle will collapse and you will be trapped.'

For several moments, smoke billowed from the vents. Then the vehicle settled on its axles. A face appeared at the grille, forked tongue slithering through the mesh.

'You think we're stupid, elf? We're gonna burn clean through this pile of junk.'

Holly stepped closer, turning up the speakers.

'Listen to me, goblin. You are stupid, let's just accept that and move on. If you continue to fireball that vehicle, the roof will melt and fall on you like shells from a human gun. You may be fireproof, but are you bulletproof?'

The goblin licked his lidless eyes, thinking it over.

'You lie, elf! We will blow a hole right through this prison. You will be next.'

The wagon's panels began to lurch and buckle as the goblins renewed their attack.

'Not to worry,' said Grub, from a safe distance. 'The fire extinguishers will get them.'

'They would,' corrected Holly, 'if the fire extinguishers weren't connected to the main power grid, which is shut down.'

A mobile food-preparation wagon such as this one would have to adhere to the strictest fire regulations before setting one magna wheel on the strip. In this case, several foam-packed extinguishers, which could submerge the entire interior in flame-retardant foam in a matter of seconds. The nice thing about the flame foam was that it hardened on contact with air, but the not-so-nice thing about flame foam was that the trip switch was connected to the magna strip. No power. No foam.

Holly drew her Neutrino 2000 from its holster. 'I'll just have to trip this switch myself.'

Captain Short sealed her helmet and climbed into the wagon's cab. She avoided touching metal wherever possible, because even though microfilaments in her LEP jumpsuit were designed to disperse extra heat, microfilaments didn't always do what they were designed to do.

The goblins were on their backs, pumping fireball after fireball into the roof panels.

'Knock it off!' she ordered, pointing her laser's muzzle through the mesh.

Three of the goblins ignored her. One, possibly the leader, turned his scaly face to the grille. Holly saw that he had eyeball tattoos. This act of supreme stupidity probably would have guaranteed him promotion had the B'wa Kell not been effectively disbanded.

'You will not be able to get us all, elf,' he said, smoke leaking from his mouth and slitted nostrils. 'Then one of us will get you.'

The goblin was right, even if he didn't realize why. Holly suddenly remembered that she could not fire during a lockdown. Regulations stated that there were to be no unshielded power surges in case Haven was being probed.

Her hesitation was all the proof the goblin needed.

'I knew it!' he crowed, tossing a casual fireball at the grille. The mesh glowed red, and sparks cascaded against Holly's visor. Over the goblins' heads, the roof sagged dangerously. A few more seconds and it would collapse.

Holly unclipped a piton dart from her belt, screwing it into the launcher above the Neutrino's main barrel. The launcher was spring-loaded, like an old-fashioned spear gun, and would not give off a heat flash: nothing to alarm any sensors.

The goblin was highly amused, as goblins often are just before incarceration, which explains why so many are incarcerated.

'A dart? You going to prod us all to death, little elf?'

Holly aimed at a clip protruding from the fire-foam nozzle in the rear of the wagon.

'Would you please be quiet?' she said, and launched

the dart. It flew over the goblin's head, jamming itself between the rods of the nozzle clip; the piton cord stretched the length of the wagon.

'Missed me,' said the goblin, waggling his forked tongue. It was a testament to the goblin's stupidity that he could be trapped in a melting vehicle during a lockdown with an LEP officer firing at him, and still think he had the upper hand.

'I told you to be quiet!' said Holly, pulling sharply on the piton cord and snapping the clip.

Eight hundred kilograms of extinguisher foam blasted from the diffuser nozzle at over two hundred miles per hour. Needless to say, all fireballs went out. The goblins were pinned down by the force of the already hardening foam. The leader was pressed so forcibly against the grille that his tattooed eyes were easily legible. One said 'Mummy', the other 'Duddy'. A misspelling, though he probably didn't know it.

'Ow,' he said. More from disbelief than pain. He didn't say anything else, because his mouth was full of congealing foam.

'Don't worry,' said Holly. 'The foam is porous, so you will be able to breathe, but it's also completely fireproof, so good luck trying to burn your way out.'

Grub was still examining his hangnail when Holly emerged from the van. She removed her helmet, wiping the soot from the visor with the sleeve of her jumpsuit. It was supposed to be non-stick; maybe she should send it in for another coating.

'Everything all right?' asked Grub.

'Yes, Corporal. Everything is all right. No thanks to you.'

Grub had the audacity to look offended. 'I was securing the perimeter, Captain. We can't all be action heroes.'

That was typical Grub, an excuse for every occasion. She could deal with him later. Now it was vital that she get to Police Plaza and find out why the Council had shut down the city.

'I think we should get back to HQ,' Grub offered. 'The intelligence boys might want to interview me if the humans are invading.'

'I think *I* should get back to HQ,' said Holly. 'You stay here and keep an eye on the suspects until the power comes back on. Do you think you can handle that? Or are you too incapacitated with that hangnail?'

Holly's auburn hair stood in sweat-slicked spikes, and her round hazel eyes dared Grub to argue.

'No, Holly … Captain. You leave it to me. Everything is under control.'

I doubt it, thought Holly, setting off at a run towards Police Plaza.

The city was in complete chaos. Every citizen was on the street staring at his or her dead appliance in disbelief. For some of the younger fairies, the loss of their mobile phones was too much to bear. They sank to the streets, sobbing gently.

Police Plaza was mobbed by enquiring minds, like moths drawn to a light. In this case, one of the only lights in town. Hospitals and emergency vehicles would still have juice but, otherwise, the LEP headquarters was the only government building still functioning.

Holly forced her way through the crowd, into the lobby area. The public service queues ran down the steps and out the door. Today everyone was asking the same question: What's happened to the power?

The same question was on Holly's lips as she burst into the Situations booth, but she kept it to herself. The room was already packed with the force's complement of captains, along with the three regional commanders and all seven Council members.

'Aaah,' said Chairman Cahartez. 'The last captain.'

'I didn't get my emergency juice,' explained Holly. 'Non-regulation vehicle.'

Cahartez adjusted his official conical hat. 'No time for excuses, Captain, Mister Foaly has been holding off on his briefing until you got here.'

Holly took her seat at the captain's table, beside Trouble Kelp.

'Grub OK?' he whispered.

'He got a hangnail.'

Trouble rolled his eyes. 'No doubt he'll make a complaint.'

The centaur Foaly trotted through the doors, clutching armfuls of disks. Foaly was the LEP's technical genius, and his security innovations were the main reason why humans had not yet discovered the subterranean fairy hideaway. Maybe that was about to change.

The centaur expertly loaded the disks on to the operating system, opening several windows on a wall-size plasma screen. Various complicated-looking algorithms and wave patterns appeared on the screen.

He cleared his throat noisily. 'I advised Chairman Cahartez to initiate lockdown on the basis of these readings.'

Recon's Commander Root sucked on an unlit fungus cigar. 'I think I'm speaking for the whole room here, Foaly, when I say that all I see is lines and squiggles. Doubtless it makes sense to a smart pony like yourself, but the rest of us are going to need some plain Gnommish.'

Foaly sighed. 'Simply put. Really simply. We got pinged. Is that plain enough?'

It was. The room resonated with stunned silence. Pinged was an old naval term from back in the days when sonar was the preferred method of detection.

Getting pinged was slang for being detected. Someone knew the fairy folk were down here.

Root was the first to recover his voice. 'Pinged. Who pinged us?'

Foaly shrugged. 'Don't know. It only lasted a few seconds. There was no recognizable signature, and it was untraceable.'

'What did they get?'

'Quite a bit. Everything North European. Scopes, Sentinel. All our cam-cams. Downloaded information on every one of them.'

This was catastrophic news. Someone or something knew all about fairy surveillance in Northern Europe, after only a few seconds.

'Was it human,' asked Holly, 'or alien?'

Foaly pointed to a digital representation of the beam. 'I can't say for certain. If it is human, it's something brand new. This came out of nowhere. No one has been developing technology like this as far as I know. Whatever it is, it read us like an open book. My security encryptions folded like they weren't even there.'

Cahartez took off his official hat, no longer concerned with protocol. 'What does this mean for the People?'

'It's difficult to say. There are best and worst case scenarios. Our mysterious guest could learn all about us whenever he wishes and do with our civilization what he will.'

'And the best case scenario?' asked Trouble.

Foaly took a breath. 'That was the best case scenario.'

Commander Root called Holly into his office. The room stank of cigar smoke in spite of the purifier built into the desk. Foaly was already there, his fingers a blur over the commander's keyboard.

'The signal originated in London somewhere,' said the centaur. 'We only know that because I happened to be looking at the monitor at the time.' He leaned back from the keyboard, shaking his head. 'This is incredible. It's some kind of hybrid technology. Almost like our ion systems, but not quite – just a hair's breadth away.'

'The how is not important now,' said Root. 'It's the who I'm worried about.'

'What can I do, sir?' asked Holly.

Root stood and walked to a map of London on the wall plasma screen.

'I need you to sign out a surveillance pack, go topside and wait. If we get pinged again, I want someone on site, ready to go. We can't record this thing, but we can certainly get a visual on the signal. As soon as it shows up on the screen we'll feed you the coordinates and you can investigate.'

Holly nodded. 'When is the next hotshot?'

Hotshot was LEP-speak for the magma flares that Recon officers ride to the surface in titanium eggs. Pod pilots referred to this seat-of-the-pants procedure as 'Riding the Hotshots'.

'No such luck,' replied Foaly. 'Nothing in the pipes for the next two days. You'll have to take a shuttle.'

'What about the lockdown?'

'I've restored power to Stonehenge and our satellite arrays. We'll have to risk it; you need to get above ground and we need to stay in contact. The future of our civilization could depend on it.'

Holly felt the weight of responsibility settle on her shoulders. This *future of our civilization* thing was happening more and more lately.

En Fin, Knightsbridge

 THE sonic blast from Butler's grenade had crashed through the kitchen door, sweeping aside stainless-steel implements like stalks of grass. The aquarium had shattered, leaving the flagstones slick with water, perspex and surprised lobsters. They skittered through the debris, claws raised.

The restaurant staff were on the floor, bound and saturated, but alive. Butler did not untie them. He did not need hysteria right now. Time enough to deal with them once all threats had been neutralized.

An assassin stirred, suspended halfway through a dividing wall. The manservant checked her eyes. They were crossed and unfocused. No threat there. Butler pocketed the old lady's weapon just the same. You couldn't be too careful — something he was learning all over again. If Madame Ko could have seen this afternoon's

41

display, she would have had his graduation tattoo lasered for sure.

The room was clear, but still something was bothering the bodyguard. His soldier's sense grated like two broken bones. Once again Butler flashed back to Madame Ko, his sensei from the Academy. *The bodyguard's primary function is to protect his principal. The principal cannot be shot if you are standing in front of him.* Madame Ko always referred to employers as principals. One did not become involved with principals.

Butler wondered why this particular maxim had occurred to him. Out of the hundreds Madame Ko had drummed into his skull, why this one? It was obvious really. He had broken the first rule of personal protection by leaving his principal unguarded. The second rule: *Do not develop an emotional attachment to the principal* was pretty much in smithereens too. Butler had become so attached to Artemis that it was obviously beginning to affect his judgement.

He could see Madame Ko before him, nondescript in her khaki suit, for all the world an ordinary Japanese housewife. But how many housewives of any nationality could strike so quickly that the air hissed? *You are a disgrace, Butler. A disgrace to your name. It would better suit your talents to get a job mending shoes. Your principal has already been neutralized.*

Butler moved as though in a dream. The very air

seemed to hold him back as he raced for the kitchen doors. He knew what would have happened. Arno Blunt was a professional. Vain perhaps — a cardinal sin among bodyguards — but a professional nevertheless. Professionals always inserted earplugs if there was any danger of gunfire.

The tiles were slick beneath his feet, but Butler compensated by leaning forward and digging his rubber-soled toes into the surface. His intact eardrums picked up irregular vibrations from the restaurant. Conversation. Artemis was speaking with someone. Arno Blunt, no doubt. It was already too late.

Butler came through the service door at a speed that would have shamed an Olympian. His brain began calculating odds the moment pictures arrived from his retinas: Blunt was in the act of firing. Nothing could be done about that now. There was only one option. Without hesitation, Butler took it.

In his right hand, Blunt held a silenced pistol.

'You first,' he said. 'Then the ape.'

Arno Blunt cocked the gun, took aim briefly and fired.

Butler came from nowhere. He seemed to fill the entire room, flinging himself in the bullet's path. From a greater distance, the Kevlar in his bulletproof vest might have held, but at point-blank range, the Teflon-coated bullet drilled through the waistcoat like a hot poker through snow. It entered Butler's chest a centimetre below the heart. It was a fatal wound. And this time Captain Short was not around to save him with her fairy magic.

The bodyguard's own momentum, combined with the force of the bullet, sent Butler crashing into Artemis, pinning him to the dessert trolley. Nothing of the boy was visible, save one Armani loafer.

Butler's breathing was shallow and his vision gone, but he was not dead yet. His brain's electricity was rapidly running out, but the bodyguard held on to a single thought: protect the principal.

Arno Blunt drew a surprised breath, and Butler fired six shots at the sound. He would have been disappointed with the spread had he been able to see it. But one of the bullets found its mark, clipping Blunt's temple. Unconsciousness was immediate, concussion inevitable. Arno Blunt joined the rest of his team, on the floor.

Butler ignored the pain squashing his torso like a giant fist. Instead he listened for movement. There was nothing locally, just the scratch of lobster claws on the tiles. And if one of the lobsters decided to attack, Artemis was on his own.

Nothing more could be done. Either Artemis was safe, or he was not. If not, Butler was in no condition to fulfil the terms of his contract. This realization brought tremendous calm. No more responsibility. Just his own life to live, for a few seconds at any rate. And anyway,

Artemis wasn't just a principal. He was part of the bodyguard's life. His only true friend. Madame Ko might not like this attitude, but there wasn't much she could do about it now. There wasn't much anybody could do.

Artemis had never liked desserts. And yet, he found himself submersed in eclairs, cheesecake and pavlova. His suit would be absolutely destroyed. Of course, Artemis's brain was only throwing up these facts so he could avoid thinking about what had happened. But a ninety-kilogram deadweight is a hard thing to ignore.

Luckily for Artemis, Butler's impact had actually driven him through to the trolley's second shelf, while the bodyguard remained on the ice-cream ledge above. As far as Artemis could tell, the Black Forest gateau had cushioned his impact sufficiently to avoid serious internal injury. Still, he had no doubt that a visit to the chiropractor would be called for. Possibly for Butler too, though the man had the constitution of a troll.

Artemis struggled out from underneath his manservant. With each movement, malignant cream horns exploded in his direction.

'Really, Butler,' grumbled the teenager. 'I must begin choosing my business associates more carefully. Hardly a day goes by when we aren't the victims of some plot.'

Artemis was relieved to see Arno Blunt unconscious on the restaurant floor.

'Another villain dispatched. Good shooting, Butler, as usual. And one more thing, I have decided to wear a bulletproof vest to all future meetings. That should make your job somewhat easier, eh?'

It was at this point that Artemis noticed Butler's shirt. The sight knocked the air from his chest like an invisible mallet. Not the hole in the material, but the blood leaking from it.

'Butler, you're injured. Shot. But the Kevlar?'

The bodyguard didn't reply, nor did he have to. Artemis knew science better than most nuclear physicists. Truth be told, he often posted lectures on the Internet under the pseudonym Emmsey Squire. Obviously the bullet's momentum had been too great for the jacket to withstand. It had possibly been coated with Teflon for extra penetration.

A large part of Artemis wanted to drape his arms across the bodyguard's frame and cry as he would for a brother. But Artemis repressed that instinct. Now was the time for quick thinking.

Butler interrupted his train of thought.

'Artemis ... is that you?' he said, the words coming in short gasps.

'Yes, it's me,' answered Artemis, his voice trembling.

'Don't worry. Juliet will protect you. You'll be fine.'

'Don't talk, Butler. Lie still. The wound is not serious.'

⊕🖳🍳🄱🗲•⊕🖳🗖•🖳🔺💈🕸🍳🄱🗲•1💈🗩🦂🌙•

Butler spluttered. It was as close as he could get to a laugh.

'Very well, it is serious. But I will think of something. Just stay still.'

With his last vestige of strength, Butler raised a hand.

'Goodbye, Artemis,' he said. 'My friend.'

Artemis caught the hand. The tears were streaming now. Unchecked.

'Goodbye, Butler.'

The Eurasian's sightless eyes were calm. 'Artemis, call me – Domovoi.'

The name told Artemis two things. Firstly, his lifelong ally had been named after a Slavic guardian spirit. Secondly, graduates of the Madame Ko Academy were instructed never to reveal first names to their principals. It helped to keep things clinical. Butler would never have broken this rule … unless it no longer mattered.

'Goodbye, Domovoi,' sobbed the boy. 'Goodbye, my friend.'

The hand dropped. Butler was gone.

'No!' shouted Artemis, staggering backwards.

This wasn't right. This was not the way things should end. For some reason, he had always imagined that they would die together – facing insurmountable odds, in some exotic location. On the lip of a reactivated Vesuvius perhaps, or on the banks of the mighty Ganges. But together, as friends. After all they had been through,

Butler simply could not be defeated at the hands of some grandstanding second-rate muscleman.

Butler had almost died before. The year before last, he had been mauled by a troll from the deep tunnels below Haven City. Holly Short had saved him then, using her fairy magic. But now there were no fairies around to save the bodyguard. Time was the enemy here. If Artemis had more of it, he could figure out how to contact the LEP and persuade Holly to use her magic once again. But time was running out. Butler had perhaps four minutes before his brain shut down. Not long enough, even for an intellect such as Artemis's — he needed to buy some more time. Or steal some.

Think, boy, think. Use what the situation provides. Artemis shut off the wellspring of tears. He was in a restaurant, a fish restaurant. Useless! Worthless! Perhaps in a medical facility he could do something. But here? What was here? An oven, sinks, utensils. Even if he did have the proper tools, he had not yet completed his medical studies. It was too late for conventional surgery at any rate — unless there was a method of heart transplant that took less than four minutes.

The seconds were ticking by. Artemis was growing angry with himself. Time was against them. Time was the enemy. Time needed to be stopped. The idea sparked in Artemis's brain in a flash of neurons. Perhaps he couldn't stop time, but he could halt Butler's passage through it.

The process was risky, certainly, but it was the only chance they had.

Artemis popped the dessert trolley's brake with his foot, and began hauling the contraption towards the kitchen. He had to pause several times to drag moaning assassins from the vehicle's path.

Emergency vehicles were approaching, making their way down Knightsbridge. Obviously the sonic grenade's detonation would have attracted attention. There were only moments left before he would have to fabricate some plausible story for the authorities ... Better not to be there ... Fingerprints wouldn't be a problem, as the restaurant would have had dozens of customers. All he had to do was get out of there before London's finest arrived.

The kitchen was forged from stainless steel. Hobs, hoods and work surfaces were littered with fallout from the sonic grenade. Fish flapped in the sink, crustaceans clicked across the tiles and beluga dripped from the ceiling.

There! At the back, a line of freezers, essential in any seafood bistro. Artemis put his shoulder against the trolley, steering it to the rear of the kitchen.

The largest of the freezers was of the custom-built pull-out variety, often found in large restaurants. Artemis hauled open the drawer, quickly evicting the salmon, sea bass and hake that were encrusted in the ice shavings.

Cryogenics. It was their only chance. The science of

freezing a body until medicine had evolved sufficiently to revive it. Generally dismissed by the medical community, it nevertheless made millions each year from the estates of rich eccentrics who needed more than one lifetime to spend their money. Cryogenic chambers were generally built to very exact specifications, but there was no time for Artemis's usual standards now. This freezer would have to do as a temporary solution. It was imperative that Butler's head be cooled to preserve the brain cells. So long as his brain functions were intact, he could theoretically be revived, even if there were no heartbeat.

Artemis manoeuvred the trolley until it overhung the open freezer; then, with the help of a silver platter, he levered Butler's body into the steaming ice. It was tight, but the bodyguard fitted with barely a bend of the legs. Artemis heaped loose ice on top of his fallen comrade, and then adjusted the thermostat to four below zero to avoid tissue damage. Butler's blank face was just visible through a layer of ice.

'I'll be back,' the boy said. 'Sleep well.'

The sirens were close now. Artemis heard the screech of tyres.

'Hold on, Domovoi,' whispered Artemis, closing the freezer drawer.

Artemis left through the back door, mingling with the crowds of locals and sightseers. The police would have someone photographing the crowd, so he did not linger at the cordon, or even glance back towards the restaurant. Instead, he made his way to Harrods and found himself a table at the gallery cafe.

Once he had assured the waitress that he was not looking for his mummy, and produced sufficient cash to pay for his pot of Earl Grey tea, Artemis pulled out his mobile, selecting a number from the speed-dial menu.

A man answered on the second ring.

'Hello. Make it quick, whoever you are. I'm very busy at the moment.'

The man was Detective Inspector Justin Barre of New Scotland Yard. Barre's gravelly tones were caused by a hunting knife across the gullet during a bar fight in the nineties. If Butler hadn't been on hand to stop the bleeding, Justin Barre would never have risen beyond Sergeant. It was time to call in the debt.

'Detective Inspector Barre. This is Artemis Fowl.'

'Artemis, how are you? And how's my old partner, Butler?'

Artemis kneaded his forehead. 'Not well at all, I'm afraid. He needs a favour.'

'Anything for the big man. What can I do?'

'Did you hear something about a disturbance in Knightsbridge?'

There was a pause. Artemis heard paper rip as a fax was torn off the roll.

'Yes, it just came in. A couple of windows were shattered in some restaurant. Nothing major. Some tourists are a bit shell-shocked. Preliminary reports say it was some kind of localized earthquake, if you can believe that. We've got two cars there right now. Don't tell me Butler was behind it?'

Artemis took a breath. 'I need you to keep your men away from the freezers.'

'That's a strange request, Artemis. What's in the freezers that I shouldn't see?'

'Nothing illegal,' promised Artemis. 'Believe me when I say this is life or death for Butler.'

Barre didn't hesitate. 'This is not exactly in my jurisdiction, but consider it done. Do you need to get whatever I'm not supposed to see out of the freezers?'

The officer had read his mind. 'As soon as possible. Two minutes are all I need.'

Barre chewed it over. 'OK. Let's synchronize schedules. The forensics team is going to be in there for a couple of hours. Nothing I can do about that. But at six-thirty precisely, I can guarantee there won't be anyone on duty. You have five minutes.'

'That will be more than sufficient.'

'Good. And tell the big man that we're quits.'

Artemis kept his voice even. 'Yes, Detective Inspector. I'll tell him.'

If I get the opportunity, he thought.

ICE AGE CRYOGENICS INSTITUTE, OFF HARLEY STREET, LONDON

The Ice Age Cryogenics Institute was not actually on London's Harley Street. Technically, it was tucked away in Dickens Lane, a side alley on the famous medical boulevard's southern end. But this did not stop the facility's MD, one Doctor Constance Lane, from putting Harley Street on all Ice Age stationery. You couldn't buy credibility like that. When the upper classes saw those magic words on a business card they fell over themselves to have their frail frames frozen.

Artemis Fowl was not so easily impressed. But then he had little choice; Ice Age was one of three cryogenic centres in the city, and the only one with free units. Though Artemis did consider the neon sign a bit much: 'Pods to Rent'. Honestly.

The building itself was enough to make Artemis squirm. The facade was lined with brushed aluminium, obviously designed to resemble a spaceship, and the doors were of the whoosh *Star Trek* variety. Where was culture? Where was art? How did a monstrosity like this get planning permission in historic London?

A nurse, complete with white uniform and three-pointed hat, was manning the reception. Artemis doubted she was an actual nurse — something about the cigarette between her false nails.

'Excuse me, miss?'

The nurse barely glanced up from her gossip magazine.

'Yes? Are you looking for someone?'

Artemis clenched his fists behind his back.

'Yes, I would like to see Doctor Lane. She is the surgeon, is she not?'

The nurse ground out her cigarette in an overflowing ashtray.

'This is not another school project, is it? Doctor Lane says no more projects.'

'No. Not another school project.'

'You're not a lawyer, are you?' asked the nurse suspiciously. 'One of those geniuses who gets a degree while they're still in nappies?'

Artemis sighed. 'A genius, yes. A lawyer, hardly. I am, mademoiselle, a customer.'

And suddenly the nurse was all charm.

'Oh, a customer! Why didn't you say so? I'll show you right in. Would sir care for tea, coffee or perhaps something stronger?'

'I am thirteen years old, mademoiselle.'

'A juice?'

'Tea would be fine. Earl Grey if you have it. No sugar, obviously; it might make me hyperactive.'

The nurse was quite prepared to accept sarcasm from an actual paying customer, and directed Artemis to a lounge where the style was, again, space age. Plenty of shining velour and eternity mirrors.

Artemis had half finished a cup of something that was most definitely not Earl Grey when Doctor Lane's door swung open.

'Do come in,' said a tall woman uncertainly.

'Shall I walk?' asked Artemis. 'Or will you beam me up?'

The office walls were lined with frames. Along one side were the doctor's degrees and certificates. Artemis suspected that many of these certificates could be obtained over the weekend. Along the wall were several photographic portraits. Above these read the legend 'Love Lies Sleeping'. Artemis almost left then, but he was desperate.

Doctor Lane sat behind her desk. She was a very glamorous woman, with flowing red hair and the tapered fingers of an artist. Her smock was Dior. Even Constance Lane's smile was perfect — too perfect. Artemis looked closer and realized that her entire face was the handiwork of a plastic surgeon. Obviously, this woman's life was all about cheating time. He had come to the right place.

'Now, young man, Tracy says you wish to become a customer?' The doctor tried to smile, but the stretching made her face shine like a balloon.

'Not personally, no,' replied Artemis. 'But I do wish to rent one of your units. Short term.'

Constance Lane pulled a company pamphlet from the drawer, ringing some figures in red.

⊖♕∥♌◗◯⊛ ⨯⃫⊱⊛ · ⊛♌⊶ · ▢◯⊖⟁ · ⨯⃫⊱⨝ ·

'Our rates are quite steep.'

Artemis did not even glance at the numbers.

'Money is no object. We can set up a wire transfer right now from my Swiss bank. In five minutes you can have a hundred thousand pounds sitting in your personal account. All I need is a unit for a single night.'

The figure was impressive. Constance thought of all the nips and tucks it would buy. But she was still reluctant ...

'Generally minors are not allowed to commit relatives to our chambers. It's the law actually.'

Artemis leaned forward.

'Doctor Lane. Constance. What I'm doing here is not exactly legal, but no one is being hurt either. One night and you're a rich woman. This time tomorrow and I was never here. No bodies, no complaints.'

The doctor's hand fingered her jaw line.

'One night?'

'Just one. You won't even know we're here.'

Constance took a hand mirror from her desk drawer, studying her reflection closely.

'Call your bank,' she said.

STONEHENGE, WILTSHIRE

Two LEP chutes emerged in the south of England. One in London itself, but that was closed to the public due to the fact that Chelsea Football Club had built their grounds five hundred metres above the shuttle port.

The other port was in Wiltshire, beside what humans referred to as Stonehenge. Mud People had several theories as to the origins of the structure. These ranged from spaceship landing port to pagan centre of worship. The truth was far less glamorous. Stonehenge had actually been an outlet for a flat-bread-based food. Or, in human terms, a pizza parlour.

A gnome called Bog had realized how many tourists forgot their sandwiches on above-ground jaunts, and so had set up shop beside the terminal. It was a smooth operation. You drove up to one of the windows, named your toppings, and ten minutes later you were stuffing your face. Of course, Bog had to shift his operation below ground once humans began talking in full sentences. And anyway, all that cheese was making the ground soggy. A couple of the service windows had even collapsed.

It was difficult for fairy civilians to get visas to visit Stonehenge because of the constant activity on the surface. Then again, hippies saw fairies every day and it never made the front page. As a police officer, Holly didn't have a visa problem; one flash of the Recon badge opened a hole right through to the surface.

But being a Recon officer didn't help if there was no magma flare scheduled. And the Stonehenge chute had been dormant for over three centuries. Not a spark. In the absence of a hotshot to ride, Holly was forced to travel aboard a commercial shuttle.

The first available shuttle was heavily booked, but luckily there was a late cancellation so Holly wasn't forced to bump a passenger.

The shuttle was a fifty-seater luxury cruiser. It had been commissioned especially by the Brotherhood of Bog to visit their patron's site. These fairies, mostly gnomes, dedicated their lives to pizza and every year on the anniversary of Bog's first day in business, they chartered a shuttle and took a picnic above ground. The picnic consisted of pizza, tuber beer and pizza-flavoured ice cream. Needless to say, they did not remove their rubber pizza bonnets for the entire day.

So, for sixty-seven minutes, Holly sat wedged between two beer-swilling gnomes singing the pizza song:

> *Pizza, pizza,*
> *Fill up your face,*
> *The thicker the pastry,*
> *The better the base!*

There were a hundred and fourteen verses. And it didn't get any better. Holly had never been happier to see the Stonehenge landing lights.

The actual terminal was pretty comprehensive,

boasting a three-lane visa clearance booth, entertainment complex and duty-free shopping. The current souvenir craze was a Mud Man hippy doll that said, 'Peace, man,' when you pressed its tummy.

Holly badged her way through the customs queue, taking a security elevator to the surface. Stonehenge had become easier to exit recently, because the Mud People had put up fencing. The humans were protecting their heritage, or so they thought. Strange that Mud People seemed more concerned about the past than the present.

Holly strapped on her wings, and once the control booth had given her the go-ahead, she cleared the airlock, soaring to a height of seven thousand feet. There was plenty of cloud cover, but nevertheless she activated her shield. Nothing could spot her now; she was invisible to human and mechanical eyes. Only rats and two species of monkey could see through a fairy shield.

Holly switched on the on-board navigator in the wings' computer and let the rig do the steering for her. It was nice to be above ground again, and at sunset too. Her favourite time of day. A slow smile spread across her face. In spite of the situation, she was content. This was what she was born to do. Recon. With the wind against her visor and a challenge between her teeth.

Knightsbridge, London

It had been almost two hours since Butler had been shot. Generally the grace period between heart failure and brain damage is about four minutes, but that period can be extended if the patient's body temperature is lowered sufficiently. Drowning victims, for example, can be resuscitated for up to an hour after their apparent death. Artemis could only pray that his makeshift cryogenic chamber could hold Butler in stasis until he could be transferred to one of Ice Age's pods.

Ice Age Cryogenics had a mobile unit for transporting clients from the private clinics where they expired. The van was equipped with its own generator and full surgery. Even if cryogenics was considered crackpot medicine by many physicians, the vehicle itself would meet the strictest standards of equipment and hygiene.

'These units cost almost a million pounds apiece,' Doctor Constance Lane informed Artemis, as they sat in the stark white surgery. A cylindrical cryo pod was strapped to a trolley between them.

'The vans are custom-made in Munich, specially armoured too. This thing could drive over a landmine and come out smiling.'

For once, Artemis was not interested in gathering information.

'That's very nice, Doctor, but can it go any faster? My

associate's time is running out. It has already been one hundred and twenty seven-minutes.'

Constance Lane tried to frown, but there wasn't enough slack skin across her brow.

'Two hours. Nobody has ever been revived after that long. Then again, no one has *ever* been revived from a cryogenic chamber.'

The Knightsbridge traffic was, as usual, chaotic. Harrods was running a one-day sale, and the block was crowded with droves of tired customers on their way home. It took a further seventeen minutes to reach En Fin's delivery entrance and, as promised, there were no policemen present, except one. Detective Inspector Justin Barre himself was standing sentry at the rear door. The man was huge, a descendant of the Zulu nation, according to Butler. It was not difficult to imagine him at Butler's side in some faraway land.

Incredibly, they found a parking space, and Artemis climbed down from the van.

'Cryogenics,' said Barre, noting the vehicle's inscription. 'Do you think you can do anything for him?'

'You looked in the freezer then?' said Artemis.

The officer nodded. 'How could I resist? Curiosity is my business. I'm sorry I checked now; he was a good man.'

'*Is* a good man,' insisted Artemis. 'I am not ready to give up on him yet.'

Barre stood aside to admit two uniformed Ice Age paramedics.

'According to my men, a group of armed bandits attempted to rob the establishment, but they were interrupted by an earthquake. And if that's what really happened, I'll eat my badge. I don't suppose you can throw any light on the situation?'

'A competitor of mine disagreed with a business strategy. It was a violent disagreement.'

'Who pulled the trigger?'

'Arno Blunt. A New Zealander. Bleached hair, rings in his ears, tattoos on his body and neck. Most of his teeth are missing.'

Barre took a note. 'I'll circulate the description to the airports. You never know, we might catch him.'

Artemis rubbed his eyes.

'Butler saved my life. The bullet was meant for me.'

'That's Butler all right,' said Barre, nodding. 'If there's anything I can do ... ?'

'You'll be the first to know,' said Artemis. 'Did your officers find anyone on the scene?'

Barre consulted his notebook. 'Some customers and staff. They all checked out, so we let them go. The thieves escaped before we arrived.'

'No matter. Better I deal with the culprits myself.'

Barre made a concerted effort to ignore the activity in the kitchen behind him.

'Artemis, can you guarantee this is not going to come back to haunt me? Technically, we're looking at a homicide.'

Artemis looked Barre in the eye, which was quite an effort.

'Detective Inspector, no body, no case. And I guarantee that by tomorrow Butler will be alive and kicking. I shall instruct him to call you, if that would set your mind at rest.'

'It would.'

The paramedics rolled Butler past on a trolley. A frosting of ice covered his face. Tissue damage was already turning his fingers blue.

'Any surgeon who could fix this would have to be a real magician!'

Artemis glanced downwards.

'That's the plan, Detective Inspector. That's the plan.'

Doctor Lane administered glucose injections in the van.

'These are to stop the cells collapsing,' she informed Artemis, massaging Butler's chest to circulate the medication. 'Otherwise the water in his blood will freeze in spikes and puncture the cell walls.'

Butler was lying in an open cryo unit, with its own gyroscopes. He had been dressed in a special silver freezer suit, and cold packs were heaped on his body like sachets of sugar in a bowl.

Constance was unaccustomed to people actually paying attention when she explained the process, but this pale youth absorbed facts faster than she could present them.

'Won't the water freeze anyway? Glucose can't prevent that.'

Constance was impressed. 'Why, yes it will. But in small pieces, so it can float safely between cells.'

Artemis jotted a note in his hand-held computer. 'Small pieces, I understand.'

'The glucose is only a temporary measure,' continued the doctor. 'The next step is surgery; we need to completely wash out his veins, and replace the blood with a preservative. Then we can lower the patient's temperature to minus thirty degrees. We'll have to do that back at the institute.'

Artemis shut down his computer. 'No need for that. I just need him held in stasis for a few hours. After that it won't make any difference.'

'I don't think you understand, young man,' said Doctor Lane. 'Current medical practices have not evolved to the point where this kind of injury can be healed. If I don't do a complete blood substitution soon, there will be severe tissue damage.'

The van jolted as a wheel crashed into one of London's numerous potholes. Butler's arm jerked and, for a moment, Artemis could pretend he was alive.

64

'Don't worry about that, Doctor.'

'But …'

'A hundred thousand pounds, Constance. Just keep repeating that figure to yourself. Park the mobile unit outside and forget all about us. In the morning we'll be gone. Both of us.'

Doctor Lane was surprised.

'Park outside? You don't even want to come in?'

'No, Butler stays outside,' said Artemis. 'My … ah … surgeon, has a problem with dwellings. But may I enter for a moment to use your phone? I need to make a rather special phone call.'

LONDON AIRSPACE

The lights of London were spread out below Holly like the stars of some turbulent galaxy. England's capital was generally a no-fly area for Recon officers, because of the four airports feeding planes into the sky. Five years ago, Captain Trouble Kelp had narrowly missed being impaled by a Heathrow–JFK airbus. Since then, all flight plans involving airport cities had to be cleared personally by Foaly.

Holly spoke into her helmet mike.

'Foaly. Any flights coming in I should know about?'

'Let me just bring up the radar. OK, let's see. I'd drop

down to five hundred feet if I were you. There's a 747 coming in from Malaga in a couple of minutes. It won't hit you, but your helmet computer could interfere with its navigation systems.'

Holly dipped her flaps until she was at the correct altitude. Overhead, the giant jet screamed across the sky. If it hadn't been for Holly's sonic filter sponges, both her eardrums would have popped.

'OK. One jet full of tourists successfully avoided. What now?'

'Now we wait. I won't call again unless it's important.'

They didn't have to wait long. Less than five minutes later Foaly broke radio silence.

'Holly. We got something.'

'Another probe?'

'No. Something from Sentinel. Hold on, I'm sending the file to your helmet.'

A sound file appeared in Holly's visor. Its wave resembled a seismograph's readout.

'What is it, a phone tap?'

'Not exactly,' said Foaly. 'It's one of a billion throwaway files that Sentinel sends us every day.'

The Sentinel system was a series of monitoring units that Foaly had piggybacked to obsolete US and Russian satellites. Their function was to monitor all human telecommunications. Obviously, it would be impossible to review every phone call made each day. So the computer was programmed to pick up on certain key words. If, for example, the words 'fairy', 'haven' and 'underground' appeared in a conversation, the computer would flag the call. The more People-related phrases that appeared, the more urgent the rating.

'This call was made in London minutes ago. It's loaded with keywords. I've never heard anything like it.'

'Play,' said Holly clearly, using voice command. A vertical line cursor began scrolling across the sound wave.

'People,' said a voice, hazy with distortion. 'LEP, magic, Haven, shuttle ports, sprites, B'wa Kell, trolls, time-stop, Recon, Atlantis.'

'That's it?'

'That's not enough? Whoever made that call could be writing our biography.'

'But it's just a string of words. It makes no sense.'

'Hey, there's no point arguing with me,' said the centaur. 'I just collect information. But there has to be a connection to the probe. Two things like this don't just happen on the same day.'

'OK. Do we have an exact location?'

'The call came from a cryogenics institute in London. Sentinel quality is not enough to run a voice-recognition scan. We just know it came from inside the building.'

'Who was our mystery Mud Man calling?'

'Strange thing. He was calling *The Times* newspaper crossword hotline.'

'Maybe those words were the answers to today's crossword?' said Holly hopefully.

'No. I checked the correct solution. Not a fairy-related word in sight.'

Holly set her wings to manual. 'OK. Time to find out what our caller is up to. Send me the institute's coordinates.'

Holly suspected that it was a false alarm. Hundreds of these calls came in every year. Foaly was so paranoid that he believed the Mud People were invading every time someone mentioned the word 'magic' on a phone line. And with the recent trend for human fantasy movies and video games, magical phrases cropped up quite a lot. Thousands of police hours were wasted staking out the dwellings of residents where these phone calls originated, and it usually turned out to be some kid playing on his PC.

More than likely this phantom phone call was the result of a crossed line, or some Hollywood hack pitching a screenplay, or even an undercover LEP operative trying to phone home. But then, today of all days, everything had to be checked.

Holly kicked up her legs behind her, dropping into a steep dive. Diving was against Recon regulations. All approaches were supposed to be controlled and gradual, but what was the point of flying if you couldn't feel the slipstream tugging at your toes?

Ice Age Cryogenics Institute, London

Artemis leaned against the cryogenics mobile unit's rear bumper. It was funny how quickly a person's priorities could change. This morning he had been worried about which loafers to wear with his suit, and now all he could think about was the fact that his dearest friend's life hung in the balance. And the balance was rapidly shifting.

Artemis wiped a coating of frost from the spectacles he'd retrieved from his bodyguard's jacket. These were no ordinary spectacles. Butler had 20/20 vision. These particular eye glasses had been specially tooled to accommodate filters taken from an LEP helmet. Anti-shield filters. Butler had carried them since Holly Short almost got the jump on him at Fowl Manor.

'You never know,' he'd said. 'We're a threat to LEP security, and some day Commander Root could be replaced with someone who isn't quite so fond of us.'

Artemis wasn't convinced. The fairies were, by and large, a peaceful people. He couldn't believe they would harm anyone, even a Mud Person, on the basis of past crimes. After all, they had parted friends. Or, at least, not enemies.

Artemis presumed the call would work – there was no reason to believe it wouldn't: several government security agencies monitored phone lines using the key word system, recording conversations that could compromise national security. And if humans were doing it, it was a safe bet that Foaly was two steps ahead.

Artemis donned the glasses, climbing into the vehicle's cabin. He had placed the call ten minutes ago. Presuming Foaly got working on a trace straight away, it could still be another two hours before the LEP could get an operative on the surface. That would make it almost five hours since Butler's heart had stopped. The record for a revival was two hours and fifty minutes for an Alpine skier frozen in an avalanche. There had never been a revival after three hours. Maybe there shouldn't be.

Artemis glanced at the tray of food sent out by Doctor Lane. Any other day he would have complained about virtually everything on the plate, but now the meal was simply sustenance to keep him awake until the cavalry arrived. Artemis took a long drink from a polystyrene cup of tea. It sloshed audibly around his empty stomach. Behind him, in the van's surgery, Butler's cryo unit hummed like a common household freezer. Occasionally the computer emitted electronic beeps and whirrs as the machine ran self-diagnostics. Artemis was reminded of the weeks spent in Helsinki waiting for his father to regain consciousness. Waiting to see what the fairy magic would do to him …

Excerpt from Artemis Fowl's diary. Disk 2. Encrypted.

Today my father spoke to me. For the first time in over two years I heard his voice, and it is exactly as I remembered it. But not everything was the same.

It had been over two months since Holly Short used her healing magic on his battered body, and still he lay in his Helsinki hospital bed. Immobile, unresponsive. The doctors could not understand it.

'He should be awake,' they informed me. 'His brainwaves are strong, exceptionally so. And his heart beats like a horse. It is incredible; this man should be at death's door, yet he has the muscle tone of a twenty-year-old.'

Of course, it is no mystery to me. Holly's magic has overhauled my father's entire being, with the exception of his left leg, which was lost when his ship went down off the coast of Murmansk. He has received an infusion of life, body and mind.

The effect of the magic on his body does not worry me, but I cannot help but wonder what effect this positive energy will have on my father's mind. For my father, a change like this could be traumatic. He is the Fowl patriarch, and his life revolves around moneymaking.

For sixteen days we sat in my father's hospital room, waiting for some sign of life. I had, by then, learned to read the instruments and noticed immediately the morning that my father's brainwaves began spiking. My diagnosis was that he would soon regain consciousness, and so I called the nurse.

We were ushered from the room to admit a medical team of at least a dozen. Two heart specialists, an anaesthetist, a brain surgeon, a psychologist and several nurses.

In fact, my father had no need of medical attention. He simply sat up, rubbed his eyes and uttered one word: 'Angeline'.

Mother was admitted. Butler, Juliet and I were forced to wait for several more agonizing minutes until she reappeared at the door.

'Come in, everyone,' she said. 'He wants to see you.'

And suddenly I was afraid. My father, the man whose shoes I had been trying to fill for two years, was awake. Would he still live up to my expectations? Would I live up to his?

I entered hesitantly. Artemis Fowl the First was propped up by several pillows. The first thing that I noticed was his face. Not the scar traces — which were already almost completely healed, but the expression. My father's brow, usually a thunderhead of moody contemplation, was smooth and carefree.

After such a long time apart, I didn't know what to say.

My father had no such doubts.

'Arty,' he cried, stretching his arms towards me. 'You're a man now. A young man.'

I ran into his embrace, and while he held me close all plots and schemes were forgotten. I had a father again.

Ice Age Cryogenics Institute, London

Artemis's memories were interrupted by a sly movement on the wall above. He peered out the rear window and fixed his gaze on the spot, watching through filtered eyes. There was a fairy crouching on a third-storey window sill: a Recon officer, complete with wings and helmet. After only fifteen minutes! His ruse had worked. Foaly had intercepted the call and sent someone to investigate. Now all that remained was to hope this particular fairy was full to the brim with magic and willing to help.

This had to be handled sensitively. The last thing he wanted to do was spook the Recon officer. One wrong move and he'd wake up in six hours, with absolutely no recollection of the day's events. And that would be fatal for Butler.

Artemis opened the van door slowly, stepping down into the yard. The fairy cocked its head, following his movements. To his dismay, Artemis saw the creature draw a platinum handgun.

'Don't shoot,' said Artemis, raising his hands. 'I am unarmed. And I need your help.'

The fairy activated its wings, descending slowly until its visor was level with Artemis's eyes.

'Do not be alarmed,' continued Artemis. 'I am a friend to the People. I helped to defeat the B'wa Kell. My name is –'

The fairy unshielded, her opaque visor sliding up.

'I know what your name is, Artemis,' said Captain Holly Short.

'Holly,' said Artemis, grasping her by the shoulders. 'It's you.'

Holly shrugged off the human's hands. 'I know it's me. What's going on here? I presume you made the call?'

'Yes, yes. No time for that now. I can explain later.'

Holly opened the throttle on her wings, rising to a height of four metres.

'No, Artemis. I want an explanation now. If you needed help, why didn't you call on your own phone?'

Artemis forced himself to answer the question.

'You told me that Foaly had pulled surveillance on my communications, and anyway I wasn't sure you'd come.'

Holly considered it.

'OK. Maybe I wouldn't have.' Then she noticed. 'Where's Butler? Watching our backs as usual, I suppose.'

Artemis didn't answer, but his expression told Holly exactly why the Mud Boy had summoned her.

Artemis pressed a button, and a pneumatic pump opened the cryo pod's lid. Butler lay inside, encased in a centimetre of ice.

'Oh no,' sighed Holly. 'What happened?'

'He stopped a bullet that was meant for me,' replied Artemis.

'When are you going to learn, Mud Boy?' snapped the fairy. 'Your little schemes have a tendency to get people hurt. Usually the people who care about you.'

Artemis didn't answer. The truth was the truth after all.

Holly peeled away a cold pack from the bodyguard's chest.

'How long?'

Artemis consulted the clock on his mobile phone.

'Three hours. Give or take a few minutes.'

Captain Short wiped away the ice, laying her hand flat on Butler's chest.

'Three hours. I don't know, Artemis. There's nothing here. Not a flicker.'

Artemis faced her across the cryo pod.

'Can you do it, Holly? Can you heal him?'

Holly stepped back. 'Me? I can't heal him. We need a professional warlock to even attempt something like this.'

'But you healed my father.'

'That was different. Your father wasn't dead. He wasn't even critical. I hate to say it, but Butler is gone. Long gone.'

Artemis pulled a gold medallion from a leather thong around his neck. The disc was perforated by a single circular hole. Dead centre.

'Remember this? You gave it to me for ensuring your trigger finger got reattached to your hand. You said it would remind me of the spark of decency inside me. I'm trying to do something decent now, Captain.'

'It's not a question of decency. It just can't be done.'

Artemis drummed his fingers on the trolley. Thinking.

'I want to talk to Foaly,' he said finally.

'I speak for the People, Fowl,' said Holly testily. 'We don't take orders from humans.'

'Please, Holly,' said Artemis. 'I can't just let him go. It's Butler.'

Holly couldn't help herself. After all, Butler had saved all their hides on more than one occasion.

'Very well,' she said, fishing a spare com set from her belt. 'But he's not going to have any good news for you.'

Artemis hooked the speaker over one ear, adjusting the mike stem so it wound across his mouth.

'Foaly? Are you listening?'

'Are you kidding?' came the reply. 'This is better than human soap operas.'

Artemis composed himself. He would have to present a convincing case or Butler's last chance was gone.

'All I want is a healing. I accept that it may not work, but what does it cost to try?'

'It's not that straightforward, Mud Boy,' replied the centaur. 'Healing isn't a simple process. It requires talent and concentration. Holly is pretty good, I grant you, but for something like this we need a trained team of warlocks.'

'There's no time,' snapped Artemis. 'Butler has already been under too long. This has to be done now, before the glucose is absorbed into his bloodstream. There is already tissue damage to the fingers.'

'Maybe his brain too?' suggested the centaur.

'No. I got his temperature down in minutes. The cranium has been frozen since the incident.'

'Are you sure about that? We don't want to bring Butler's body back and not his mind.'

'I'm sure. The brain is fine.'

Foaly didn't speak for several moments.

'Artemis, if we agree to try this, I have no idea what the results would be. The effect on Butler's body could be catastrophic, not to mention his mind. An operation of this kind has never been attempted on a human.'

'I understand.'

'Do you, Artemis? Do you really? Are you prepared to accept the consequences of this healing? There could be any number of unforeseeable problems. Whatever emerges from this pod is yours to care for. Will you accept this responsibility?'

'I will,' said Artemis, without hesitation.

'Very well, then it's Holly's decision. Nobody can force her to use her magic – it's up to her.'

Artemis lowered his eyes. He could not bring himself to look at the LEP elf.

'Well, Holly. Will you do it? Will you try?'

Holly brushed the ice from Butler's brow. He had been a good friend to the People.

'I'll try,' she said. 'No guarantees, but I'll do what I can.'

Artemis's knees almost buckled with relief. Then he was in control again. Time enough for weak knees later.

'Thank you, Captain. I realize this could not be an easy decision to take. Now, what can I do?'

Holly pointed to the rear doors. 'You can get out. I need a sterile environment. I'll come and get you when it's over. And whatever happens, whatever you hear, don't come in until I call.'

Holly unclipped her helmet camera, suspending it from the cryo pod's lid to give Foaly a better view of the patient.

'How's that?'

'Good,' replied Foaly. 'I can see the whole upper body. Cryogenics. That Fowl is a genius, for a human. Do you realize that he had less than a minute to come up with this plan? That's one smart Mud Boy.'

Holly scrubbed her hands thoroughly in the medi-sink.

'Not smart enough to keep himself out of trouble. I can't believe I'm doing this. A three-hour healing. This has got to be a first.'

'Technically it's only a two-minute healing, if he got the brain down to below zero straight away. But ...'

'But what?' asked Holly, rubbing her fingers briskly with a towel.

'But the freezing interferes with the body's own bio-rhythms and magnetic fields – things even the People don't understand fully. There's more than skin and bone at stake here. We have no idea what a trauma like this could do to Butler.'

Holly stuck her head under the camera.

'Are you sure this is a good idea, Foaly?'

'I wish we had time for discussion, Holly, but every second costs our old friend a couple of brain cells. I'm going to talk you through it. The first thing we need to do is to take a look at the wound.'

Holly peeled off several cold packs, unzipping the foil suit. The entry wound was small and black, hidden in the centre of a pool of blood, like a flower's bud.

'He never had a chance. Right under the heart. I'm going to zoom in.'

Holly closed her visor, using the helmet's filters to magnify Butler's wound.

'There are fibres trapped in there. Kevlar, I'd say.'

Foaly groaned over the speakers. 'That's all we need. Complications.'

'What difference do fibres make? And this really is not the time for jargon. I need plain Gnommish.'

'OK. Surgery for morons it is. If you poke your fingers into that wound, the magic will reproduce Butler's cells, complete with their new strands of Kevlar. He'll be dead, but completely bulletproof.'

Holly could feel the tension creeping up her back.

'So, I need to do what?'

'You need to make a new wound, and let the magic spread from there.'

Oh great, thought Holly, a new wound. Just slice open an old friend.

'But he's as hard as rock.'

'Well then, you're going to have to melt him down a little. Use your Neutrino 2000, low setting, but not too much. If that brain wakes up before we want it to, he's finished.'

Holly drew her Neutrino, adjusting the output to minimum.

'Where do you suggest I melt?'

'The other pectoral. Be ready to heal; that heat is going to spread rapidly. Butler needs to be healed before oxygen gets to his brain.'

Holly pointed the laser at the bodyguard's chest.

'Just say the word.'

'In a bit closer. Fifteen centimetres approximately. A two-second burst.'

Holly raised her visor, taking several deep breaths. A Neutrino 2000 being used as a medical instrument. Who would have thought it?

Holly pulled her trigger to the first click. One more click would activate the laser.

'Two seconds.'

'OK. Go.'

Click. An orange beam of concentrated heat spilled from the Neutrino's snout, blossoming across Butler's chest. Had the bodyguard been awake, he would have been knocked unconscious. A neat circle of ice evaporated, rising to condense on the surgery's ceiling.

'Now,' said Foaly, his voice high-pitched with urgency. 'Narrow the beam and focus it.'

Holly manipulated the gun controls expertly with her thumb. Narrowing the beam would intensify its power, but the laser would have to be focused at a certain range to avoid slicing right through Butler's body.

'I'm setting it for fifteen centimetres.'

'Good, but hurry; that heat is spreading.'

The colour had returned to Butler's chest and the ice was melting across his body. Holly pulled the trigger again, this time carving a crescent-shaped slit in Butler's flesh. A single drop of blood oozed from between the wound's edges.

'No steady flow,' said Foaly. 'That's good.'

Holly holstered her weapon. 'Now what?'

'Now get your hands in deep, and give it every drop of magic you've got. Don't just let it flow; push the magic out.'

᛫᛫᛫᛫᛫᛫᛫᛫᛫᛫᛫᛫

Holly grimaced. She never liked this bit. No matter how many healings she performed, she could never get used to sticking her fingers into other people's insides. She lined her thumbs up, back to back, and slid them into the incision.

'Heal,' she breathed, and the magic scurried down her fingers. Blue sparks hovered over Butler's wound, then disappeared inside, like shooting stars diving behind the horizon.

'More, Holly,' urged Foaly. 'Another shot.'

Holly pushed again, harder. The flow was thick at first, a roiling mass of blue streaks; then, as her magic ebbed, the flow grew weaker.

'That's it,' she panted. 'I have barely enough left to shield on the way home.'

'Well then,' said Foaly, 'stand back until I tell you, because all hell is about to break loose.'

Holly backed up to the wall. Nothing much happened for several moments, then Butler's back arched, throwing his chest into the air. Holly heard a couple of vertebrae groaning.

'That's the heart started,' noted Foaly. 'The easy bit.'

Butler flopped back into the pod, blood flowing from his most recent wound. The magical sparks knitted together, forming a vibrating lattice over the bodyguard's torso. Butler bounced on the trolley, like a bead in a rattle, as the magic reshaped his atoms. His pores vented mist as toxins were expelled from his system. The coating of ice around him dissolved instantly, causing clouds of steam and then rain, as the water particles condensed on the metal ceiling. Cold packs popped like balloons, sending crystals ricocheting around the surgery. It was like being in the centre of a multicoloured storm.

'You need to get in there now!' said Foaly in Holly's ear.

'What?'

'Get in there. The magic is spreading up his spinal column. Hold his head still for the healing, or any damaged cells could be replicated. And once something's been healed, we can't undo it.'

Great, thought Holly. Hold Butler still. No problem. She battled her way through the debris, cold-pack crystals impacting against her visor.

The human's frame continued thrashing in the cryo pod, shrouded by a cloud of steam.

Holly clamped a hand on either side of Butler's head. The vibrations travelled the length of her arms and through her body.

'Hold him, Holly. Hold him!'

Holly leaned across the pod, placing the weight of her body on the manservant's head. In all the confusion, she couldn't tell if her efforts were having any effect whatsoever.

'Here it comes!' said Foaly in her ear. 'Brace yourself!'

)I⊷•⊗▢⟐⍵•⌐⏧⥾•⊙⍵•⅄⏉⏁⍵⊗•

The magical lattice spread along Butler's neck and across his face. Blue sparks targeted the eyes, travelling along the optic nerve, into the brain itself. Butler's eyes flew open, rolling in their sockets. His mouth was reactivated too, spewing out long strings of words in various languages, none of which made any sense.

'His brain is running tests,' said Foaly. 'Just to check everything's working.'

Each muscle and joint was tested to its limit, rolling, swivelling and stretching. Hair follicles grew at an accelerated rate, covering Butler's normally shaven dome with a thick growth of hair. Nails shot out of his fingers like tiger claws, and a raggedy beard snaked from his chin.

Holly could only hang on. She imagined that this was how it must feel to be a rodeo cowboy straddling a particularly bad-tempered bull.

Eventually the sparks dissipated, spiralling into the air like embers on a breeze. Butler calmed and settled, his body sinking into fifteen centimetres of water and coolant. His breathing was slow and deep.

'We did it,' said Holly, sliding off the pod on to her knees. 'He's alive.'

'Don't start celebrating just yet,' said Foaly. 'There's still a long way to go. He won't regain consciousness for a couple of days at least, and even then who knows what shape his mind will be in. And, of course, there's the obvious problem.'

Holly raised her visor. 'What obvious problem?'

'See for yourself.'

Captain Short was almost afraid to look at whatever lay in the pod. Grotesque images crowded her imagination. What kind of misshapen mutant human had they created?

The first thing she noticed was Butler's chest. The bullet hole itself had completely disappeared, but the skin had darkened, with a red line amongst the black. It looked like a capital 'I'.

'Kevlar,' explained Foaly. 'Some of it must have replicated. Not enough to kill him, thankfully, but enough to slow down his breathing. Butler won't be running any marathons with those fibres clinging to his ribs.'

'What's the red line?'

'At a guess, I'd say dye. There must have been writing on the original bulletproof jacket.'

Holly glanced around the surgery. Butler's vest lay discarded in a corner. The letters 'FBI' were printed in red across the chest. There was a small hole in the centre of the 'I'.

'Ah well,' said the centaur. 'It's a small price to pay for his life. He can pretend it's a tattoo. They're very popular among the Mud People these days.'

Holly had been hoping the Kevlar-reinforced skin was the 'obvious problem' to which Foaly had been referring. But there was something else. The something else became immediately apparent when her gaze landed on the bodyguard's face. Or, more accurately, the hair sprouting from his face.

'Oh gods,' she breathed. 'Artemis is not going to like this.'

Artemis paced the yard while his bodyguard underwent magical surgery. Now that his plan was actually in progress, doubts began to chew at the edges of his mind, like slugs on a leaf. Was this the right thing to do? What if Butler wasn't himself? After all, his father had been undeniably different on the day he had finally come back to them. He would never forget that first conversation …

Excerpt from Artemis Fowl's diary. Disk 2. Encrypted.

The doctors in Helsinki were determined that they should pump my father full of vitamin supplements. He was just as determined that they shouldn't. And a determined Fowl usually gets his way.

'I am perfectly fine,' he insisted. 'Please allow me some time to reacquaint myself with my family.'

The doctors withdrew, disarmed by his personality. I was surprised by this approach. Charm had never been my father's weapon of choice. He had previously achieved his aims by bulldozing over anybody stupid enough to stand in his way.

Father was sitting in the hospital room's only armchair, his shortened leg resting on a footstool. My mother was perched on the armrest, resplendent in white faux fur.

Father caught me looking at his leg.

'Don't worry, Arty,' he said. 'I'm being measured for a prosthetic tomorrow. Doctor Hermann Gruber is being flown in from Dortmund.'

I had heard of Gruber. He worked with the German Paralympics squad. The best.

'I'm going to ask for something sporty. Maybe with speed stripes.'

A joke. That wasn't like my father.

My mother ruffled my father's hair.

'Stop teasing, darling. This is difficult for Arty, you know. He was only a baby when you left.'

'Hardly a baby, Mother,' I said. 'I was eleven, after all.'

My father smiled at me fondly. Perhaps now would be an appropriate time for us to talk, before his good mood wore off to be replaced by the usual gruffness?

'Father, things have changed since your disappearance. I have changed.'

Father nodded solemnly. 'Yes, you are right. We need to talk about the business.'

Ah yes. Back to business. This was the father I remembered.

'I think you will find that the family bank accounts are healthy, and I trust you will approve of the stocks portfolio. It has yielded an eighteen per cent dividend in the past financial year. Eighteen per cent is quite exemplary in the current market; I haven't failed you.'

⚛ ✴ ⚙ Ʊ ⊕ • ☉ ↻ • ⊗ ⚛ • ⏚ ⧖ ⊅ ⟩∣ • ⬡ ⊕ • ⊕ ◻ •

'I have failed you, son,' said Artemis Senior, 'if you think bank accounts and stocks are all that's important. You must have learned that from me.' He pulled me close to him. 'I haven't been the perfect father, Arty, far from it. Too busy with the family business. I was always taught that it was my duty to manage the Fowl empire. A criminal empire, as we both know. If any good has come out of my abduction, it's that I have reassessed my priorities. I want a new life for us all.'

I could not believe what I was hearing. One of my most persistent memories was of Father repeatedly quoting the family motto, 'aurum potestas est' — 'Gold is power'. And now, here he was, turning his back on Fowl principles. What had the magic done to him?

'Gold isn't all-important, Arty,' he continued. 'Neither is power. We have everything we need right here. The three of us.'

I was utterly surprised. But not unpleasantly so.

'But, Father. You have always said ... This isn't you. You're a new man.'

Mother joined the conversation. 'No, Arty. Not a new man. An old one. The one I fell in love with and married, before the Fowl empire took over. And now I have him back; we're a family again.'

I looked at my parents — how happy they were together. A family? Was it possible that the Fowls could be a normal family?

Artemis was yanked back to the present by a commotion from inside the Ice Age mobile unit. The vehicle began to rock on its axles, blue light crackling from beneath the door.

Artemis did not panic. He had seen healings before. Last year, when Holly reattached her index finger, the magical fallout had shattered half a ton of ice – and that was for one little finger. Imagine the damage Butler's system could do repairing a critical injury.

The pandemonium continued for several minutes, popping two of the van's tyres, and completely wrecking the suspension. Luckily the institute was locked up for the night or Doctor Lane would certainly be adding automobile repairs to her bill.

Eventually the magical storm subsided, and the vehicle settled like a rollercoaster car after the ride. Holly opened the rear door, leaning heavily against the frame. She was exhausted, drained. A sickly pallor glowed through her coffee complexion.

'Well?' demanded Artemis. 'Is he alive?'

Holly didn't answer. A strenuous healing often resulted in nausea and fatigue. Captain Short took several deep breaths, resting on the rear bumper.

'Is he alive?' repeated the youth.

Holly nodded. 'Alive. Yes, he's alive. But …'

'But what, Holly? Tell me!'

Holly tugged off her helmet. It slipped from her fingers, rolling across the yard.

'I'm sorry, Artemis. I did the best I could.'

It was possibly the worst thing she could have said.

*

Artemis climbed into the van. The floor was slick with water and coloured crystals. Smoke leaked from the fractured grille of the air-conditioning system, and the overhead neon strip flickered like lightning in a bottle.

The cryo pod lay off-kilter in one corner, its gyroscopes leaking fluid. One of Butler's arms flopped over the unit's edge, throwing a monster shadow on the wall.

The cryo pod's instruments panel was still operating. Artemis was relieved to see the heartbeat icon blipping gently in the display. Butler was alive! Holly had done it again! But something had been worrying the fairy captain. There was a problem.

As soon as Artemis looked inside the pod it became immediately apparent what that problem was. The manservant's newly grown hair was heavily streaked with grey: Butler had gone into the cryo chamber forty years of age; the man before Artemis now was at least fifty. Possibly older. In the space of just over three hours Butler had grown old.

Holly appeared at Artemis's shoulder.

'He's alive at least,' said the fairy.

Artemis nodded. 'When will he wake up?'

'A couple of days. Maybe.'

'How did this happen?' asked the boy, brushing a lock of hair from Butler's brow.

Holly shrugged. 'I'm not exactly sure. That's Foaly's area.'

Artemis took the spare com set from his pocket, hooking the speaker wire over his ear.

'Any theories, Foaly?'

'I can't be sure,' the centaur replied. 'But I'm guessing that Holly's magic wasn't enough. Some of Butler's own life force was needed for the healing. About fifteen years' worth by the looks of it.'

'Can anything be done?'

'Afraid not. A healing can't be undone. If it's any consolation, he'll probably live longer than he would have done naturally. But there's no reclaiming his youth and, what's more, we can't be sure about the state of his mind. The healing could have wiped his brain cleaner than a magnetized disk.'

Artemis sighed deeply. 'What have I done to you, old friend?'

'No time for that,' said Holly briskly. 'You should both get out of here. I'm sure all the commotion will have attracted attention. Do you have transport?'

'No. We flew over on a public flight. Then took a taxi from Heathrow.'

Holly shrugged. 'I'd like to help, Artemis, but I've already given up enough time here. I'm on a mission. An extremely important mission and I have to get back to it.'

Artemis stepped away from the cryo unit.

'Holly, about your mission ...'

Captain Short turned slowly.

'Artemis ...'

'You were probed, weren't you? Something got past Foaly's defences?'

Holly pulled a large sheet of camouflage foil from her surveillance backpack.

'We need to go somewhere to talk. Somewhere private.'

The following forty-five minutes were something of a blur for Artemis. Holly wrapped both humans in the camouflage foil and clipped them on to her Moonbelt. The belt effectively reduced their weight to one fifth of the Earth's norm.

Even then it was a struggle for her mechanical wings to hoist the three of them into the night sky. Holly had to open the throttle wide just to bring them five hundred feet above sea level.

'I'm going to shield now,' she said into her mike. 'Try not to thrash about too much. I don't want to have to cut one of you loose.'

Then she was gone, and in her place hovered a slightly shimmering, Holly-shaped patch of stars. The vibrations rattled through the belt links, shaking Artemis's teeth in his head. He felt like a bug in a cocoon, trussed up in foil, with only his face exposed to the night air. Initially, the experience was almost enjoyable, riding high above the city, watching the cars flicker along the motorways. Then Holly picked up a westerly wind and threw them into the air currents over the sea.

Suddenly Artemis's universe was a maelstrom of cutting winds, buffeting passengers and startled birds. Beside him, Butler hung limply in his makeshift foil truss. The foil absorbed the local colours, reflecting the dominant hues. It was by no means a perfect recreation of the surroundings, but certainly good enough for a night flight over the sea to Ireland.

'Is this foil invisible to radar?' said Artemis into the headset. 'I don't want to be mistaken for a UFO by some eager Harrier jump-jet pilot.'

Holly considered it. 'You're right. Maybe I should take us down a bit, just in case.'

Two seconds later, Artemis deeply regretted breaking radio silence: Holly tilted her wing rig into a steep dive, sending the three of them hurtling towards the midnight waves below. She pulled up at the last moment, when Artemis could have sworn the skin was about to peel away from his face.

'Low enough for you?' asked Holly, with the barest hint of humour in her voice.

They skimmed the wave tops, spray sparking against the camouflage foil. The ocean was rough that night, and Holly followed the water patterns, dipping and climbing to match the swell's curve. A school of humpbacked whales sensed their presence and broke through the storm foam, leaping fully thirty metres across a trough before disappearing beneath the black water. There were no dolphins. The small mammals were taking shelter from the elements in the inlets and coves along the Irish coast.

Holly skirted the hull of a passenger ferry, flying close enough to feel the engine's pulse. On deck, scores of passengers vomited over the railings, narrowly missing the invisible travellers below.

'Charming,' muttered Artemis.

'Don't worry,' said Holly's voice, out of thin air. 'Almost there.'

They passed Rosslare's ferry terminal, following the coastline northwards, over the Wicklow mountains. Even in his disorientated state, Artemis could not help but marvel at their speed. Those wings were a fantastic invention. Imagine the money that could be made for a patent like that. Artemis stopped himself. Selling fairy technology was what had got Butler hurt in the first place.

They slowed sufficiently for Artemis to make out individual landmarks. Dublin squatted to the east, an aura of yellow light buzzing over its highway system. Holly skirted the city, heading for the less populated north of the county. In the centre of a large dark patch sat a single building, painted white by external spotlights: Artemis's ancestral home, Fowl Manor.

꧁口ᚨ꠨·ᚨ·꧁⊕◔ᚽᗜᏕᗜᏔ꠨·ᏕᗜᑐᎥᚩ·

Fowl Manor, Dublin, Ireland

'Now, explain yourself,' said Holly, once they had floated Butler safely to bed.

She sat on the great stairway's bottom step. Generations of Fowls glared down at her from oil portraits on the walls. The LEP captain activated her helmet mike and switched it to loudspeaker.

'Foaly, record this, would you? I have a feeling we're going to want to hear it again.'

'This entire incident began at a business meeting this afternoon,' began Artemis.

'Go on.'

'I was meeting Jon Spiro, an American industrialist.'

Holly heard keys being tapped in her ear. Undoubtedly Foaly was running a background check on this Spiro character.

'Jon Spiro,' said the centaur, almost immediately. 'A shady character, even by human standards. Mud Man security agencies have been trying to put this guy away for thirty years. His companies are eco-disasters. And that's only the tip of the iceberg: industrial espionage, abduction, blackmail, mob connections. You name it, he's gotten away with it.'

'That's the chap,' said Artemis. 'So, I set up a rendezvous with Mister Spiro.'

'What were you selling?' interrupted Foaly. 'A man

like Spiro doesn't cross the Atlantic for tea and muffins.'

Artemis frowned. 'I wasn't actually selling him anything. But I did offer to suppress some revolutionary technology, for a price, of course.'

Foaly's voice was cold: 'What revolutionary technology?'

Artemis hesitated for a beat. 'Do you remember those helmets Butler took from the Retrieval squad?'

Holly groaned. 'Oh no.'

'I deactivated the helmets' auto-destruct mechanisms and constructed a cube from the sensors and chips: the C Cube, a mini-computer. It was a simple matter to install a fibre-optic blocker so that you couldn't take control of the Cube if you detected it.'

'You gave fairy technology to a man like Jon Spiro?'

'I quite obviously didn't give it to him,' snapped Artemis. 'He took it.'

Holly pointed a finger at the youth. 'Don't bother playing the victim, Artemis. It doesn't suit you. What did you think? That Jon Spiro was going to walk away from technology that could make him the richest man on the face of the planet?'

'So it was your computer that pinged us?' said Foaly.

'Yes,' admitted Artemis. 'Unintentionally. Spiro asked for a surveillance scan, and the Cube's fairy circuits picked up LEP satellite beams.'

'Can't we block any future probes?' asked the LEP captain.

'Haven's deflectors will be useless against our own technology. Sooner or later, Spiro will find out about the People. And if that happens, I can't see a man like him just allowing us to live in harmony.'

Holly glared pointedly at Artemis.

'Remind you of anyone?'

'I am nothing like Jon Spiro,' objected the boy. 'He's a cold-blooded killer!'

'Give yourself a few years,' said Holly. 'You'll get there.'

Foaly sighed. Put Artemis Fowl and Holly Short together in a room and sooner or later there was bound to be a row.

'OK, Holly,' said the centaur. 'Let's try to act like professionals. Step one is to call off the lockdown. Our next priority is to retrieve the Cube before Spiro can unlock its secrets.'

'We do have some time,' said Artemis. 'The Cube is encrypted.'

'How encrypted?'

'I built an Eternity Code into its hard drive.'

'An Eternity Code,' said Foaly. 'I'm impressed.'

'It wasn't that difficult. I invented an entirely new base language, so Spiro will have no frame of reference.'

Holly was feeling a bit left out. 'And how long will it take to crack this Eternity Code?'

Artemis couldn't resist raising an eyebrow.

'Eternity,' he said. 'In theory, but with Spiro's resources, quite a bit less.'

Holly ignored the tone. 'OK then, we're safe. No need to go hunting Spiro if all he has is a box of useless circuits.'

'Far from useless,' countered Artemis. 'The chip design alone will lead his research and development team in interesting directions. But you are right about one thing, Holly, there is no need to go hunting Spiro. Once he realizes that I am still alive, he will come looking for me. After all, I am the only one who can unlock the full potential of the C Cube.'

Holly dropped her head into her hands. 'So, any moment now a team of hit men could come blasting in here, looking for the key to your Eternity Code. It's at times like these we could do with someone like Butler.'

Artemis plucked the wall phone from its cradle.

'There's more than one Butler in the family,' he said.

CHAPTER 4: RUNNING IN THE FAMILY

 FOR her eighteenth birthday, Juliet Butler asked for, and received, a ribbed Judo crash vest, two weighted throwing knives and a World Wrestling Grudge Match video – items that did not generally feature on the average teenage girl's wish list. Then again, Juliet Butler was not the average teenage girl.

Juliet was extraordinary in many ways. For one thing, she could hit a moving target with any weapon you cared to name and, for another, she could throw most people a lot further than she trusted them.

Of course, she didn't learn all of this watching wrestling videos. Juliet's training began at age four. After kindergarten each day, Domovoi Butler would escort his little sister to the Fowl Estate dojo, where he instructed her in the various forms of martial arts. By the time she was eight, Juliet was a third dan black belt in seven disciplines. By eleven years of age, she was beyond belts.

Traditionally, all Butler males enrolled in Madame Ko's Personal Protection Academy on their tenth birthday, spending six months of every year learning the bodyguard's craft, and the other six guarding a low-risk principal. The female Butlers generally went into the service of various wealthy families around the world. However, Juliet decided she would combine both roles, spending half the year with Angeline Fowl, and the other half honing her martial arts skills in Madame Ko's camp. She was the first Butler female to enrol in the Academy, and only the fifth female ever to make it past the physical exam. The camp was never located in the same country for more than five years. Butler had done his training in Switzerland and Israel, but his younger sister received her instruction in the Utsukushigahara Highlands in Japan.

Madame Ko's dormitory was a far cry from the luxurious accommodation in Fowl Manor. In Japan, Juliet slept on a straw mat, owned nothing apart from two rough cotton robes, and consumed only rice, fish and protein shakes.

The day began at five thirty when Juliet and the other acolytes ran four miles to the nearest stream, catching fish with their bare hands. Having cooked and presented the fish to their sensei, the acolytes strapped empty twenty-gallon barrels to their backs and climbed to the snowline. When their barrel was filled with snow the acolyte would roll it back to base camp, and then pound the snow with bare feet until it melted and could be used by the sensei to bathe. Then the day's training could begin.

Lessons included *Cos Ta'pa*, a martial art developed by Madame Ko herself, specially tailored for bodyguards, whose primary aim was not self-defence, but defence of the principal. Acolytes also studied advanced weaponry, information technology, vehicular maintenance and hostage-negotiation techniques.

By her eighteenth birthday, Juliet could break down and reassemble ninety per cent of the world's production weapons blindfolded, operate any vehicle, do her make-up in under four minutes and, in spite of her stunning Asian and European gene mix, blend into any crowd like a native. Her big brother was very proud.

The final step in her training was a field simulation in a foreign environment. If she passed this test, Madame Ko would have Juliet's shoulder marked with a blue diamond tattoo. The tattoo, identical to the one on Butler's shoulder, symbolized not only the graduate's toughness, but also the multifaceted nature of his or her training. In personal protection circles, a bodyguard bearing the blue diamond needed no further reference.

Madame Ko had chosen the city of Sfax in Tunisia for Juliet's final assessment. Her mission was to guide the principal through the city's tumultuous market or medina. Generally, a bodyguard would advise his principal against venturing into such a densely populated area, but Madame Ko pointed out that principals rarely listened to advice, and it was best to be prepared for every eventuality. And, as if Juliet wasn't under enough pressure, Madame Ko herself decided to act as surrogate principal.

It was exceptionally hot in North Africa. Juliet squinted through her wraparound sunglasses, concentrating on following the diminutive figure bobbing through the crowd before her.

'Hurry,' snapped Madame Ko. 'You will lose me.'

'In your dreams, Madame,' replied Juliet, unperturbed. Madame Ko was simply trying to distract her with conversation. And there were already enough distractions in the local environment. Gold hung in shimmering ropes from a dozen stalls; Tunisian rugs flapped from wooden frames, the perfect cover for an assassin. Locals pressed uncomfortably close, eager for a look at this attractive female, and the terrain was treacherous – one false step could lead to a twisted ankle and failure.

Juliet processed all this information automatically, factoring it into every move. She placed a firm hand on the chest of a teenager grinning at her, skipped over an oily puddle reflecting rainbow patterns and followed Madame Ko down yet another alley in the medina's endless maze.

Suddenly there was a man in her face. One of the market traders.

'I have good carpets,' he said in broken French. 'You come with me. I show you!'

Madame Ko kept going. Juliet attempted to follow her, but the man blocked her path.

'No, thank you. I am so not interested. I live outdoors.'

'Very funny, *mademoiselle*. You make good joke. Now come and see Ahmed's carpets.'

The crowd began to take notice, swirling to face her, like the tendrils of a giant organism. Madame Ko was moving further away. She was losing the principal.

'I said no. Now back off, Mister Carpet Man. Don't make me break a nail.'

The Tunisian was unaccustomed to taking orders from a female, and now his friends were watching.

'I give good bargain,' he persisted, pointing at his stall. 'Best rugs in Sfax.'

Juliet dodged to one side, but the crowd moved to cut her off.

It was at this point that Ahmed lost any sympathy that Juliet might have had for him. Up to now, he had simply been an innocent local in the wrong place at the wrong time. But now ...

'Let's go,' said the Tunisian, wrapping an arm around the blonde girl's waist. Not an idea that would make it on to his top ten of good ideas.

'Oh, bad move, Carpet Man!'

Faster than the eye could blink, Ahmed was wrapped in the folds of a nearby carpet and Juliet was gone. Nobody had a clue what had happened until they replayed the incident on the screen of Kamal the chicken man's camcorder. In slo-mo, the traders saw the Eurasian girl hoist Ahmed by the throat and belt, and lob him bodily into a carpet stall. It was a move that one of the gold merchants recognized as a Slingshot, a manoeuvre made popular by the American wrestler Papa Hog. The traders laughed so much that several of them became dehydrated. It was the funniest thing to happen all year. The clip even won a prize on Tunisia's version of the *World's Funniest Videos*. Three weeks later, Ahmed moved to Egypt.

Back to Juliet. The bodyguard-in-training ran like a sprinter out of the blocks, dodging around stunned merchants and hanging a hard right down an alley. Madame Ko couldn't have gone far. She could still complete her assignment.

Juliet was furious with herself. This was exactly the kind of stunt her brother had warned her about.

'Watch out for Madame Ko,' Butler had advised. 'You never know what she'll cook up for a field assignment. I heard that she once stampeded a herd of elephants in Calcutta, just to distract an acolyte.'

The trouble was that you couldn't be sure. That carpet merchant might have been in Madame Ko's employ, or he might have been an innocent civilian, who happened to stick his nose in where it didn't belong.

The alley narrowed so that the human traffic ran single file. Makeshift clothes lines zigzagged at head height; *gutras* and *abayas* hung limp and steaming in the heat. Juliet ducked below the laundry, dodging around dawdling shoppers. Startled turkeys hopped as far out of the way as their string leads would allow.

And suddenly she was in a clearing. A dim square surrounded by three-storey houses. Men lounged on the upper balconies, puffing on fruit-flavoured water pipes. Underfoot was a priceless chipped mosaic, depicting a Roman bath scene.

In the centre of the square, lying with her knees hugged to her chest, was Madame Ko. She was being assaulted by three men. These were no local traders. All three wore special-forces black, and attacked with the assurance and accuracy of trained professionals. This was no test. These men were actually trying to kill her sensei.

Juliet was unarmed; this was one of the rules. To smuggle arms into the African country would automatically mean life imprisonment. Luckily, it seemed as though her adversaries were also without weapons, though hands and feet would certainly be sufficient for the job they had in mind.

Improvisation was the key to survival here. There was no point in attempting a straight assault. If these three had subdued Madame Ko, then they would be more than a match for her in regular combat. Time to try something a bit unorthodox.

Juliet leaped on the run, snagging a clothes line on her way past. The ring resisted for a second, then popped out of the dried plaster. The cable played out behind her, sagging with its load of rugs and headscarves. Juliet veered left as far as the line's other anchor would allow, and then swung round towards the men.

'Hey, boys!' she yelled, not from bravado, but because this would work better head on.

The men looked up just in time to get a faceful of sopping camel hair. The heavy rugs and garments wrapped themselves around their flailing limbs, and the nylon cable caught them below the chins. In under a second the three were down. And Juliet made certain they stayed down with pinches to the nerve clusters at the base of their necks.

'Madame Ko!' she cried, searching the laundry for her sensei. The old woman lay shuddering in an olive dress, a plain headscarf covering her face.

Juliet helped the woman to her feet.

'Did you see that move, Madame? I totally decked those morons. I bet they never saw anything like that before. Improvisation. Butler always says it's the key. You know, I think my eyeshadow distracted them. Glitter green. Never fails ...'

Juliet stopped talking because there was a knife at her throat. The knife was wielded by Madame Ko herself, who was in fact not Madame Ko, but some other tiny Oriental lady in an olive dress. A decoy.

'You are dead,' said the lady.

'Yes,' agreed Madame Ko, stepping from the shadows. 'And if you are dead, then the principal is dead. And you have failed.'

Juliet bowed low, joining her hands.

'That was a sly trick, Madame,' she said, trying to sound respectful.

Her sensei laughed. 'Of course. That is the way of life. What did you expect?'

'But those assassins; I completely kicked their b— ; I defeated them comprehensively.'

Madame Ko dismissed the claim with a wave. 'Luck. Fortunately for you, these were not assassins, but three graduates of the Academy. What was that nonsense with the wire?'

'It's a wrestling trick,' said Juliet. 'It's called the Clothes Line.'

'Unreliable,' said the Japanese lady. 'You succeeded because fortune was with you. Fortune is not enough in our business.'

'It wasn't my fault,' protested Juliet. 'There was this guy in the market. Totally in my face. I had to put him asleep for a while.'

Madame Ko tapped Juliet between the eyes. 'Quiet, girl. Think for once. What should you have done?'

Juliet bowed an inch lower. 'I should have incapacitated the merchant immediately.'

'Exactly. His life means nothing. Insignificant compared to the principal's safety.'

'I can't just kill innocent people,' protested Juliet.

Madame Ko sighed. 'I know, child. And that is why you are not ready. You have all the skill, but you lack focus and resolve. Perhaps next year.'

Juliet's heart plummeted. Her brother had earned the blue diamond at eighteen years of age. The youngest graduate in the Academy's history. She had been hoping to equal that feat. Now she would have to try again in twelve months. It was pointless to object any further. Madame Ko never reversed a decision.

A young woman in acolyte's robes emerged from the alley, holding a small briefcase.

'Madame,' she said, bowing. 'There is a call for you on the satellite phone.'

Madame Ko took the offered handset and listened intently for several moments.

'A message from Artemis Fowl,' she said eventually.

Juliet itched to straighten from her bow, but it would be an unforgivable breach of protocol.

'Yes, Madame?'

'The message is: Domovoi needs you.'

Juliet frowned. 'You mean Butler needs me.'

'No,' said Madame Ko, without a trace of emotion. 'I mean Domovoi needs you. I am just repeating what was told to me.'

And suddenly Juliet could feel the sun pounding on her neck, and she could hear the mosquitoes whining in her ears like dentist drills, and all she wanted to do was straighten up and run all the way to the airport. Butler would never have revealed his name to Artemis. Not unless … No, she couldn't believe it. She couldn't even allow herself to think it.

Madame Ko tapped her chin thoughtfully. 'You are not ready. I should not let you leave. You are too emotionally involved to be an effective bodyguard.'

'Please, Madame,' said Juliet.

Her sensei considered it for two long minutes.

'Very well,' she said. 'Go.'

Juliet was gone before the word finished echoing around the square, and heaven help any carpet merchant who blocked her path.

CHAPTER 5: THE METAL MAN AND THE MONKEY

THE SPIRO NEEDLE, CHICAGO, ILLINOIS, USA

 JON Spiro took the Concorde from Heathrow to O'Hare International Airport in Chicago. A stretch limousine ferried him downtown to the Spiro Needle, a sliver of steel and glass rising eighty-six storeys above the Chicago skyline. Spiro Industries was located on floors fifty through to eighty-five. The eighty-sixth floor was Spiro's personal residence, accessible either by private lift or helipad.

Jon Spiro hadn't slept for the entire journey, too excited by the little cube sitting in his briefcase. The head of his technical staff was equally excited when Spiro informed him what this harmless-looking box was capable of, and immediately scurried off to unravel the C Cube's secrets. Six hours later he scurried back to the conference room for a meeting.

'It's useless,' said the scientist, whose name was Doctor Pearson.

Spiro swirled an olive in his martini glass.

'I don't think so, Pearson,' he said. 'In fact, I know that little gizmo is anything but useless. I think that maybe you're the useless one in this equation.'

Spiro was in a terrible mood. Arno Blunt had just called to inform him of Fowl's survival. When Spiro was in a dark mood people had been known to disappear off the face of the earth, if they were lucky.

Pearson could feel the stare of the conference room's third occupant bouncing off his head. This was not a woman you wanted angry with you: Pearson knew that if Jon Spiro decided to have him thrown out the window, this particular individual would have no problem signing an affidavit swearing that he had jumped.

Pearson chose his words carefully. 'This device –'

'The C Cube. That's what it's called. I told you that, so use the name.'

'This C Cube undoubtedly has enormous potential. But it's encrypted.'

Spiro threw the olive at his head scientist. It was a humiliating experience for a Nobel Prize winner.

'So break the encryption. What do I pay you guys for?'

Pearson could feel his heart rate speeding up. 'It's not that simple. This code. It's unbreakable.'

'Let me get this straight,' said Spiro, leaning back in his ox-blood leather chair. 'I'm putting two hundred million a year into your department, and you can't break one lousy code, set up by a kid?'

Pearson was trying not to think about the sound his body would make hitting the pavement. His next sentence would save him or damn him.

'The Cube is voice-activated, and coded to Artemis Fowl's voice patterns. Nobody can break the code. It's not possible.'

Spiro did not respond; it was a signal to continue.

'I've heard of something like this. We scientists theorize about it. An Eternity Code, it's called. The code has millions of possible permutations and, not only that, it's based on an unknown language. It seems as though this boy has created a language that is spoken only by him. We don't even know how it corresponds to English. A code like this is not even supposed to exist. If Fowl is dead, then I'm sorry to say, Mister Spiro, the C Cube died with him.'

Jon Spiro stuck a cigar into the corner of his mouth. He did not light it. His doctors had forbidden it. Politely.

'And if Fowl were alive?'

Pearson knew a lifeline when it was being thrown to him.

'If Fowl were alive, he would be a lot easier to break than an Eternity Code.'

⌨🖥🖱 ▫🖱🐟 🐚🐟🐠🐟🐟 🐟🐟

'OK, Doc,' said Spiro. 'You're dismissed. You don't want to hear what's coming next.'

Pearson gathered his notes and hurried for the door. He tried not to look at the face of the woman at the table. If he didn't hear what came next, he could kid himself that his conscience was clear. And if he didn't actually see the woman at the conference table, then he couldn't pick her out of a line-up.

'It looks like we have a problem,' said Spiro to the woman in the dark suit.

The woman nodded. Everything she wore was black. Black power suit, black blouse, black stilettos. Even the Rado watch on her wrist was jet black.

'Yes. But it's my kind of problem.'

Carla Frazetti was god-daughter to Spatz Antonelli, who ran the downtown section of the Antonelli crime family. Carla operated as liaison between Spiro and Antonelli, possibly the two most powerful men in Chicago. Spiro had learned early in his career that businesses allied to the Mob tended to flourish.

Carla checked her manicured nails.

'It seems to me that you only have one option: you nab the Fowl kid and squeeze him for this code.'

Spiro sucked on his unlit cigar, thinking about it.

'It's not that straightforward. The kid runs a tight operation. Fowl Manor is like a fortress.'

Carla smiled. 'This is a thirteen-year-old kid we're talking about, right?'

'He'll be fourteen in six months,' said Spiro defensively. 'Anyway, there are complications.'

'Such as?'

'Arno is injured. Somehow Fowl blew his teeth out.'

'Ouch,' said Carla, wincing.

'He can't even stand in a breeze, never mind head up an operation.'

'That's a shame.'

'In fact, the kid incapacitated all my best people. They're on a dental plan too. It's going to cost me a fortune. No, I need some outside help on this one.'

'You want to contract the job to us?'

'Exactly. But it's got to be the right people. Ireland is an old-world kind of place. Wise guys are going to stick out a mile. I need guys who blend in and can persuade a kid to accompany them back here. Easy money.'

Carla winked. 'I read you, Mister Spiro.'

'So, you got guys like that? Guys who can take care of business without drawing attention to themselves?'

'The way I see it, you need a metal man and a monkey?'

Spiro nodded, familiar with Mob slang. A metal man carried the gun, and a monkey got into hard-to-reach places.

'We have two such men on our books. I can guarantee

they won't attract the wrong kind of attention in Ireland. But it won't be cheap.'

'Are they good?' asked Spiro.

Carla smiled. One of her incisors was inset with a tiny ruby.

'Oh, they're good,' she replied. 'These guys are the best.'

THE METAL MAN

THE INK BLOT TATTOO PARLOUR, DOWNTOWN CHICAGO

Loafers McGuire was having a tattoo done. A skull's head in the shape of the ace of spades. It was his own design and he was very proud of it. So proud, in fact, that he'd wanted the tattoo on his neck. Inky Burton, the tattooist, managed to change Loafers' mind, arguing that neck tattoos were better than a name tag when the cops wanted to ID a suspect. Loafers relented. 'OK,' he'd said. 'Put it on my forearm.'

Loafers had a tattoo done after every job. There wasn't much skin left on his body that still retained its original colour. That was how good Loafers McGuire was at his job.

Loafers' real name was Aloysius, and he hailed from

the Irish town of Kilkenny. He'd come up with the nickname Loafers himself, because he thought it sounded more Mob-like than Aloysius. All his life, Loafers had wanted to be a mobster, just like in the movies. When his efforts to start a Celtic mafia had failed Loafers came to Chicago.

The Chicago Mob welcomed him with open arms. Actually, one of their enforcers grabbed him in a bear-hug. Loafers sent the man and six of his buddies to the Mother of Mercy Hospital. Not bad for a guy five feet tall. Eight hours after stepping off the plane, Loafers was on the payroll.

And here he was, two years and several jobs later, already the organization's top metal man. His specialities were robbery and debt collection. Not the usual line of work for five-footers. But then, Loafers was not the usual five-footer.

Loafers leaned back in the tattooist's adjustable chair.

'You like the shoes, Inky?'

Inky blinked sweat from his eyes. You had to be careful with Loafers. Even the most innocent question could be a trap. One wrong answer and you could find yourself making your excuses to Saint Peter.

'Yeah. I like 'em. What are they called?'

'Loafers!' snapped the tiny gangster. 'Loafers, idiot. They're my trademark.'

'Oh yeah, loafers. I forgot. Cool, havin' a trademark.'

Loafers checked the progress on his arm.

'You ready with that needle yet?'

'Just ready,' replied Inky. 'I'm finished painting on the guidelines. I just gotta put in a fresh needle.'

'It's not gonna hurt, is it?'

Of course it is, moron, thought Inky. I'm sticking a needle in your arm.

But out loud he said, 'Not too much. I gave your arm a swab of anaesthetic.'

'It better not hurt,' warned Loafers. 'Or you'll be hurting shortly afterwards.'

Nobody threatened Inky except Loafers McGuire. Inky did all the Mob's tattoo work. He was the best in the state.

Carla Frazetti pushed through the door. Her black-suited elegance seemed out of place in the dingy establishment.

'Hello, boys,' she said.

'Hello, Miss Carla,' said Inky, blushing deeply. You didn't get too many ladies in the Ink Blot.

Loafers jumped to his feet. Even he respected the boss's god-daughter.

'Miss Frazetti. You could have beeped me. No need for you to come down to this dump.'

'No time for that. This is urgent. You leave straight away.'

'I'm leaving? Where am I going?'

'Ireland. Your Uncle Pat is sick.'

Loafers frowned.

'Uncle Pat? I don't have an Uncle Pat.'

Carla tapped the toe of one stiletto.

'He's sick, Loafers. Real sick, if you catch my drift.'

Loafers finally caught on.

'Oh, I get it. So I gotta pay him a visit.'

'That's it. That's exactly how sick he is.'

Loafers used a rag to clean the ink off his arm.

'OK, I'm ready. Are we going straight to the airport?'

Carla linked the tiny gangster.

'Soon, Loafers. But first we need to pick up your brother.'

'I don't have a brother,' protested Loafers.

'Of course you do. The one with the keys to Uncle Pat's house. He's a regular little monkey.'

'Oh,' said Loafers. 'That brother.'

Loafers and Carla took the limo out to the East Side. Loafers was still in awe of the sheer size of American buildings. In Kilkenny there was nothing over five storeys, and Loafers himself had lived all his life in a suburban bungalow. Not that he would ever admit that to his Mob friends. For their benefit he had reinvented himself as an orphan, who spent his youth in and out of various remand homes.

'Who's the monkey?' he asked.

Carla Frazetti was fixing her jet-black hair in a compact mirror. It was short and slicked back.

'A new guy. Mo Digence. He's Irish, like you. It makes things very convenient. No visas, no papers, no elaborate cover story. Just two short guys home for the holidays.'

Loafers bristled.

'What do you mean two short guys?'

Carla snapped the compact shut.

'Who are you talking to, McGuire? Because you couldn't be talking to me. Not in that tone.'

Loafers paled, his life flashing before him.

'I'm sorry, Miss Frazetti. It's just the short thing. I've been listening to it my whole life.'

'What do you want people to call you? Lofty? You're short, Loafers. Get over it. That's what gives you your edge. My godfather always says there's nothing more dangerous than a short guy with something to prove. That's why you've got a job.'

'I suppose.'

Carla patted him on the shoulder.

'Cheer up, Loafers. Compared to this guy, you're a regular giant.'

Loafers perked up considerably. 'Really? Just how short is Mo Digence?'

'He's short,' said Carla. 'I don't know the exact centimetres, but any shorter and I'd be changing his diaper and stuffing him in a stroller.'

Loafers grinned. He was going to enjoy this job.

THE MONKEY

Mo Digence had seen better days. Less than four months ago he had been living it up in a Los Angeles penthouse with over a million dollars in the bank. But now his funds had been frozen by the Criminal Assets Bureau and he was working for the Chicago Mob on a commission basis. Spatz Antonelli was not known for the generosity of his commissions. Of course, Mo could always leave Chicago and go back to LA, but there was a police task force there with his name on it, just waiting for him to return to the scene of the crime. In fact, there was no safe haven for Mo above ground or below it, because Mo Digence was actually Mulch Diggums, kleptomaniac dwarf and fugitive from the LEP.

Mulch was a tunnel dwarf, who decided that a life in the mines was not for him and put his mining talents to another use: namely, relieving Mud People of their valuables and selling them on the fairy black market. Of course, entering another's dwelling without permission meant forfeiting your magic, but Mulch didn't care. Dwarfs didn't have much power anyway, and casting spells had always made him nauseous.

Dwarfs have several physical features that make them ideal burglars. They can dislocate their jaws, ingesting several kilos of soil a second. It is stripped of any beneficial minerals, then ejected at the other end. They have also developed the ability to drink through their pores, an attribute that can be very handy during cave-ins. It also transforms the pores into living suction cups, a convenient tool in any burglar's arsenal. Finally, dwarf hair is actually a network of living antennae, similar to feline whiskers, which can do everything from trap beetles to bounce sonar waves off a tunnel wall.

Mulch had been a rising star in the fairy underworld – until Commander Julius Root got hold of his file. Since then, he had spent over three hundred years in and out of prison. He was currently on the run for stealing several gold bars from the Holly Short ransom fund. There was no safe haven below ground any more, even among his own kind. So Mulch was forced to pass himself off as human, and take whatever work he could get from the Chicago Mob.

There were hazards associated with impersonating a human. Of course, his size drew attention from everyone who happened to glance downwards. But Mulch quickly discovered that Mud People could find a reason to distrust almost anyone. Height, weight, skin colour, religion. It was almost safer to be different in some way.

The sun was a bigger problem. Dwarfs are extremely photosensitive, with a burn time of less than three minutes. Luckily, Mulch's job generally involved night work, but when he was forced to venture abroad in daylight hours the dwarf made certain that every centimetre of exposed skin was covered with long-lasting sun block.

Mulch had rented a basement apartment in an early twentieth-century brownstone. It was a bit of a fixer-upper, but this suited the dwarf just fine. He stripped out the floorboards in the bedroom, dumping two tons of topsoil and fertilizer on to the rotten foundations. Mould and damp already clung to the walls, so no need to remodel anything there. In a matter of hours, insect life was thriving in the room. Mulch would lie back in his pit and snag cockroaches with his beard hair. Home sweet home. Not only was the apartment beginning to resemble a tunnel cave, but if the LEP came a callin', he could be fifty metres below ground in the blink of an eye.

In the coming days, Mulch would come to regret not taking that route as soon as he heard the knock at the door.

There was a knock at the door. Mulch crawled out of his tunnel bed and checked the video buzzer. Carla Frazetti was checking her hair in the brass knocker.

The boss's god-daughter? In person. This must be a big job. Perhaps the commission would be enough to set him up in another state. He'd been in Chicago for nearly three months now, and it was only a matter of time before the LEP picked up his trail. He would never leave the US though. If you had to live above ground, it might as well be somewhere with cable TV and a lot of rich people to steal from.

Mulch pressed the intercom panel.

'Just a minute, Miss Frazetti, I'm getting dressed.'

'Hurry it up, Mo,' snapped Carla, her voice crackly through the cheap speakers. 'I'm getting old here.'

Mulch threw on a robe he had fashioned from old potato sacks. He found the texture of the cloth, reminiscent of Haven Penitentiary pyjamas, to be weirdly comforting. He gave his beard a quick comb to dislodge any straggling beetles, and answered the door.

Carla Frazetti swept past him into the lounge, settling into the room's only armchair. There was another person on the doorstep, hidden beneath the camera's field. Mulch made a mental note. Redirect the CCTV lens. A fairy could sneak right in under it, even if he or she wasn't shielded.

The man gave Mulch a dangerous squint. Typical Mob behaviour. Just because these people were murdering gangsters, didn't mean they had to be rude.

'Don't you have another chair?' asked the small human, following Miss Frazetti into the lounge.

Mulch closed the door. 'I don't get many visitors. Actually, you're the first. Usually Bruno beeps me and I come into the chop shop.'

Bruno the Cheese was the Mob's local supervisor. He ran his business from a local hot-car warehouse. Legend had it that he hadn't been out from behind his desk during work hours in fifteen years.

'Quite a look you've got going here,' said Loafers sarcastically. 'Mould and woodlice. I like it.'

Mulch ran a fond finger along a green strip of damp. 'That mould was just sitting behind the wallpaper when I moved in. Amazing what people cover up.'

Carla Frazetti took a bottle of White Petals perfume from her bag and sprayed the air around her person.

'OK, enough conversation. I have a special job for you, Mo.'

Mulch forced himself to stay calm. This was his big chance. Maybe he could find a nice damp hell hole and settle down for a while.

'Is this the kind of job where there's a big pay-off if you do it right?'

'No,' replied Carla. 'This is the kind of job where there's a painful pay-off if you do it wrong.'

Mulch sighed. Didn't anyone talk nicely any more?

'So why me?' he asked.

Carla Frazetti smiled, her ruby winking in the gloom.

'I'm going to answer that question, Mo. Even though I'm not used to explaining myself to the hired help. Especially not a monkey like yourself.'

Mulch swallowed. Sometimes he forgot how ruthless these people were. Never for long.

'You've been chosen for this assignment, Mo, because of the outstanding job you did with that Van Gogh.'

Mulch smiled modestly. The museum alarm had been child's play. There hadn't even been any dogs.

'But also because you have an Irish passport.'

A gnome fugitive hiding out in NYC had run him up some Irish papers on a stolen LEP copier. The Irish had always been Mulch's favourite humans, so he had decided to be one. He should have known it would lead to trouble.

'This particular job is in Ireland, which might be a problem, generally. But for you two it'll be like a paid holiday.'

Mulch nodded at Loafers. 'Who's the mutt?'

Loafers' squint narrowed. Mulch knew that if Miss Frazetti gave the word, the man would kill him on the spot.

'The mutt is Loafers McGuire, your partner. He's a metal man. It's a two-tiered job. You open the doors. Loafers escorts the mark back here.'

Escorting the mark. Mulch understood what that term meant, and he didn't want any part of it. Robbery was one thing, but kidnapping was another. Mulch knew that he couldn't actually turn down this assignment. What he could do was ditch the metal man at the first opportunity and head to one of the southern states. Apparently Florida had some lovely swamps.

'So, who's the mark?' said Mulch, pretending that it mattered.

'That's need-to-know information,' said Loafers.

'And let me guess, I don't need to know.'

Carla Frazetti pulled a photograph from her coat pocket.

'The less you know, the less you have to feel guilty about. This is all you need. The house. This photograph is all we have for the moment; you can case the joint when you get there.'

Mulch took the photo. What he saw on the paper hit him like a gas attack. It was Fowl Manor. Therefore Artemis was the target. This little psychopath was being sent to kidnap Artemis.

Frazetti sensed his discomfort. 'Something wrong, Mo?'

Don't let it show on your face, thought Mulch. Don't let them see.

'No. It's … eh … That's quite a set-up. I can see alarm boxes and outdoor spots. It's not going to be easy.'

'If it was easy, I'd do it myself,' said Carla.

Loafers took a step forward, looking down at Mulch. What's the matter, little man? Too tough for you?'

Mulch was forced to think on his feet. If Carla Frazetti thought he wasn't up to the job, then they would send somebody else. Somebody with no qualms about leading the Mob to Artemis's door. Mulch was surprised to realize that he couldn't let that happen. The Irish boy had saved his life during the goblin rebellion, and was the closest thing he had to a friend – which was pretty pathetic when you thought about it. He had to take the job, if only to make sure that it didn't go according to plan.

'Hey, don't worry about me. A building hasn't been built that Mo Digence can't crack. I just hope Loafers is man enough for the job.'

Loafers grabbed the dwarf by the lapels. 'What's that supposed to mean, Digence?'

Mulch generally avoided insulting people who were likely to kill him, but it might be useful to establish Loafers as a hothead now. Especially if he was going to blame him for things going wrong later.

'It's one thing being a midget monkey, but a midget metal man? How good can you be at close quarters?'

Loafers dropped the dwarf and ripped open his shirt to reveal a chest rippling with a tapestry of tattoos.

'That's how good I am, Digence. Count the tattoos. Count 'em.'

Mulch shot Miss Frazetti a loaded look. The look said: You're going to trust this guy?

'That's enough!' said Carla. 'The testosterone in here is starting to stink worse than the walls. This is a very important job. If you two can't handle it, I'll bring in another team.'

Loafers buttoned his shirt. 'OK, Miss Frazetti. We can handle it. This job is as good as done.'

Carla stood, brushing a couple of centipedes from the hem of her jacket. The insects didn't bother her unduly. She'd seen a lot worse in her twenty-five years.

'Glad to hear it. Mo, put some clothes on and grab your monkey kit. We'll wait in the limo.'

Loafers poked Mulch in the chest. 'Five minutes. Then we're coming in to get you.'

Mulch watched them go. This was his last chance to duck out. He could chew through the bedroom foundations and be on a southbound train before Carla Frazetti knew he was gone.

Mulch thought about it seriously. This kind of thing was totally against his nature. It wasn't that he was a bad fairy, it was simply that he wasn't accustomed to helping other people. Not unless there was something in it for him. Deciding to help Artemis Fowl was a completely selfless act. Mulch shuddered. A conscience was the last thing he needed right now. Next thing you knew, he'd be selling cookies for the Girl Guides.

CHAPTER 6: ASSAULT ON FOWL MANOR

EXCERPT FROM ARTEMIS FOWL'S DIARY. DISK 2. ENCRYPTED

 MY father had finally regained consciousness. I was, of course, relieved, but his last words to me that day were chasing themselves around in my mind.

'Gold isn't all-important, Arty,' he had said. 'Neither is power. We have everything we need right here. The three of us.'

Was it possible that the magic had transformed my father? I had to know. I needed to speak to him alone. So, at 3 a.m. the following morning, I had Butler bring me back to Helsinki's University Hospital in the rented Mercedes.

Father was still awake, reading War and Peace by lamplight.

'Not many laughs,' he commented. More jokes. I tried to smile, but my face just wasn't in the mood.

Father closed the book. 'I've been expecting you, Arty. We need to talk. There are a few things we have to straighten out.'

I stood stiffly at the foot of the bed. 'Yes, Father. I agree.'

Father's smile was tinged with sadness. 'So formal. I remember being the same with my own father. I sometimes think that he didn't know me at all, and I worry that the same thing will happen to us. So I want us to talk, son, not about bank accounts. Not stocks and shares. Not corporate takeovers. I don't want to talk business, I want to talk about you.'

I had been afraid of this. 'Me? You are the priority here, Father.'

'Perhaps, but I cannot be happy until your mother's mind is put at rest.'

'At rest?' I asked, as though I didn't know where this was going.

'Don't play the innocent, Artemis. I've called a few of my law-enforcement contacts around Europe. Apparently you have been active in my absence. Very active.'

I shrugged, unsure whether I was being scolded or praised.

'Not so long ago I would have been very impressed by your antics. Such audacity and still a minor. But now, speaking as a father, things have to change, Arty. You must reclaim your childhood. It is my wish, and your mother's, that you return to school after the holidays and leave the family's business to me.'

'But, Father!'

'Trust me, Arty. I've been in business a lot longer than you. I have promised your mother that the Fowls are on the straight and narrow from now on. All of the Fowls. I have another chance, and I will not waste it on greed. We are a family now. A proper one.

From now on the Fowl name will be associated with honour and honesty. Agreed?'

'Agreed,' I said, clasping his hand.

But what of my meeting with Chicago's Jon Spiro? I decided to proceed as planned. One last adventure – then the Fowls could be a proper family. After all, Butler would accompany me. What could go wrong?

FOWL MANOR

Butler opened his eyes. He was home. Artemis was asleep in the armchair beside the bed. The boy looked a hundred years old. It wasn't surprising after all he'd been through. That life was over now though. All of it.

'Anybody home?' said the manservant.

Artemis was instantly alert.

'Butler, you've come back to us.'

Butler struggled on to his elbows. It was quite an effort.

'It's a surprise to me. I never expected to see you, or anyone, ever again.'

Artemis poured a glass of water from the bedside jug.

'Here, old friend. Just rest.'

Butler drank slowly. He was tired, but it was more than that. He had felt battle fatigue before, but this went deeper.

'Artemis, what has happened? I shouldn't be alive at all. And if I accept that I am alive, then I should be experiencing massive amounts of pain right about now.'

Artemis crossed to the window, looking out over the estate.

'Blunt shot you. It was a fatal wound, and Holly wasn't around to help, so I froze you until she arrived.'

Butler shook his head. 'Cryogenics? Only Artemis Fowl. You used the fish freezers, I suppose?'

Artemis nodded.

'I trust I am not part freshwater trout now, eh?'

When Artemis turned to face his friend, he was not smiling.

'There were complications.'

'Complications?'

Artemis took a breath. 'It was a difficult healing – no way to predict the outcome. Foaly warned that it might be too much for your system, but I insisted we press on.'

Butler sat up. 'Artemis. It's all right. I'm alive. Anything is better than the alternative.'

Artemis was not reassured. He took a pearl-handled mirror from the locker.

'Prepare yourself, and take a look.'

Butler took a deep breath and looked. He stretched his jaw and pinched the bags beneath his eyes.

'Just how long was I out?' he asked.

TRAnSATLAnTiC BOEinG 747

Mulch had decided that the best way to undermine the mission was to antagonize Loafers until he went crazy. Driving people crazy was a talent of his, and one that he did not get to exercise often enough.

The two diminutive individuals were seated side by side in a 747, watching the clouds shoot past below. First class: one of the perks of working for the Antonellis.

Mulch sipped delicately from a champagne flute.

'So, Slippers ...'

'That's Loafers.'

'Oh yes, Loafers. What's the story behind all the tattoos?'

Loafers rolled up his sleeve, revealing a turquoise snake with drops of blood for eyes. Another of his own designs.

'I get one done after every job.'

'Oh,' said Mulch. 'So if you paint a kitchen, then you get a tattoo?'

'Not that kind of job, stupid.'

'What kind of job then?'

Loafers ground his teeth. 'Do I have to spell it out for you?'

Mulch pinched some peanuts from a passing tray.

'No point. I never got no schoolin'. Plain English will be fine.'

'You can't be this stupid! Spatz Antonelli doesn't hire morons.'

Mulch gave a smarmy wink. 'You sure about that?'

Loafers patted his shirt, hoping to find a weapon of some kind.

'You wait until this is over, smart alec. Me and you will settle our differences.'

'You keep telling yourself that, Boots.'

'Loafers!'

'Whatever.'

Mulch hid behind the airline magazine. This was too easy. The mobster was half-crazed already. A few more hours in Mulch's company should be enough to have Loafers McGuire foaming at the mouth.

DUBLIN AIRPORT, IRELAND

Mulch and Loafers passed through Irish customs without incident. After all, they were simply citizens returning home for the holidays. It wasn't as if they were a Mob team up to no good. How could they be? Whoever heard of little people being involved in organized crime? Nobody. But maybe that was because they were very good at it.

Passport control provided Mulch with another opportunity to infuriate his partner.

The officer was doing his best not to notice Mulch's height, or lack of it.

'So, Mister Digence, home to visit the family?'

Mulch nodded. 'That's right. My mother's folks are from Killarney.'

'Oh, really?'

'O'Reilly, actually. But what's a vowel between friends?'

'Very good. You should be on the stage.'

'It's funny you should mention that –'

The passport officer groaned. Ten more minutes and his shift would have been over.

'I was being sarcastic actually …' he muttered.

'– because my friend Mister McGuire and I are also doing a stint in the Christmas pantomime. It's *Snow White*. I'm Doc, and he's Dopey.'

The passport officer forced a smile. 'Very good. Next.'

Mulch spoke for the entire queue to hear.

'Of course, Mister McGuire there was born to play Dopey, if you catch my drift.'

Loafers lost it right there in the terminal.

'You little freak!' he screamed. 'I'll kill you! You'll be my next tattoo. You'll be my next tattoo!'

Mulch tutted as Loafers disappeared beneath half a dozen security guards.

'Actors,' he said. 'Highly strung.'

*

They released Loafers three hours later after a full search and several phone calls to the parish priest in his home town. Mulch was waiting in the pre-ordered rental car, a specially modified model with elevated accelerator and brake pedals.

'Your temper is seriously jeopardizing this operation,' commented the dwarf, straight-faced. 'I'll have to phone Miss Frazetti if you can't control yourself.'

'Drive,' said the metal man hoarsely. 'Let's get this over with.'

'OK then. But you're on your very last chance. One more episode like that and I'm going to have to crush your head between my teeth.'

Loafers noticed his partner's teeth for the first time. They were tombstone-shaped blocks of enamel, and there seemed to be an awful lot of them for just one mouth. Was it possible that Digence could actually do what he threatened? No, Loafers decided. He was just a bit spooked after the customs interrogation. Still, there was something about the dwarf's smile. A glint that spoke of hidden and frightening talents. Talents that the metal man would prefer to stay hidden.

Mulch took care of the driving while Loafers made a couple of calls on his mobile phone. It was a simple matter for him to contact a few old associates and arrange for a weapon, a silencer and two headsets to be left in a duffel bag behind the motorway exit sign for Fowl Manor. Loafers' associates even took credit cards, so there was no need for the usual macho trade-off that generally accompanied black-market transactions.

Loafers checked the weapon's action and sights in the car. He felt in control again.

'So, Mo,' said Loafers, chuckling as if that simple rhyme was the funniest joke he had ever made. And sadly, it was. 'Have you put together a plan yet?'

Mulch didn't take his eyes from the road. 'Nope. I thought you were the head honcho here. Plans are your department. I just break and enter.'

'That's right. I am the head honcho, and believe me Master Fowl is going to realize that too when I'm finished talking to him.'

'*Master* Fowl?' said Mulch innocently. 'We're here for some kid?'

'Not just some kid,' revealed Loafers, against orders. 'Artemis Fowl. Heir to the Fowl criminal empire. He has something in his head that Miss Frazetti wants. So we're supposed to impress upon the little brat how important it is that he come with us and spill the beans.'

Mulch's grip tightened on the wheel. He should have made his move before now. But the trick was not to incapacitate Loafers, it was persuading Carla Frazetti not to send another team.

Artemis would know what to do. He had to get to the

boy before Loafers did. A mobile phone and a visit to the bathroom were all he needed. A pity he had never bothered purchasing a phone, but there had never been anybody to call before. Besides, you could never be too careful with Foaly. That centaur could triangulate a chirping cricket.

'We better stop for supplies,' said Loafers. 'It could take days to check this place out.'

'No need. I know the layout. I burgled it before, in my youth. Piece of cake.'

'And you didn't mention this before because …'

Mulch made a rude gesture at a lorry driver hogging both lanes.

'You know the way it is. I work on commission. The commission is calculated on a hardship basis. The second I say I turned this place over before, ten grand is cut off my fee.'

Loafers didn't argue. It was true. You always exaggerated the difficulty of the job. Anything to squeeze a few more bucks out of your employer.

'So, you can get us in there?'

'I can get *me* in there. Then I come back out for you.'

Loafers was suspicious. 'Why don't I just come with you? It would be a lot easier than hanging around in broad daylight.'

'Firstly, I'm not going in until after dark. And secondly, sure you can come with me, if you don't mind crawling

138

through the septic tank and up nine metres of effluent pipe.'

Loafers had to open a window at the thought of it.

'OK. You come get me. But we stay in contact over the headsets. Anything goes wrong and you let me know.'

'Yes, sir, boss,' said Mulch, screwing the earpiece into a hairy ear and clipping the mike to his jacket. 'Wouldn't want you to miss your appointment intimidating a kid.'

The sarcasm made a slight whistling noise as it flew over Loafer's head.

'That's right,' said the Kilkenny man. 'I *am* the boss. And you *don't* want to make me late for my appointment.'

Mulch had to concentrate to stop his beard hair curling. Dwarf hair is very mood-sensitive, especially to hostility, and it was flowing out of this man's every pore. Mulch's bristles had never been wrong yet. This little partnership was not going to end well.

Mulch parked in the shadow of the Fowl Estate's boundary wall.

'You certain this is the place?' asked Loafers.

Mulch pointed a stubby finger at the ornate iron gate.

'You see there where it says Fowl Manor?'

'Yes.'

'I'd say this was probably the place.'

Even Loafers couldn't miss a direct jibe like that.

'You better get me in there, Digence, or ...'

ᛒᚩᚹ · ᚱ · ᚠᚪᚻᚾ · ᚩᚾᚱ · ᚩᛒ · ᚱ ·

Mulch showed him the teeth. 'Or what?'

'Or Miss Frazetti will be extremely annoyed,' completed Loafers lamely, well aware that he was losing the hard-man-banter battle. Loafers resolved to teach Mo Digence a lesson as soon as possible.

'We wouldn't want to annoy Miss Frazetti,' said Mulch. He climbed down from the elevated seat and reclaimed his gear bag from the trunk. There were certain unorthodox burglary tools in the bag, supplied by his fairy contact in New York. Hopefully none of them would be needed. Not the way he intended gaining entrance to the manor.

Mulch rapped on the passenger window. Loafers buzzed it open.

'What?'

'Remember, you stay here until I come and get you.'

'That sounds like an order, Digence. Are you giving me orders now?'

'Me?' said Mulch, revealing the full expanse of his teeth. 'Giving orders? I wouldn't dream of it.'

Loafers buzzed the window back up.

'You better not be,' he said as soon as there was a layer of toughened glass between him and those teeth.

Inside Fowl Manor, Butler had just finished clipping and shaving. He was beginning to look like his old self again. His older self.

'Kevlar, you say?' he repeated, examining the darkened tissue on his chest.

Artemis nodded. 'Apparently some fibres were trapped in the wound. The magic replicated them. According to Foaly, the new tissue will restrict your breathing, but it isn't dense enough to be bulletproof, except for a small-calibre bullet.'

Butler buttoned his shirt. 'Everything is different, Artemis. I can't guard you any more.'

'I won't need guarding. Holly was right. My grand schemes generally lead to people getting hurt. As soon as we have dealt with Spiro I intend to concentrate on my education.'

'As soon as we have dealt with Spiro? You make it sound like a foregone conclusion. Jon Spiro is a dangerous man, Artemis. I thought you would have learned that.'

'I have, old friend. Believe me, I won't underestimate him again. I have already begun to formulate a plan. We should be able to retrieve the C Cube and neutralize Mister Spiro, providing Holly agrees to help.'

'Where is Holly? I need to thank her. Again.'

Artemis glanced out of the window. 'She has gone to complete the Ritual. You can guess where.'

Butler nodded. They had first encountered Holly at a sacred fairy site in the south-east while she was conducting the power-restoring Ritual. Although 'encountered' was not the term Holly used. 'Abducted' was closer to the truth.

'She should be back within the hour. I suggest you rest until then.'

Butler shook his head. 'I can rest later. Right now, I have to check the grounds. It's unlikely that Spiro could put a team together so quickly. But you never know.'

The bodyguard crossed to a wall panel that linked his room to the security-system control booth. Artemis could see that each step was an effort. With Butler's new chest tissue, just climbing the stairs would seem like a marathon.

Butler split-screened his monitor so he could view all the CCTVs simultaneously. One of the screens interested him more than the others, so he punched it up on the monitor.

'Well, well,' he chuckled. 'Look who's dropped in to say hello.'

Artemis crossed to the security panel. There was a very small individual making rude gestures at the kitchen-door camera.

'Mulch Diggums,' said Artemis. 'Just the dwarf I wanted to see.'

Butler transferred Mulch's image to the main screen.

'Perhaps. But why does he want to see you?'

Melodramatic as always, the dwarf insisted on a sandwich before explaining the situation. Unfortunately for Mulch,

142

it was Artemis who volunteered to prepare it for him. He emerged from the pantry with what resembled nothing more than an explosion on a plate.

'It's more difficult than it looks,' explained the boy.

Mulch cranked open his massive jaws, pouring the whole pile down in one swallow. After several minutes' chewing, he reached an entire hand into his mouth and dislodged a chunk of roast turkey.

'Next time more mustard,' he said, brushing some crumbs from his shirt and, in the process, inadvertently switching on the mike clipped there.

'You're welcome,' said Artemis.

'You should be thanking me, Mud Boy,' said Mulch. 'I came all the way from Chicago to save your life. Surely that's worth one lousy sandwich? And when I say sandwich I mean it in the loosest sense of the word.'

'Chicago? Jon Spiro sent you?'

The dwarf shook his head. 'Possibly, but not directly. I work for the Antonelli family. Of course, they have no idea that I am an actual fairy dwarf; they think I'm simply the best cat burglar in the business.'

'Chicago's district attorney has linked the Antonellis to Spiro in the past. Or rather, he's tried to.'

'Whatever. Anyway, the plan is that I break in here, and then my partner encourages you to accompany us to Chicago.'

Butler was leaning against the table. 'Where is your partner now, Mulch?'

'Outside the gate. He's the small angry one. Glad to see you're alive by the way, big man. There was a rumour going around the underworld that you were dead.'

'I was,' said Butler, heading for the security booth. 'But I'm better now.'

Loafers took a small spiral pad from his breast pocket. In it he had recorded any quips that he felt had really worked in dangerous situations. Snappy dialogue, that was the trademark of a good gangster – according to the movies at any rate. He flicked through the pages, smiling fondly.

'*It's time to close your account. Permanently.*' – Larry Ferrigamo. Bent banker. 9th August.

'*I'm afraid your hard drive has just been wiped.*' – David Spinski. Computer hacker. 23rd September.

'*I'm doing this 'cause I knead the dough.*' – Morty the Baker. 17th July.

It was good material. Maybe he would write his memoirs some day.

Loafers was still chuckling when he heard Mo talking in his earpiece. At first he thought the monkey was speaking to him, but then he realized that his so-called partner was spilling the beans to their pigeon.

'You should be thanking me, Mud Boy,' said Digence. 'I came all the way from Chicago to save your life.'

To save his life! Mo was working for the other side and the little idiot had forgotten about his mike.

Loafers climbed out of the car, being careful to lock it. He would lose the deposit if the rental was stolen, and Miss Frazetti would take it out of his commission. There was a small pedestrian entrance in the wall beside the main gate. Mo Digence had left it open. Loafers slipped through and hurried down the avenue, careful to stay in the shadow of the trees.

In his ear, Mo kept rabbiting on. He laid out their entire plan to the Fowl kid without so much as the threat of torture. It was completely voluntary. Digence had somehow been working for the Irish kid all along. And what's more, Mo was not Mo, he was Mulch. What kind of a name was that? Mulch, who was apparently a fairy dwarf. This was getting weirder and weirder. Maybe the fairy dwarfs were some kind of gang. Although it wasn't much of a gang name. The *fairy dwarfs* were hardly going to strike terror into the hearts of the competition.

Loafers trotted up the avenue, past a line of elegant silver birches and an honest-to-God croquet pitch. Two peacocks strutted around the edge of a water feature. Loafers snorted. Water feature! In the days before TV gardeners it would have been called a pond.

Loafers was wondering where the delivery entrance was when he saw the sign: 'Deliveries at rear'. Thank you very much. He checked his silencer and load one more time, and tiptoed across the gravel driveway.

Artemis sniffed the air. 'What's that smell?'

Mulch poked his head round the refrigerator door.

'Me, I'm afraid,' he mumbled, an unfeasible amount of food revolving inside his mouth. 'Sunblock. Disgusting, I know, but I'd smell a whole lot worse without it. Think bacon strips on a flat rock in Death Valley.'

'A charming image.'

'Dwarfs are subterranean creatures,' explained Mulch. 'Even during the Frond Dynasty we lived under-ground …'

Frond was the first elfin king. During his reign, fairies and humans had shared the earth's surface.

'… Being photosensitive makes it difficult to exist among humans. To be honest, I'm a bit fed up of this life.'

'Your wish is my command,' said a voice. It was Loafers. He was standing at the kitchen door, brandishing a very large gun.

In fairness to Mulch, he recovered well.

'I thought I told you to wait outside.'

'It's true, you did. But I decided to come in anyway. And guess what? No septic tank, no effluent pipe. The back door is wide open.'

Mulch tended to grind his teeth when he thought. It sounded like nails being scraped down a chalkboard.

'Ah … yes. A stroke of luck there. I took advantage of it, but unfortunately I was interrupted by the boy. I had just gained his confidence when you burst in.'

'Don't bother,' said Loafers. 'Your mike is on. I heard the whole thing, Mo. Or should I say Mulch, the fairy dwarf?'

Mulch swallowed the half-chewed mass of food. Once again his big mouth had got him into trouble — maybe it could get him out of trouble too. It was just possible that he could unhinge his jaw and swallow the little hit man. He'd eaten bigger. A quick burst of dwarf gas should be enough to propel him across the room. He'd just have to hope that the gun didn't go off before he could pass it.

Loafers caught the look in Mulch's eye.

'That's right, little man,' he said, cocking his pistol. 'You go for it. See how far you get.'

Artemis was thinking too. He knew that he was safe for the moment. The newcomer would not harm him against orders. But Mulch's time was running out and there was no one to save him. Butler was too weak to intervene even if he had been here. Holly was away completing the Ritual. And Artemis himself was not the best in physical situations. He would have to negotiate.

'I know what you're here for,' he began. 'The Cube's secrets. I'll tell you, but not if you harm my friend.'

Loafers waved the gun barrel. 'You'll do whatever I

ask, when I ask. Possibly you'll cry like a girl too. Sometimes that happens.'

'Very well. I'll tell you what you want to know. Just don't shoot anyone.'

Loafers swallowed a grin. 'Sure. That's fine. You just come with me, nice and quiet, and I won't hurt a soul. You have my word.'

Butler entered the kitchen. His face was slick with perspiration and his breath came in short gasps.

'I checked the monitor,' he said. 'The car is empty, the other man must be …'

'Here,' completed Loafers. 'Old news to everyone except you, Grandad. Now, no sudden moves and you might not have a heart attack.'

Artemis saw Butler's eyes flitting around the room. He was searching for an angle. Some way to save them. Maybe yesterday's Butler could have done it, but today's Butler was fifteen years older and not yet fully recovered from magical surgery. The situation was desperate.

'You could tie the others up,' ventured Artemis. Then we could leave together.'

Loafers smacked his own head. 'What a great idea! Then maybe I could agree to some other delaying tactic, on account of me being a complete amateur.'

Loafers felt a shadow fall across his back. He spun round to see a girl standing in the doorway. Another witness. Carla Frazetti would be getting the bill for all these sundries. This whole job had been misrepresented from the start.

'OK, miss,' said Loafers. 'Go join the others. And don't do anything stupid.'

The girl at the door flicked her hair over one shoulder, blinking her glittering green eyelids.

'I don't do stupid things,' she said. Then her hand flicked out, brushing against Loafer's weapon. She grabbed the pistol's slide and deftly twisted it from the stock. The gun was now completely useless, except for hammering nails.

Loafers jerked backwards. 'Hey, hey. Watch it. I don't want to wound you by accident. This gun could go off.'

That's what he thought.

Loafers continued brandishing his piece of harmless metal.

'Back off, little girl. I won't say it again.'

Juliet dangled the slide under his nose. 'Or what? You'll shoot me with this?'

Loafers stared cross-eyed at the piece of metal.

'Hey, that looks just like …'

Then Juliet hit him in the chest so hard he crashed through the breakfast bar.

Mulch stared over at the unconscious mobster, then at the girl in the doorway.

'Hey, Butler. Just a shot in the dark here, but I'd say that's your sister.'

⊖⚭⚇ • ⊕⚘ • ▢⚗⚸ ⚹ • ⊕▢⚲ ⚵ • ⊖⚮ ➤ • ↝

'You're right,' said the manservant, hugging Juliet tightly. 'How on earth did you guess?'

CHAPTER 7: BEST-LAID PLANS

 IT was time for consultation. That night, the group sat in the manor's conference room, facing two monitors that Juliet had brought down from the security booth. Foaly had hijacked the monitors' frequency and was broadcasting live images of Commander Root and himself.

Much to his own annoyance, Mulch was still present. He had been attempting to weasel some kind of reward from Artemis when Holly returned and cuffed him to a chair.

Root's cigar smoke was hazing the screen. 'Looks like the gang's all here,' he said, using the fairy gift of tongues to speak English. 'And guess what. I don't like gangs.'

Holly had placed her headset in the centre of the

conference table, so all the room's occupants could be picked up.

'I can explain, Commander.'

'Oh, I'll just bet you can. But, strangely, I have a premonition that your explanation is going to cut no ice with me whatsoever, and I will have your badge in my drawer by the end of this shift.'

Artemis tried to intervene. 'Really, Commander. Holly – Captain Short – is only here because I tricked her.'

'Is that a fact? And then, pray tell, why is she still there? Doing lunch, are we?'

'This is no time for sarcasm, Commander. We have a serious situation here. Potentially disastrous.'

Root exhaled a cloud of greenish smoke. 'What you humans do to each other is your own affair. We are not your personal police force, Fowl.'

Foaly cleared his throat. 'We're involved whether we like it or not: Artemis was the one who pinged us. And that's not the worst of it, Julius.'

Root glanced across at the centaur. Foaly had called him by his first name. Things must be serious.

'Very well, Captain,' he said. 'Continue with your briefing.'

Holly opened a report on her hand-held computer.

'Yesterday I responded to a recording from the Sentinel warning system. The call was sent by Artemis Fowl, a Mud Man well known to the LEP for his part in the B'wa Kell uprising. Fowl's associate Butler had been mortally injured on the orders of another Mud Man, Jon Spiro, and he requested my assistance with a healing.'

'Which you refused, and then requested technical back-up to perform a mind wipe, as per regulations.'

Holly could have sworn the screen was heating up.

'No. Taking into account Butler's considerable assistance during the goblin revolution, I performed the healing and transported Butler and Fowl back to their domicile.'

'Tell me you didn't fly them ...?'

'There was no alternative. They were wrapped in cam foil.'

Root rubbed his temples. 'One foot. If there was so much as one foot sticking out, we could be all over the Internet by tomorrow. Holly, why do you do this to me?'

Holly didn't reply. What could she say?

'There's more. We have detained one of Spiro's employees. A nasty piece of work.'

'Did he see you?'

'No. But he heard Mulch say that he was a fairy dwarf.'

'No problem,' said Foaly. 'Do a block mind wipe and send him home.'

'It's not that simple. The man is an assassin. He could be sent back to finish the job. I think we need to relocate him. Believe me. He won't be missed here.'

'OK,' said Foaly. 'Sedate him, do the wipe and get rid of anything that might trigger his memories. Then send him somewhere he can't do any harm.'

The commander took several long puffs to calm himself.

'OK. Tell me about the probe. And if Fowl is responsible, is the alert over?'

'No. The human businessman Jon Spiro stole the fairy technology from Artemis.'

'Which Artemis stole from us,' noted Foaly.

'This Spiro character is determined to acquire the technology's secret and he's not particular how he gets it,' continued Holly.

'And who knows the secret?' asked Root.

'Artemis is the only one who can operate the C Cube.'

'Do I want to know what a C Cube is?'

Foaly took up the narrative. 'Artemis cobbled together a microcomputer from old LEP technology. Most of it is obsolete below ground but, by human standards, it's approximately fifty years ahead of their developmental schedule.'

'And therefore worth a fortune,' concluded the commander.

'And therefore worth an absolute fortune,' agreed Foaly.

Suddenly Mulch was listening. 'A fortune? Exactly how much of a fortune?'

154

Root was relieved to have someone to shout at. 'Shut your mouth, convict! This doesn't concern you. You just concentrate on enjoying your last few breaths of free air. This time tomorrow you'll be shaking hands with your cell mate, and I hope he's a troll.'

Mulch was unbowed. 'Give me a break, Julius. Every time there's a Fowl situation I'm the one who saves your sorry hide. I have no doubt that whatever plan Artemis concocts will feature yours truly. Probably in some ridiculously dangerous capacity.'

Root's complexion went from rosé to full-bodied red. 'Well, Artemis? Do you plan on using the convict?'

'That depends.'

'On what?'

'On whether or not you give me Holly.'

Root's head disappeared behind a fog of cigar smoke. With the red tip glowing, he looked like a steam train coming out of a tunnel. Some of the smoke drifted across to Foaly's screen.

'It doesn't look good,' commented the centaur.

Eventually Root calmed down sufficiently to talk.

'Give you Holly? Gods, give me patience. Have you any idea the amount of red tape I'm ignoring just for this conference?'

'Quite a lot, I'd imagine.'

'A mountain of the stuff, Artemis. A mountain. I wouldn't be talking to you at all if it weren't for the B'wa

Kell thing. If this ever leaked out, I'd end up directing sewage-treatment subs in Atlantis.'

Mulch winked at the screen. 'I probably shouldn't have heard that.'

The commander ignored him. 'You have thirty seconds, Artemis. Sell it to me.'

Artemis rose, standing directly before the screen.

'Spiro has fairy technology. It is unlikely that he will be able to use it, but it will put his scientists on to ion technology. The man is a megalomaniac, with no respect for life or the environment. Who knows what ghastly machine he will construct from fairy technology? There is also the definite chance that his new technology will lead him to discover Haven itself and, if that happens, the life of every creature on the planet, and under it, is at risk.'

Root wheeled his chair off-camera, reappearing in Foaly's monitor. He leaned close to the centaur's ear, whispering in low tones.

'It doesn't look good,' said Holly. 'I could be on the next shuttle home.'

Artemis drummed his fingers on the table. It was difficult to see how he could take on Spiro without fairy assistance.

After several moments, the commander reappeared in his own screen.

'This is serious. We cannot afford to risk that this Spiro person will activate another probe. However small the possibility, there's still a chance. I will have to put together an insertion team. The works: a fully tooled-up Retrieval team.'

'A full team?' protested Holly. 'In an urban area? Commander, you know what Retrieval is like. This could turn into a disaster. Let me take a crack at it.'

Root considered it. 'It will take forty-eight hours to clear an operation, so that's what you have. I can cover for you for a couple of days. I can't let you have Foaly. He'll have enough to do putting this operation together. But Diggums can help if he wants; it's his choice. I might drop a couple of the burglary charges, but he's still facing five to ten for the bullion robbery. That's all I can do. If you fail, then the Retrieval team is waiting in the wings.'

Artemis thought about it. 'Very well.'

Root took a breath. 'There is a condition.'

'I thought as much,' said Artemis. 'You want a mind wipe. Correct?'

'That's right, Artemis. You are becoming a severe liability to the People. If we are to assist you in this matter, then you and your staff would have to submit to mind wipes.'

'And if we don't?'

'Then we go straight to plan B, and you get wiped anyway.'

'No offence, Commander, but this is a technical matter …'

Foaly stepped in. 'There are two kinds of mind wipe. A block wipe, which takes out everything in the chosen period. Holly could do that with the equipment in her bag. And a fine-tune wipe, which only deletes certain memories. This is a more specialized procedure, but there is less danger of a drop in IQ. We do a fine-tune wipe on all of you. I detonate a data charge in your computer system that automatically deletes any fairy-related files. Also, I will need your permission to do a sweep of your house just in case there is any fairy memorabilia lying around. In practical terms, you will wake up the day after this operation with absolutely no record or memory of the fairy People.'

'You're talking about nearly two years of memories.'

'You won't miss them. Your brain will invent some new ones to fill the gaps.'

It was a tough decision. On the one hand, his knowledge of the People was now a large part of Artemis's psychological make-up. On the other, he could no longer put people's lives at risk.

'Very well,' said the teenager. 'I accept your offer.'

Root tossed the cigar into a nearby incinerator. 'OK then. We have a deal. Captain Short, keep a channel open at all times.'

'Yes, sir.'

'Holly.'

'Commander?'

'Be careful on this one. Your career won't survive

another blow.'

'Understood, sir,' said Holly.

'Oh, and, convict?'

Mulch sighed. 'You mean me, I suppose, Julius?'

Root scowled. 'It's over, Mulch. You won't escape again, so get your brain ready for cold food and hard walls.'

Mulch stood, presenting his back to the screen. Somehow the bum-flap on his specially adapted tunnelling trousers flopped open, presenting the commander with a lovely view of his rear end. In the dwarf world, presenting your behind was the ultimate insult, as it is in most cultures.

Commander Root terminated the link. After all, there was no come-back from an affront like that.

WEST OF WAJIR, KENYA, EAST AFRICA

Loafers McGuire woke up with a debilitating headache. It was so painful that he felt obliged to come up with some imagery, in case he had to describe it later. His head felt, he decided, like there was an angry porcupine crawling around inside his cranium. Not bad, he thought. I should put that in the book.

Then he thought, what's a book? His next thought was, who am I? Shoes, something to do with shoes.

It is always this way when memory-implant subjects

first regain consciousness. The old identity hangs around for a few moments, trying to assert itself, until outside stimuli wash it away.

Loafers sat up and the porcupine went crazy, jamming needles into every square inch of his soft brain tissue.

'Oh,' groaned Loafers, cradling his aching skull. What did all this mean? Where was he? And how did he get here?

Loafers looked at his arms. For a second, his brain projected tattoos on to the skin, but the images quickly disappeared. His skin was unblemished. Sunlight rolled across his forearms like white lightning.

All around him was scrubland. Terracotta earth stretched away to indigo hills in the distance. A golden disc of sun blasted cracks in the shimmering earth. Two figures ran through the heatwaves, elegant as cheetahs.

The men were giants, easily seven feet tall. Each carried an oval hide shield, a thin spear and a mobile phone. Their hair, necks and ears were adorned with multicoloured beads.

Loafers jumped to his feet. Feet which, he noticed, were clad in leather sandals. The men were wearing Nikes.

'Help,' he cried. 'Help me!'

The men altered their course, jogging across to the confused mobster.

'*Jambo*, brother. Are you lost?' asked one.

'I'm sorry,' said Loafers, in perfect Swahili. 'I don't

speak Swahili.'

The man glanced at his partner.

'I see. And what is your name?'

'Loafers,' said Loafers' brain. 'Nuru,' said his mouth.

'Well, Nuru. *Unatoka wapi?* Where are you from?'

The words were out before Loafers could do anything about it.

'I don't know where I'm from, but I want to go with you. To your village. That's where I should be.'

The Kenyan warriors stared down at the little stranger. He was the wrong colour, true, but he seemed sane enough.

The taller of the two unhooked a mobile phone from his leopard-skin belt. He punched in the village chieftain's number.

'*Jambo*, Chief, this is Bobby. The earth spirits have left us another one.'

Bobby laughed, looking Loafers up and down.

'Yes, he's tiny, but he looks strong and he's got a smile bigger than a peeled banana.'

Loafers stretched his smile, just in case it was a factor. For some reason, all he wanted in this world was to go to the village and live a productive life.

'OK, Chief, I'll bring him in. He can have the missionary's old hut.'

Bobby clipped the phone back on to his belt.

'Very well, brother Nuru. You're in. Follow us, and try

to keep up.'

The warriors set off at a brisk run. Loafers, henceforth to be known as Nuru, raced after them, his leather sandals flapping beneath his feet. He really would have to see about getting a pair of trainers.

One hundred and fifty feet over their heads, Captain Holly Short hovered, shielded from view, recording the entire incident.

'Relocation complete,' she said into her helmet mike. 'The subject has been adopted successfully. No apparent signs of original personality. But he will be monitored at monthly intervals, just in case.'

Foaly was on the other end of the line.

'Excellent, Captain. Return to shuttle port E77 immediately. If you open the throttle, you might just make the evening shuttle. We'll have you back in Ireland in a couple of hours.'

Holly did not need to be told twice. It wasn't often you got clearance for a speed run. She activated her radar in case of buzzards and set the stopwatch on her visor.

'Now,' she said. 'Let's see if we can't break the airspeed record.'

A record that Julius Root had set eighty years ago.

PART 2: **COUNTERATTACK**

CHAPTER 8: HOOKS, LINES AND SINKERS

EXCERPT FROM ARTEMIS FOWL'S DIARY. DISK 2. ENCRYPTED.

TODAY Father was fitted for his prosthetic limb. He joked throughout the entire process, as though he were being measured for a new suit on Grafton Street. I must admit, his good humour was infectious, and I found myself making excuses just to sit in the corner of the hospital room and enjoy his presence.

It wasn't always this way. In the past, one needed valid grounds to visit my father. Of course, he wasn't generally available, and even when he was, his time was limited. One did not burst into the Fowl study without good reason. But now I feel welcome at his side. It is a nice feeling.

My father always liked to impart wisdom, but now it is more philosophical than financial. In the old days, he would direct my attention to the latest share prices in the Financial Times.

'Look, Artemis,' he would say. 'Everything else falls, but gold stays steady. That is because there is not enough of it. And there never will be. Buy gold, boy, and keep it safe.'

I liked to listen to his pearls of wisdom, but now they are harder to understand.

On the third day of his consciousness, I fell asleep on the hospital bed while my father did his walking exercises. I woke to find him looking at me thoughtfully.

'Shall I tell you something, Arty?' he said.

I nodded, unsure what to expect.

'While I was a prisoner I thought about my life, how I had wasted it gathering riches whatever the cost to my family and others around me. In a man's life, he gets few chances to make a difference. To do the right thing. To be a hero, if you will. I intend to become involved in that struggle.'

This was not the kind of wisdom I was accustomed to hearing from my father. Was this his natural personality or the fairy magic? Or a combination of both?

'I never got involved before. I always thought the world could not be changed.'

Father's gaze was intense, burning with new passion.

'But things are different now. My priorities are different. I intend to seize the day, be the hero that every father should be.'

He sat on the bed beside me.

'And what about you, Arty? Will you make the journey with me? When the moment comes will you take your chance to be a hero?'

I couldn't respond. I didn't know the answer. I still don't.

FOWL MANOR

For two hours Artemis locked himself in his study, sitting cross-legged in the meditative position taught to him by Butler. Occasionally he would voice an idea aloud, to be picked up by a voice-activated digital recorder placed on the mat before him. Butler and Juliet knew better than to interrupt the planning process. This period was crucial to the success of their mission. Artemis had the ability to visualize a hypothetical situation and calculate the likely outcomes. It was almost a dream state, and any disturbance could send the thread of his ideas flying like vapours.

Eventually Artemis emerged, tired but satisfied. He held three CD-writable disks.

'I want you to study these files,' he said. 'They contain details of your assignment. When you have memorized the contents destroy the disks.'

Holly took the disks.

'A CD. How quaint. We have these in museums.'

'There are several computers in the study,' continued Artemis. 'Use any terminal you wish.'

Butler was empty-handed.

'Nothing for me, Artemis?' he asked.

⚷◗◌⊕⚷•⚹∪♌◗♭⚷•⊕♌⚸⚚⚷•⚹•

168

Artemis waited until the others had gone.

'I needed to give you your instructions verbally,' he began. 'I don't want to risk Foaly picking them up from the computer.'

Butler sighed deeply, sinking into a leather armchair by the fireplace.

'I'm not going with you. Am I?'

Artemis sat on the chair's arm. 'No, old friend. But I have an important task for you.'

'Really, Artemis,' said Butler. 'I've skipped right over my midlife crisis. You don't have to invent a job just to make me feel useful.'

'No, Butler. This is of vital importance. It concerns the mind wipes. If my plan succeeds, we will have to submit to them. I see no way to sabotage the process itself, so I must ensure that something survives Foaly's search. Something that will trigger our memories of the People. Foaly once told me that a strong enough stimulus can result in total recall.'

Butler shifted his position in the chair, wincing. His chest was still giving him trouble. Not surprising really. He had been alive less than two days.

'Any ideas?'

'We need to lay a couple of false trails. Foaly will be expecting that.'

'Of course. A hidden file on the server. I could send an e-mail to ourselves, but not pick it up. Then the first time we check our mail, all this information will come through.'

Artemis handed the bodyguard a folded sheet of A4.

'No doubt we will be mesmerized and questioned. In the past we have hidden from the *mesmer* behind mirrored sunglasses. We won't get away with that on this occasion. So, we need to come up with something else. Here are the instructions.'

Butler studied the plans.

'It's possible. I know someone in Limerick. The best man in the country for this kind of specialized work.'

'Excellent,' said Artemis. 'After that, you need to put everything we have on the People on a disk. All documents, videos, schematics. Everything. And don't forget my diary. The whole story is there.'

'And where do we hide this disk?' asked Butler.

Artemis untied the fairy pendant from around his neck.

'I'd say this was about the same size as the disk. Wouldn't you?'

Butler tucked the gold medallion into his jacket pocket.

'It soon will be,' he said.

Butler prepared them a meal. Nothing fancy. Vegetarian spring rolls, followed by mushroom risotto with crème caramel to finish. Mulch opted for a bucket of diced worms and beetles, sautéed in a rainwater and moss vinaigrette.

'Has everybody studied their files?' Artemis asked, when the group had adjourned to the library.

'Yes,' said Holly. 'But I seem to be missing a few key pieces.'

'Nobody has the entire plan. Just the parts concerning them. I think it's safer that way. Do we have the equipment I specified?'

Holly dumped the contents of her pack on the rug.

'A complete LEP surveillance kit, including camouflage foil, mikes, video clips and a first aid box.'

'Plus we still have two intact LEP helmets and three laser handguns left over from the siege,' added Butler. 'And, of course, one of the prototype Cubes from the lab.'

Artemis passed the cordless phone to Mulch.

'Very well then. We may as well get started.'

THE SPIRO NEEDLE

Jon Spiro sat in his opulent office, staring glumly at the C Cube on his desk. People thought it was easy being him. How little they knew. The more money you had, the more pressure you were under. He had eight hundred employees in this building alone, all relying on him for a pay cheque. They wanted yearly salary reviews, medical plans, baby-care centres, regular coffee breaks, double pay for overtime and even stock options, for heaven's sake. Sometimes Spiro missed the times when a troublesome worker was thrown out of a high window and that was the end of him. These days, if you threw someone out of a window, they'd phone their lawyer on the way down.

But this Cube could be the answer to his prayers. A once-in-a-lifetime deal, the brass ring. If he could get this weird little gizmo working, the sky was the limit. Literally. The world's satellites would be his to command. He would have complete control over spy satellites, military lasers, communications networks and, most important of all, television stations. He could feasibly rule the world.

His secretary buzzed from reception.

'Mister Blunt to see you, sir.'

Spiro jabbed the intercom button.

'OK, Marlene, send him in. And tell him he better look sorry.'

Blunt did indeed look sorry when he pushed through the double doors. The doors themselves were imposing enough. Spiro had them stolen from the ballroom of the sunken *Titanic*. They were a perfect example of power gone mad.

Arno Blunt was not quite so cocky as he had been in

London. Then again, it is difficult to look arrogant when your forehead is a mass of bruises and your mouth is full of gums and nothing else.

Spiro winced at the sight of his sunken cheeks.

'How many teeth did you lose?'

Blunt touched his jaw gingerly.

'All ob 'em. Dendish shaid de roods are shaddered.'

'It serves you right,' said Spiro matter-of-factly. 'What do I gotta do, Arno? I hand you Artemis Fowl on a platter and you mess it up. Tell me what happened. And I don't want to hear about any earthquakes. I want the truth.'

Blunt wiped a blob of drool from the corner of his mouth.

'I doh undershtan ih. Shomeshin explohduh. I dunno wha'. Shome kinna shoun grenay. Buh I dell you shomeshin. Budlah ish dead. I shod him in de heart. No way he'sh geddin uh affer da.'

'Oh, shut up!' snapped Spiro. 'You're giving me a headache. The sooner you get those new teeth, the better.'

'My gumsh wi be healed suffishendly by hish afernoo.'

'I thought I told you to shut up!'

'Shorry, bosh.'

'You've put me in a very difficult situation, Arno. Because of your incompetence I had to hire a team from the Antonellis. Carla is a smart girl; she could decide that they deserve a percentage. It would cost me billions.'

Arno tried his best to look remorseful.

'And don't bother with the puppy dog look, Blunt. It doesn't cut any ice with me. If this deal goes south, you'll be losing a lot more than a couple of teeth.'

Arno decided to change the subject.

'Sho, di' your shiendishds geh de Gube worging?'

'No,' said Spiro, twisting his gold identity bracelet. 'Fowl has it sealed up tight. An Eternity Code, or some such thing. That idiot, Pearson, couldn't get a peep out of it.'

It was at that moment, dramatically, that a voice emanated from the C Cube's micro-speaker mesh.

'Mister Spiro?' said the voice. 'This is Ireland calling. Do you read, Mister Spiro?'

Jon Spiro was not a man who spooked easily. He hadn't seen a horror movie yet that could make him jump in his seat, but the voice coming out of that speaker almost knocked him off his chair. The quality was incredible. Close your eyes and you'd swear that the person speaking was standing right in front of you.

'You wan' me do anshwer da?'

'I told you to shut up! Anyway, I don't know how to answer this thing.'

'I can hear you, Mister Spiro,' said the voice. 'You don't need to do anything. Just talk. The box does the rest.'

Spiro noticed that a digital wave meter had appeared on the Cube's screen. When he spoke it registered.

174

'OK then. We got communication. Now, who the hell are you? And how did you get this box working?'

'The name is Mo Digence, Mister Spiro. I'm the monkey from Carla Frazetti's team. I don't know what kind of box you have at your end; I just have a plain old telephone.'

'Well, who dialled the number then?'

'A little kid I have here by the scruff of the neck. I impressed upon him how important it was that I talk to you.'

'And how did you know to talk to me? Who gave you my name?'

'Again, the kid. He was very eager to tell me everything after he saw what I did to the metal man.'

Spiro sighed. If the metal man was damaged, he would have to pay the Antonellis a fine.

'What did you do to the metal man?'

'Nothing permanent. But he won't be aiming any guns at kids for a while.'

'Why did you feel it necessary to damage your own partner, Digence?'

There was a pause on the other end while Mulch got the supposed sequence of events sorted out.

'It was like this, Mister Spiro. Our instructions were to escort the kid across to the US. But Loafers goes crazy and starts waving a gun about. I figured this was the wrong way to go, so I stopped him. Forcibly. Anyway, the kid gets so scared that he tells me everything I want to know. And here I am now having a conversation with you.'

Spiro rubbed his hands together. 'You did the right thing, Digence. There'll be a bonus in this for you. I'll see to it personally.'

'Thanks, Mister Spiro. Believe me, the pleasure was mine.'

'Is the Fowl kid there?'

'Right beside me. A little pale, but not a scratch on him.'

'Put him on,' ordered Spiro, all traces of depression vanishing.

'Spiro, it's me.' Artemis's voice was aloof, but with an unmistakable tremor.

Spiro squeezed the air, as though it were Artemis's neck.

'Not so cocky now, kid? It's like I told you, you don't have the guts for this job. Me, on the other hand, if I don't get what I want, then I'll have Mo put you out of my misery. Do we understand each other?'

'Yes. Loud and clear.'

'Good,' said Spiro, clamping a huge Cuban cigar between his teeth. It would be chewed to a pulp, but not lit. 'Now, talk. What do I have to do to get this Cube working?'

Artemis's voice sounded even shakier than before. 'It's not that simple, Mister Spiro. The C Cube is coded.

Something called an Eternity Code. I can remotely access certain basic functions: the phone, MP3 player and so on, but to disable the code completely and unlock the Cube's potential, I need to have it here in front of me. If you could just bring the Cube here ...'

Spiro spat out the cigar.

'Hold it right there, Fowl. Just how stupid do you think I am? I'm going to bring this priceless technology back to Europe? Forget it! If you're going to disable this thing, you're going to do it here. In the Spiro Needle!'

'But my tools? My lab?'

'I got tools here. And a lab. The best in the world. You do it here.'

'Yes. Whatever you say.'

'That's right, kid. Whatever I say. I want you to fuel up the Lear jet that I happen to know you have, and do a quick hop across to O' Hare Airport. I'll have a chopper waiting for you.'

'I don't suppose I have a choice.'

'That's right, kid. You don't. But do this right and I might just let you go. Did you get all that, Digence?'

'Loud and clear, Mister Spiro.'

'Good. I'm counting on you to get the kid here safely.'

'Consider it done.'

The line went dead.

Spiro chuckled.

'I think I'm going to celebrate,' he said, punching the

intercom button. 'Marlene, send in a pot of coffee, and no low-caffeine junk either. I want the real thing.'

'But, Mister Spiro, your doctors said …'

Spiro waited for his secretary to realize who she was arguing with.

'I'm sorry, sir. Right away, sir.'

Spiro leaned back in his chair, lacing his fingers behind his head.

'You see, Blunt. This is going to turn out fine, in spite of your incompetence. I got that kid just where I want him.'

'Yesh, shir. Mashderfully done, shir.'

Spiro laughed. 'Shut up, you clown. You sound like some cartoon character.'

'Yesh. Mosh amushing, shir.'

Spiro licked his lips, anticipating his coffee.

'For a supposed genius, that kid sure is gullible. Do this right and I might just let you go? He fell for that one hook, line and sinker.'

Blunt tried to grin. It was not a pretty sight.

'Yesh, Mishduh Shpiro. Hoo, line an' shinkuh.'

FOWL MANOR

Artemis hung up the phone, his face flushed with the thrill of the sting.

⚜ ✸ · ✸ ▢ · ∪ ⟩ ◗ ∞ ⚛ · § · ⫯ ▢ ⚔ | ⫯ ·

'What do you think?' he asked.

'I think he bought it,' replied Butler.

'Hook, line and sinker,' added Mulch. 'You have a jet? I presume there's a kitchen.'

Butler drove them to Dublin Airport in the Bentley. It was to be his final act in this particular operation. Holly and Mulch huddled in the back, glad of the tinted glass.

The Butler siblings sat up front, dressed in corresponding black Armani suits. Juliet had jazzed hers up with a pink cravat and glitter make-up. The family resemblance was clear: the same narrow nose and full lips. The same eyes, jumping in their sockets like roulette balls in the wheel. Watching, always watching.

'You don't need a traditional gun on this trip,' said Butler. 'Use an LEP blaster. They don't need reloading, they shoot in a straight line forever and they're non-lethal. I gave Holly a couple from my stash.'

'Got it, Dom.'

Butler took the airport exit.

'Dom. I haven't been called that in so long. Being a bodyguard becomes your world. You forget to have your own life. Are you sure that's what you want, Juliet?'

Juliet was twining her hair in a tight braid. At the end of the plait she attached an ornamental jade ring. Ornamental and dangerous.

'Where else would I get to bodyslam people outside of

a wrestling ring? Bodyguarding fits the bill, for the moment.'

Butler lowered his voice. 'Of course, it's completely against protocol for you to have Artemis as your principal. He already knows your first name and, truth be told, I think he's a little fond of you.'

Juliet slapped the jade ring against her palm.

'This is just temporary. I'm not anybody's bodyguard just yet. Madame Ko doesn't like my style.'

'I'm not surprised,' said Butler, pointing to the jade ring. 'Where did you get that?'

Juliet smiled. 'My own idea. A nice little surprise for anyone who underestimates females.'

Butler pulled into the set-down area.

'Listen to me, Juliet,' he said, catching his sister's hand. 'Spiro is dangerous. Look what happened to me, and, in all modesty, I was the best. If this mission weren't so vital to humans and fairies, I wouldn't let you go at all.'

Juliet touched her brother's face.

'I will be careful.'

They climbed on to the walkway. Holly hovered, shielded, just above the throngs of business travellers and holidaymakers. Mulch had applied a fresh layer of sunblock, and the stink repelled every human who was unfortunate enough to pick up his scent.

Butler touched Artemis's shoulder.

'Are you going to be all right?'

Artemis shrugged. 'I honestly don't know. Without you by my side I feel as though one of my limbs is missing.'

'Juliet will keep you safe. She has an unusual style, but she is a Butler, after all.'

'It's one mission, old friend. Then there will be no more need for bodyguards.'

'It's a pity Holly couldn't have simply mesmerized Spiro through the Cube.'

Artemis shook his head.

'It wouldn't have worked. Even if we could have set up a link, a fairy needs eye-to-eye contact to mesmerize a strong mind like Spiro's. I don't want to take any chances with this man. He needs to be put away. Even if the fairies relocated him, he could do some damage.'

'What about your plan?' Butler asked. 'From what you told me, it's quite convoluted. Are you sure it's going to work?'

Artemis winked – a very unusual display of levity.

'I'm sure,' he said. 'Trust me. I'm a genius.'

Juliet piloted the Lear jet across the Atlantic. Holly sat in the co-pilot's chair, admiring the hardware.

'Nice bird,' she commented.

'Not bad, fairy girl,' said Juliet, switching to autopilot. 'Not a patch on fairy craft, I'd bet?'

'The LEP doesn't believe in comfort,' said Holly.

〰〰〰

'There's barely enough room in an LEP shuttle to swing a stink worm.'

'If you wanted to swing a stink worm.'

'True.' Holly studied the pilot. 'You've grown a lot in two years. The last time I saw you, you were a little girl.'

Juliet smiled. 'A lot can happen in two years. I spent most of that time wrestling big hairy men.'

'You should see fairy wrestling. Two pumped-up gnomes having it out in a zero G chamber. Not a pretty sight. I'll send you a videodisc.'

'No, you won't.'

Holly remembered the mind wipes.

'You're right,' she said. 'No, I won't.'

In the passenger section of the Lear jet, Mulch was reliving his glory days.

'Hey, Artemis,' he said, through a mouthful of caviar. 'Remember the time I nearly blew Butler's head off with a blast of gas?'

Artemis did not smile. 'I remember, Mulch. You were the spanner in an otherwise perfect works.'

'To tell you the truth, it was an accident. I was just nervous. I didn't even realize the big guy was there.'

'That makes me feel better. Scuppered by a bowel problem.'

'And do you remember the time I saved your neck in Koboi Laboratories? If it hadn't been for me, you'd be locked up in Howler's Peak right now. Can't you do anything without me?'

Artemis sipped mineral water from a crystal flute.

'Apparently not, though I live for the day.'

Holly made her way back through the aisle.

'We'd better get you kitted out, Artemis. We land in thirty minutes.'

'Good idea.'

Holly emptied the bag's contents on to the central table.

'OK, what do we need for now? The throat mike and an iris-camera.'

The LEP captain selected what looked like a circular adhesive bandage from the pile. She peeled back the adhesive layer and stuck the material to Artemis's neck. It immediately turned the colour of his skin.

'Memory latex,' explained Holly. 'It's almost invisible. Maybe an ant crawling up your neck might notice it, but apart from that ... The material is also X-ray proof, so the mike is undetectable. It will pick up whatever is said within a ten-metre radius, and I record it on my helmet chip. Unfortunately, we can't risk an earpiece – too visible. So we can hear you, but you won't be able to hear us.'

Artemis swallowed, feeling the mike ride on his Adam's apple.

'And the camera?'

'Here we go.'

Holly removed a contact lens from a jar of fluid.

'This thing is a marvel. We've got hi-resolution, digital quality, recordable picture with several filter options, including magnification and thermal.'

Mulch sucked a chicken bone dry.

'You're starting to sound like Foaly.'

Artemis stared at the lens.

'A technological marvel it may be, but it's hazel.'

'Of course it's hazel. My eyes are hazel.'

'I'm glad to hear it, Holly. But my eyes are blue, as you well know. This iris-cam will not do.'

'Don't look at me like that, Mud Boy. You're the genius.'

'I can't go in there with one brown eye and one blue eye. Spiro will notice.'

'Well, you should have thought of that while you were meditating. It's a little late now.'

Artemis pinched the bridge of his nose. 'You're right, of course. I am the mastermind here. Thinking is my responsibility, not yours.'

Holly squinted suspiciously. 'Was that an insult, Mud Boy?'

Mulch spat the chicken bone into a nearby bin.

'I have to tell you, Arty, a cock-up this early in the proceedings doesn't exactly fill me with confidence. I hope you're as clever as you keep telling everyone you are.'

'I never tell anybody *exactly* how clever I am. They would be too scared. Very well, we will have to risk the hazel iris-cam. With any luck, Spiro might not notice. If he does, I can invent some excuse.'

Holly placed the camera on the tip of her finger, sliding the lens under Artemis's lid.

'It's your decision, Artemis,' she said. 'I just hope you haven't met your match in Jon Spiro.'

11 P.M., O'HARE AIRPORT, CHICAGO

Spiro was waiting for them at O' Hare's private hangar. He wore a fur-collared greatcoat over his trademark white suit. Halogen lamps blasted the tarmac, and the downdraught from the chopper blades snagged his coat tails. It was all very cinematic.

All we need now is background music, thought Artemis as he descended the motorized steps.

As per instructions, Mulch was putting on the gangster act.

'Move it, kid,' he snarled, quite convincingly. 'We don't want to keep Mister Spiro waiting.'

Artemis was about to respond when he realized that he was supposed to be the 'terrified kid'. It wasn't going to be easy. Being humble was a real problem for Artemis Fowl.

'I said move it!' repeated the dwarf, stressing the point with a firm shove.

Artemis stumbled the last few steps, almost colliding with a grinning Arno Blunt. And this was no ordinary grin. Blunt's teeth had been replaced by a custom-crafted porcelain set. The tips had been filed to sharp points. The bodyguard looked for all the world like a human shark hybrid.

Blunt caught Artemis's stare.

'You like 'em? I got other sets too. One is all flat. For crushing stuff.'

A cynical sneer was forming on Artemis's mouth before he remembered his role, replacing the sneer with a set of quivering lips. He was basing his performance on the effect Butler usually had on people.

Spiro was not impressed.

'Nice acting, sonny. But pardon me if I doubt the great Artemis Fowl has fallen to pieces quite so easily. Arno, check the plane.'

Blunt nodded curtly, ducking inside the private jet. Juliet was dressed in a flight attendant's uniform and was straightening the headrest covers. For all her athletic ability, she was finding it difficult not to fall out of her high heels.

'Where's the pilot?' growled Blunt, living up to his name.

'Master Artemis flies the plane,' replied Juliet. 'He's been flying it since he was eleven years old.'

'Oh, really? Is that legal?'

Juliet put on her best innocent face. 'I don't know about legal, Mister. I just serve the drinks.'

Blunt grunted, charming as ever, and had a quick poke about the jet's interior. Eventually he decided to accept the flight attendant's word. Lucky for him, because had he decided to argue, two things would have happened. First, Juliet would have clobbered him with the jade ring. And second, Holly, who was lying shielded in an overhead locker, would have blasted him into unconsciousness with her Neutrino 2000. Of course, Holly could simply have mesmerized the bodyguard, but after what he had done to Butler, a blasting seemed more appropriate.

Blunt stuck his head through the hatch.

'No one in there except some dumb attendant.'

Spiro was not surprised.

'I didn't think so. But they're here somewhere. Believe it or not, Digence, Artemis Fowl did not get suckered by a goon like you. He's here because he wants to be here.'

Artemis was not surprised by this deduction. It was only natural that Spiro should be suspicious.

'I don't know what you mean,' he said. 'I'm here because this odious little man threatened to crush my skull between his teeth. Why else would I come? The C Cube is useless to you, and I could easily construct another one.'

Spiro was not even listening.

'Yeah, yeah, whatever you say, kid. But let me tell you something. You bit off more than you could chew when you agreed to come here. The Spiro Needle has the best security on the planet. We've got stuff in there that even the military don't have. Once those doors close behind you, you're on your own. Nobody is coming to save you. Nobody. Understand?'

Artemis nodded. He understood what Spiro was saying to him. That wasn't to say that he agreed with it. Jon Spiro might have *stuff* that the military didn't have, but Artemis Fowl had *stuff* that humans had never seen.

A Sikorsky executive helicopter whisked them downtown to the Spiro Needle. They landed on a helipad on the skyscraper's roof. Artemis was familiar with helicopter controls, and realized how difficult it must be to land in the bluster of the Windy City.

'The wind speed must be treacherous at this altitude,' he said casually. Holly could record the information on her helmet chip.

'You're telling me,' shouted the pilot over the rotors' din. 'It gets over sixty miles an hour on top of the Needle. The helipad can sway up to ten metres in rough conditions.'

Spiro groaned, giving Blunt a nod. Arno reached forward and whacked the pilot's helmet.

'Shut up, you moron!' snapped Spiro. 'Why don't you

give him the blueprints to the building while you're at it?' He turned to Artemis. 'And in case you're wondering, Arty, there aren't any blueprints floating around. Anybody who goes looking in City Hall is going to find that file mysteriously missing. I have the only set, so don't bother getting one of your associates to do an Internet search.'

No surprises there. Artemis had already run several searches himself, although he hadn't really expected Spiro to be so careless.

They climbed down from the Sikorsky. Artemis was careful to point the iris-cam at any security feature that could be useful later. Butler had often told him that even a seemingly insignificant detail, like the number of steps in a stairwell, could be vital when planning an operation.

A lift brought them down from the helipad to a key-coded door. Closed-circuit cameras were strategically placed to cover the entire rooftop. Spiro moved ahead to the keypad. Artemis felt a sharp sting in his eye and suddenly the iris-cam magnified his vision by four. In spite of the distance and shadows he could easily discern the entry code.

'I hope you got that,' he muttered, feeling the mike vibrating on his throat.

Arno Blunt bent his knees, so his extraordinary teeth were a centimetre from Artemis's nose.

'Are you talking to someone?'

'Me?' said Artemis. 'Who would I be talking to? We're eighty floors up, in case you hadn't noticed.'

Blunt grabbed the teenager by the lapels, hoisting him off the tarmac.

'Maybe you're wearing a wire. Maybe you have someone listening to us right now.'

'How could I be wearing a wire, you big oaf? Your miniature hit man hasn't let me out of his sight for the entire journey. He even accompanied me to the bathroom.'

Spiro cleared his throat noisily.

'Hey there, Mister I-Gotta-Make-My-Point, that kid slips over the side and you might as well throw yourself off, because that boy is worth more to me than an army of bodyguards.'

Blunt set Artemis down.

'You're not going to be valuable forever, Fowl,' he whispered ominously. 'And when your stock falls, I'll be waiting.'

They took a mirrored lift to the eighty-fifth floor, where Doctor Pearson waited, along with two more muscle-bound minders. Artemis could tell by the look in their eyes that these two weren't exactly brain surgeons. In fact, they were as close as you could get to Rottweilers still balanced on two legs. It was probably handy to have them around to break things and not ask questions.

Spiro called one of them over.

'Pex, do you know what the Antonellis charge if you lose their personnel?'

Pex had to consider it for a moment. His lips moved as he thought.

'Yeah, wait, I got it. Twenty grand for a metal man and fifteen for a monkey.'

'That's dead, right?'

'Dead or incapaci … incatacip … broken.'

'OK,' said Spiro. 'I want you and Chips to go over to Carla Frazetti's and tell her I owe her thirty-five grand for the team. I'll wire it to her Cayman account in the morning.'

Mulch was understandably curious, and not a little apprehensive.

'Excuse me? Thirty-five grand? But I'm still alive. You only owe twenty grand for Loafers, unless the extra fifteen K is my bonus?'

Spiro sighed with almost convincing regret.

'This is the way it is, Mo,' he said, punching Mulch playfully on the shoulder. 'This deal is huge. Mammoth. We're talking telephone numbers. I can't afford any loose ends. Maybe you know something, maybe you don't. But I'm not about to take the chance that you might tip off Phonetix or one of my other competitors. I'm sure you understand.'

Mulch stretched his lips, revealing a row of tombstone teeth.

'I understand all right, Spiro. You're a back-stabbing snake. You know, the kid offered me two million dollars to cut him loose.'

'You should have taken the cash,' said Arno Blunt, propelling Mulch into Pex's gigantic arms.

The dwarf kept talking, even as he was being dragged down the corridor.

'You better bury me deep, Spiro. You better bury me real deep.'

Spiro's eyes narrowed to wet slits.

'You heard the man, boys. Before you go to Frazetti's, bury him deep.'

Doctor Pearson led the party through to the vault room. They had to pass through a small antechamber before entering the main security area.

'Please stand on the scanner pad,' said Pearson. 'We wouldn't want any bugs in here. Especially not the electronic kind.'

Artemis stepped on to the mat. It sank like a sponge beneath his feet, spurting jets of foam over his shoes.

'Anti-infection foam,' explained Pearson. 'Kills any virus you might have picked up. We're keeping some bio-technology experiments in the vault at the moment. Very susceptible to disease. The foam has the added advantage of shorting out any surveillance devices in your shoes.'

Overhead a mobile scanner bathed Artemis's frame in purple light.

'One of my own inventions,' said Pearson. 'A combination scanner. I have incorporated thermal, X-Ray and metal-detector beams. The beam basically breaks your body down into its elements and displays them on this screen here.'

Artemis saw a 3D replica of himself being traced out on the small plasma screen. He held his breath, praying that Foaly's equipment was as clever as the centaur thought it was.

On-screen, a red light pulsed on Artemis's jacket front.

'Aha,' said Doctor Pearson, plucking off a button. 'What have we here?' He cracked the button open, revealing a tiny chip, mike and power source.

'Very clever. A micro-bug. Our young friend was attempting to spy on us, Mister Spiro.'

Jon Spiro was not angry. In fact, he was delighted to have the opportunity to gloat.

'You see, kid. You may be some kind of genius, but surveillance and espionage are my business. You can't slip anything past me. And the sooner you accept that, the sooner we can get this thing over with.'

Artemis stepped off the pad. The decoy had worked, and the real bugs hadn't caused a blip in the system. Pearson was smart, but Foaly was smarter.

Artemis made sure he had a good look around the antechamber. There was more here. Every square centimetre of the metal surface contained a security or surveillance device. From what Artemis could see, an invisible ant would have trouble sneaking in. Not to mention two humans, an elf and a dwarf – assuming the dwarf survived Pex and Chips.

The vault door itself was impressive. Most corporate vaults *looked* impressive, plenty of chrome and keypads, but that was just to make an impression on stockholders. In Spiro's vault there wasn't a tumbler out of place. Artemis spotted the very latest computer lock on the face of titanium double doors. Spiro keyed in another complicated series of numbers, and the metre-thick doors slid back to reveal another barrier. The secondary door.

'Imagine you are a thief,' said Spiro, an actor introducing a play, 'and you somehow get into the building, past the electronic eyes and the locked doors. Then imagine you somehow cheat the lasers, the sensor pad and the door code, and open the first vault door – an impossible feat by the way. And while we're imagining all this, let's pretend you disable the half dozen cameras, and even then, even after all that, would you be able to do this?'

Spiro stood on a small red plate on the floor in front of the door. He placed a thumb on a gel-print scanner, held his left eyelid open and enunciated clearly.

'Jon Spiro. I am the boss, so open up quick.'

Four things happened. A retinal scanner filmed his left eye and fed the image into the computer. A print plate scanned his right thumb, and a vocal analyser scrutinized his voice's accent, timbre and intonations. Once the computer had verified all this information, the alarms were deactivated and the secondary door slid open to reveal an expansive vault.

In the very middle, in the centre of a custom-made steel column, rested the C Cube. It was enclosed in a perspex case, with at least six cameras focused on its various planes. Two burly guards stood back to back, forming a human barrier in front of the fairy technology.

Spiro could not resist a jibe. 'Unlike you,' he said, 'I look after my technology. This is the only vault of its kind in the world.'

'Live security in an airtight room. Interesting.'

'These guys are trained at high altitude. Also, we change the guards on the hour, and they all carry oxygen cylinders to keep them going. What did you think? I was going to put air vents into a vault?'

Artemis scowled. 'No need to show off, Spiro. I'm here; you win. So can we get on with it?'

Spiro punched a final number sequence into the column's keypad and the perspex panes retracted. He took the Cube from its foam nest.

'Overkill, don't you think?' commented Artemis. 'All of this is hardly necessary.'

'You never know. Some crooked businessman could attempt to relieve me of my prize.'

Artemis took a chance on some calculated sarcasm.

'Really, Spiro. Did you think I would attempt a break-in? Perhaps you thought I would fly in here with my fairy friends and magic your box away?'

Spiro laughed. 'You can bring all the fairy friends you like, Arty boy. Short of a miracle that Cube is staying right where it is.'

Juliet was an American citizen by birth, even though her brother had been born on the other side of the world. She was glad to be back in her home country. The discord of Chicago's traffic and the constant chorus of multicultural voices made her feel at home. She loved the skyscrapers and the steam vents and the affectionate sarcasm of the street vendors. If she ever got the chance to settle down, it would be in the US. On the west coast though, somewhere with sun.

Juliet and Holly were circling the Spiro Needle in a blacked out mini-van. Holly sat in the back, watching the live video feed from Artemis's iris-cam on her helmet visor.

At one point she punched the air triumphantly.

Juliet stopped at a red light. 'How are we doing?'

'Not bad,' replied the fairy, raising her visor. 'They're taking Mulch to bury him.'

'Cool. Just like Artemis said they would.'

'And Spiro has just invited all of Artemis's fairy friends into the building.'

This was a crucial development. The Book forbade fairies from entering human buildings without an invitation. Now Holly was free to break in and wreak havoc without violating fairy doctrine.

'Excellent,' said Juliet. 'We're in. I get to bodyslam the guy who shot my brother.'

'Not so fast. This building has the most sophisticated Mud Man security system I've seen. Spiro has a few tricks in there that I've never come across before.'

Juliet finally found a space opposite the Needle's main revolving doors.

'No problem for the little horsey guy, surely?'

'No, but Foaly's not supposed to help us.'

Juliet focused a set of binoculars on the door. 'I know, but it all depends on how you ask. A smart guy like Foaly – what he needs is a challenge.'

Three figures emerged from the Needle. Two large men in black and a smaller, nervous-looking individual. Mulch's feet were treading air so fast that he seemed to be performing an Irish jig. Not that he had any hope of escaping. Pex and Chips had him tighter than two badgers fighting over a bone.

'Here comes Mulch now. We better give him back-up. Just in case.'

Holly strapped on her mechanical harness, extending the wings with the touch of a button.

'I'll follow them from the air. You keep an eye on Artemis.'

Juliet ran a video lead from one of the spare helmets' hand-held computers. Artemis's point of view sprang to life on the screen.

'Do you really think Mulch needs help?' she asked.

Holly buzzed into invisibility. 'Help? I'm just going along to make sure he doesn't harm those two Mud Men.'

Inside the vault, Spiro was finished playing the gracious host.

'Let me tell you a little story, Arty,' he said, lovingly caressing the C Cube. 'There was this Irish kid who thought he was ready for the big time. So he messed with a very serious businessman.'

Don't call me Arty, thought Artemis. My father calls me Arty.

'This businessman didn't appreciate being messed with, so he messed back, and this kid is dragged kicking and screaming into the real world. So now this kid has to make a choice: does he tell the businessman what he needs to know, or does he put himself and his family in mortal danger? Well, Arty, which one is it?'

Spiro was making a serious mistake by toying with Artemis Fowl. It was difficult for adults to believe that this pale-faced thirteen-year-old could actually be a threat. Artemis had tried to take advantage of this by wearing casual clothes in place of his usual designer suit. He had also been practising an innocent, wide-eyed look on the jet, but wide-eyed was not how you wanted to look when one iris did not match the other.

Blunt prodded Artemis between the shoulder blades.

'Mister Spiro asked you a question.' His new teeth clicked as he talked.

'I'm here, am I not?' replied Artemis. 'I'll do whatever you wish.'

Spiro placed the Cube on a long steel table that ran down the centre of the vault.

'What I wish is for you to disable your Eternity Code, and get this Cube working right now.'

Artemis wished that he could make himself perspire so that his anxiety would seem more authentic.

'Right now? It's not that simple.'

Spiro grabbed Artemis by the shoulders, staring him in the eye.

'And why wouldn't it be that simple? Just punch in the code word and away we go.'

Artemis averted his mismatched eyes, staring at the floor.

'There is no straightforward code word. An Eternity

Code is built to be irreversible. I have to reconstruct an entire language. It could take days.'

'Don't you have any notes?'

'Yes. On disk. In Ireland. Your monkey wouldn't let me bring anything in case it was booby-trapped.'

'Can we access your hard drive online?'

'Yes. But I only keep my notes on disk. We could fly back to Ireland. Eighteen hours, round trip.'

Spiro wouldn't even consider that option. 'Forget it. As long as I have you here, I'm in control. Who knows what kind of reception is waiting for me in Ireland? We do it here. As long as it takes.'

Artemis sighed. 'Very well.'

Spiro replaced the Cube in its perspex case.

'Get a good night's sleep, kid, because tomorrow you're going to peel this gizmo apart like an onion. And if you don't, what's about to happen to Mo Digence will happen to you.'

Artemis wasn't unduly worried by that threat. He didn't believe Mulch to be in any danger. In fact, if anyone was in trouble, it was those two musclemen Pex and Chips.

⊖ ⊙ ∙ ⚡⚡🦀 ☽ ∙ ⚛🦵 ∙ ⊗ ◊ ◯ ⊌ ☻ 🐜 ∙ ⊖🦀⊗ ⚛ ∙

CHAPTER 9: **GHOSTS IN THE MACHINE**

VACANT LOT, MALTHOUSE INDUSTRIAL ESTATE, SOUTH CHICAGO

 JON Spiro had not hired Pex and Chips for their debating skills. In the job interview they had only been set one task. A hundred applicants were handed a walnut and asked to smash it however they could. Only two succeeded. Pex had shouted at the walnut for a few minutes, then flattened it between his giant palms. Chips opted for a more controversial method. He placed the walnut on the table, grabbed his interviewer by the ponytail and used the man's forehead to smash the nut. Both men were hired on the spot. They quickly established themselves as Arno Blunt's most reliable lieutenants for in-house work. They were not allowed outside Chicago as this could involve map reading – something Pex and Chips were not very good at.

At the moment, Pex and Chips were bonding under a full moon while Mulch dug a dwarf-sized pit in the dry clay behind an abandoned cement factory.

'You wanna guess why they call me Pex?' asked Pex, flexing his chest muscles as a hint.

Chips opened a packet of the potato chips he was forever crunching.

'I dunno. Is it, like, short for something?'

'Like what?'

'I dunno,' said Chips. He used the phrase a lot. 'Francis?'

This sounded dumb, even to Pex. 'Francis? How could Pex be short for Francis?'

Chips shrugged. 'Hey. I had an Uncle Robert and everyone called him Bobby. That don't make no sense neither.'

Pex rolled his eyes. 'It's pec-tor-als, moron. Pex is short for pectorals, on account of me having big chest muscles.'

In the pit, Mulch groaned. Listening to this mindless banter was almost as bad as having to dig a hole with a shovel. Mulch was tempted to deviate from the plan and launch himself into the flaky soil. But Artemis did not want any display of fairy powers at this stage of the proceedings. If he took off, and these goons escaped without being mesmerized, then Spiro's paranoia would be driven up another notch.

On the surface, Chips was eager to continue the game.

'Guess why they call me Chips,' he said, hiding the bag of chips behind his back.

Pex kneaded his forehead. He knew this one.

'Don't tell me,' he said. 'I can work it out.'

Mulch poked his head from the hole. 'It's because he eats chips, you idiot. Chips eats chips. You two are the thickest Mud Men I have ever met. Why don't you just kill me? At least I won't have to listen to your drivel.'

Pex and Chips were stunned. With all the mental exercise, they had almost forgotten about the little man in the hole. Plus, they were unaccustomed to prospective victims saying anything besides, 'Oh no, please, God, no.'

Pex leaned over the grave's lip. 'What do you mean *drivel*?'

'I mean that whole *Chips Pex* thing.'

Pex shook his head. 'No, I mean what does the word "drivel" mean? I've never heard that one.'

Mulch was delighted to explain. 'It means rubbish, garbage, claptrap, twaddle, baloney. Is that clear enough for you?'

Chips recognized the last one. 'Baloney? Hey, that's an insult! Are you insulting us, little man?'

Mulch clasped his hands in mock prayer. 'Finally, a breakthrough.'

The musclemen were uncertain how to react to actual abuse. There were only two people alive who insulted them regularly: Arno Blunt and Jon Spiro. But that was part of the job – you just ignored that by turning up the music in your head.

'Do we have to listen to his smart mouth?' Pex asked his partner.

'I don't think so. Maybe I should phone Mister Blunt.'

Mulch groaned. If stupidity were a crime, these two would be public enemies one and two.

'What you should do is kill me. That was the idea, wasn't it? Just kill me and get it over with.'

'What do you think, Chips? Should we just kill him?'

Chips chewed on a handful of barbecue Ruffles. 'Yeah. Course. Orders is orders.'

'But I wouldn't *just* kill me,' interjected Mulch.

'You wouldn't?'

'Oh no. After the way I just insulted your intelligence? No, I deserve something special.'

You could almost see the steam coming out of Pex's ears as his brain overheated.

'That's right, little man. We're gonna do something special to you. We don't take no insults from anybody!'

Mulch did not bother pointing out the double negative.

'You're right. I've got a smart mouth, and I deserve everything I've got coming to me.'

There followed a short silence as Pex and Chips tried to come up with something worse than the usual straight shooting.

Mulch gave them a minute, then made a polite suggestion.

'If it were me, I'd bury me alive.'

Chips was horrified.

'Bury you alive? That's terrible! You'd be screaming and clawing the dirt. I could get nightmares.'

'I promise to lie still. Anyway, I deserve it. I did call you a pair of overdeveloped, single-celled Cro-Magnons.'

'Did you?'

'Well, I have now.'

Pex was the more impulsive of the duo. 'OK, Mister Digence. You know what we're gonna do? We're going to bury you alive.'

Mulch clapped two hands to his cheeks. 'Oh, the horror!'

'You asked for it, buddy.'

'I did, didn't I?'

Pex grabbed a spare shovel from the boot. 'Nobody calls me an overdeveloped, signal bell crow magnet.'

Mulch lay down obligingly in his grave. 'No. I bet nobody does.'

Pex shovelled furiously, gymnasium-sculpted muscles stretching his suit jacket. In minutes, Mulch's form was completely covered.

⏃⏁ ⏁⊑⟒ ⟒⋏⏁⍀⏃⋏☊⟒ ⏁⍜ ⏁⊑⟒ ⟊⏃⋏⟟⏁⍜⍀

Chips was feeling a bit squeamish. 'That was horrible. Horrible. That poor little guy.'

Pex was unrepentant. 'Yeah, well, he asked for it. Calling us … all those things.'

'But buried alive?! That's like in that horror movie. Y'know, the one with all the horror.'

'I think I saw that one. With all the words going up the screen at the end?'

'Yeah, that was it. Tell you the truth, those words kinda ruined it for me.'

Pex stamped on the loose earth. 'Don't worry, buddy. There are no words in this movie.'

They climbed back into their Chevrolet automobile. Chips was still a bit upset.

'You know, it's much more real than a movie when it's real.'

Pex ignored a no-access sign and pulled on to the motorway. 'It's the smell. You can't smell stuff in a movie.'

Chips sniffed emotionally. 'Digence musta been upset right there at the end.'

'I'm not surprised.'

''Cause I could see him cryin'. His shoulders were shaking, like he was laughing. But he must have been crying. I mean, what sort of crazy whacko would laugh when he's getting buried alive?'

'He musta been crying.'

ᚩᛒᚠ· ᛪᚪᛞᚷᚫᛁᛇ· ᛞᛁ· ᚩᛞᚷ· ᚩᛇ·

Chips opened a bag of smoky bacon curls.

'Yeah. He musta been crying.'

Mulch was laughing so much that he nearly choked on the first mouthful of soil. What a pair of clowns! Then again, it was lucky for them that they *had* been clowns, otherwise they might have chosen their *own* method of execution.

Jaw unhinged, Mulch tunnelled straight down for five metres and then veered north to the cover of some abandoned warehouses. His beard hair sent out sonar signals in all directions. You couldn't be too careful in built-up areas. There was always some wildlife, and Mud People had a habit of burying things in places you wouldn't expect them. Pipes, septic tanks and barrels of industrial waste were all things he had taking an unwitting bite of in his day. And there is nothing worse than finding something in your mouth that you weren't expecting to be there, especially if it's wriggling.

It felt good to be tunnelling again. This was what dwarfs were born to do. The earth felt right between his fingers, and he soon settled into his distance rhythm. Scooping muck between his grinding teeth, breathing through slitted nostrils, and pumping waste material out the other end.

Mulch's hair antennae informed him that there were no vibrations on the surface, so he kicked upwards using the last vestiges of dwarf gas to propel him from his hole.

Holly caught him a metre from the ground.

'Charming,' she said.

'What can I tell you?' said Mulch unapologetically. 'I'm a force of nature. You were up there all that time?'

'Yes, just in case things got out of hand. You put on quite a show.'

Mulch slapped the clay from his clothes. 'A couple of Neutrino blasts could have saved me a lot of digging.'

Holly smiled in spooky imitation of Artemis. 'That's not in *the plan*. And we must stick to *the plan* now, mustn't we?'

She draped a sheet of cam foil around the dwarf's shoulders, and hooked him on to her Moonbelt.

'Take it easy now, won't you?' said Mulch anxiously. 'Dwarfs are creatures of the soil. We don't like flying; we don't even like jumping too high.'

Holly opened the throttle on her wings, heading downtown.

'I'll be just as considerate of your feelings as you are of the LEP's.'

Mulch paled. Funny how this diminutive elf was much scarier than two six-foot hit men.

'Holly, if I ever did anything to offend you, I unreservedly –'

He never finished that particular sentence, because their sudden acceleration forced the words back down his throat.

THE SPIRO NEEDLE

Arno Blunt walked Artemis to his cell. It was comfortable enough, with its own bathroom and entertainment system. There were a couple of things missing: windows and a handle on the door.

Blunt patted Artemis on the head.

'I don't know what happened in that London restaurant, but you try anything like that here, and I will turn you inside out and eat your organs.' He gnashed his pointy teeth to make the point and leaned close, whispering into Artemis's ear. Artemis could hear the teeth click with every syllable.

'I don't care what the boss says, you're not going to be useful forever, so if I were you, I'd be very nice to me.'

'If you were me,' responded Artemis, 'then I'd be you, and if I were you, then I'd hide somewhere far away.'

'Oh, really? And why would you do that?'

Artemis paused to give him the full effect of his words.

'Because Butler is coming for you. And he's extremely annoyed.'

Blunt backed off a few steps. 'No way, kid. I saw him go down. I saw the blood.'

Artemis grinned. 'I didn't say he was alive. I just said he was coming.'

'You're just messing with my mind. Mister Spiro warned me about this.'

Blunt edged out of the door, never taking his eyes off
Artemis.

'Don't worry, Blunt. I don't have him here in my
pocket. You have hours, maybe days, before the time
comes.'

Arno Blunt slammed the door so hard that the frame
shook. Artemis's grin widened. Every cloud had a silver
lining.

Artemis stepped into the shower, allowing the jet of hot
water to pound him on the forehead. In truth, he felt a
little anxious. It was one thing to formulate a plan in the
safety of one's own home. It was quite another to execute
that plan while trapped in the lion's den. And even though
he would never admit it, his confidence had taken quite a
pounding in the last few days. Spiro had outwitted him
back in London, and without apparent effort. He had
strolled into the entrepreneur's trap as naively as a tourist
down a back alley.

Artemis was well aware of his talents. He was a plotter,
a schemer, a planner of dastardly deeds. There was no
thrill greater than the execution of a perfect plan. But
lately his victories had been tainted by guilt, especially
over what had happened to Butler. Artemis had been so
close to losing his old friend that it made him queasy just
thinking about it.

Things had to change. His father would be watching

soon, hoping that Artemis would make the right choices. And if he didn't, Artemis Senior would quite possibly take those choices away from him. He remembered his father's words. *'And what about you, Arty? Will you make the journey with me? When the moment comes will you take your chance to be a hero?'*

Artemis still did not have the answer to that question.

Artemis wrapped himself in a robe monogrammed with his captor's initials. Not only was Spiro reminding him of his presence with the gold letters, but a motion-sensitive closed-circuit camera was following Artemis around the room.

Artemis focused on the challenging task of breaking into Spiro's vault and stealing back the C Cube. He had anticipated many of Spiro's security measures and packed accordingly. Although some were unforeseen and quite ingenious, Artemis had fairy technology on his side, and hopefully Foaly too. The centaur had been ordered not to help, but if Holly presented the break-in as a test, Artemis felt sure that the centaur would be unable to resist.

He sat on the bed, casually scratching his neck. The mike's latex covering had survived the shower, as Holly had assured him it would. It was comforting to know that he was not alone in his prison.

Because the microphone operated on vibrations,

Artemis did not have to speak aloud for his instructions to be transmitted.

'Good evening, friends,' he whispered, his back to the camera. 'Everything proceeds according to plan, taking it as read that Mulch made it back alive. I must warn you to expect a visit from Spiro's goons. I am certain his personnel have been monitoring the streets, and it should lull him into a false sense of security if he believes my people to be wiped out. Mister Spiro has kindly given me a tour of the facility, and hopefully you have recorded everything we need to complete our mission. I believe the local term for this kind of operation is *heist*. This is what I want you to do.'

Artemis whispered slowly, enunciating each point clearly. It was vital that his team members followed his instructions to the letter. If they did not, the entire plot could explode like an active volcano. And at the moment, he was sitting in the volcano's crater.

Pex and Chips were in a good mood. On their return to the Needle, not only had Mister Blunt handed over their five-grand bonus for the Mo Digence job, but he had also given them another assignment. The Needle's external surveillance cameras had picked up a black van parked opposite the main door. It had been there for over three hours and a review of the tapes showed the vehicle circling the building for over an hour looking for a space.

Mister Spiro had warned them to look out for suspicious vehicles, and this was certainly suspicious.

'Go down there,' Blunt had ordered from his chair in the security office. 'And if there's anything breathing inside, ask them why they're breathing outside my building.'

This was the kind of instruction that Pex and Chips understood. No asking questions, no operating complex machinery. Just open the door, scare everything, close the door. Easy. They kidded around in the lift, punching each other in the shoulder until their upper arms went numb.

'We could make big bucks tonight, partner,' said Pex, massaging his biceps to get the circulation going.

'We sure could,' enthused Chips, thinking about all the *Barney* DVDs he could buy. 'This must be worth another bonus. Five grand at least. Altogether that's …'

There followed several moments' silence while both men counted on their fingers.

'That's a lot of cash,' said Pex finally.

'A lot of cash,' agreed Chips.

Juliet had her binoculars trained on the Needle's revolving door. It would have been easier to use the Optix on a fairy helmet, but unfortunately her head had grown too large in the past couple of years. That wasn't the only thing to have changed. Juliet had transformed from gangly kid to toned athlete. She wasn't perfect bodyguard material though; there were still a few wrinkles to be ironed out. Personality wrinkles.

Juliet Butler was a fun-loving creature; she couldn't help it. She found the idea of standing po-faced at the shoulder of some opinionated politician appalling. She'd go crazy from boredom – unless Artemis asked her to stay on professionally. A person could never be bored at Artemis Fowl's side. But that was not likely to happen. Artemis had assured everyone that this was his last job. After Chicago he was going straight. If there was an after Chicago.

This stakeout business was boring too. Sitting quietly was not in Juliet's nature. Her hyperactive disposition had caused her to fail more than one class at Madame Ko's Academy.

'Be at peace with yourself, girl,' the Japanese instructor had said. 'Find that quiet place at your core and inhabit it.'

Juliet generally had to stifle a yawn when Madame Ko started on the kung fu wisdom stuff. Butler, on the other hand, ate it up. He was forever finding his *quiet place* and inhabiting it. In fact, he only came out of his *quiet place* to pulverize whoever was threatening Artemis at the time. Maybe that was why he had his blue diamond tattoo and Juliet didn't.

Two burly figures emerged from the Needle. They were grinning and punching each other on the shoulder.

214

'Captain Short, we're on,' said Juliet into a walkie-talkie tuned to Holly's frequency.

'Understood,' responded Holly from her position above the Spiro Needle. 'How many hostiles?'

'Two. Big and dumb.'

'You need back-up?'

'Negative. I'll wrap these two. You can have a word on your return.'

'OK. I'll be down in five, as soon as I've had a talk with Foaly. And, Juliet, don't mark them.'

'Understood.'

Juliet switched off the radio, climbing into the rear of the van. She swept a pile of surveillance equipment under a fold-up seat, just in case the two heavies actually managed to incapacitate her. It wasn't likely, but her brother would hide the incriminating equipment just in case. Juliet pulled off her suit jacket and placed a baseball cap backwards on her head. She then popped the rear door and clambered out on to the road.

Pex and Chips crossed State Street to the suspect van. It certainly looked suspicious, with its blacked-out windows, but the pair were not unduly concerned. Every testosterone-fuelled college freshman had blacked-out windows these days.

'Whatcha think?' Pex asked his partner.

Chips curled his fingers into fists. 'I think we don't bother knocking.'

Pex nodded. This was the plan that they generally went with. Chips would have proceeded to wrench the door from its hinges had a young lady not appeared from around the bonnet.

'You guys looking for my dad?' said the girl in perfect MTV tones. 'People are always, like, looking for him, and he's never around. Daddy is *so* not here. And I mean that spiritually.'

Pex and Chips blinked in unison. The blink being universal body language for '*Huh?*' This girl was a stunning blend of Asian and Caucasian, but she might as well have been talking Greek for all the comprehension that registered on the security men's faces. 'Spiritually' had five syllables, for heaven's sake.

'You own this van?' asked Chips, taking the offensive.

The girl twisted her ponytail. 'As much as any of us can, like, own anything. One world, one people, right, man? Ownership is, like, you know, an illusion. Maybe we don't even own our own bodies. We could be, like, the daydreams of some greater spirit.'

Pex cracked.

'Do you own the van?' he shouted, wrapping thumb and forefinger round the girl's neck.

The girl nodded. There wasn't enough air in her windpipe for speech.

'That's better. Anyone inside?'

A shake of the head this time.

Pex relaxed his grip slightly.

'How many more in the family?'

The girl answered in a whisper, using as little air as possible.

'Seven. Dad, Mom, two grandparents and the triplets: Beau, Mo and Joe. They're gone for sushi.'

Pex cheered up considerably. Triplets and grandparents, that didn't sound like any problem.

'OK. We wait. Open her up, kid.'

'Sushi?' said Chips. 'That's raw fish. You ever have that, buddy?'

Pex held the girl by the neck while she fiddled with the key.

'Yeah. I bought some in the supermarket once.'

'Was it good?'

'Yeah. I threw it in the deep-fat fryer for ten minutes. Not bad.'

The girl slid back the van door and climbed into the interior. Pex and Chips followed, ducking under the rim. Pex released the girl's neck momentarily to take the step. That was his mistake. A properly trained private soldier would never allow an untethered prisoner to lead the way into an unsecured vehicle.

The girl stumbled accidentally, dropping to both knees on the interior's carpet.

'Sushi,' said Pex. 'It's good with French fries.'

Then the girl's foot snapped back, catching him in the chest. The hired muscle collapsed, gasping, on to the floor.

'Oops,' said the girl, straightening. 'Accident.'

Chips thought he must be having some kind of waking dream, because there was no way a little pop princess clone could have decked ninety kilograms of muscle and attitude.

'You ... you just ... ,' he stuttered. 'That's impossible. No way.'

'Way,' said Juliet, pirouetting like a ballerina. The jade ring in her ponytail swung round, loaded with centrifugal force. It struck Chips between the eyeballs, like a stone from a sling. He staggered backwards, landing in a heap on a leatherette sofa.

Behind her, Pex's breath was returning. His eyeballs stopped rolling wildly and focused on his assailant.

'Hi,' said Juliet, bending over him. 'Guess what.'

'What?' said Pex.

'You're not supposed to deep-fry sushi,' said the girl, clapping the assassin on both temples with the palms of her hands. Unconsciousness was immediate.

Mulch emerged from the bathroom, buttoning the bum-flap on his tunnelling trousers.

'What did I miss?' he asked.

*

Holly hovered one hundred and fifty feet above Chicago's downtown district – known locally as the Loop after the curve of elevated track that enclosed the area. She was up there for two reasons. Firstly, they needed an X-ray scan of the Spiro Needle in order to construct 3D blueprints. And secondly, she wanted to talk to Foaly alone.

She spotted a stone eagle perched on the roof of an early twentieth-century apartment block, and alighted on its head. She would have to move perch after a few minutes, or her shield vibration would begin to pulverize the rock.

Juliet's voice sounded in her earpiece.

'Captain Short, we're on.'

'Understood,' responded Holly. 'How many hostiles?'

'Two. Big and dumb.'

'You need back-up?'

'Negative. I'll wrap these two. You can have a word on your return.'

'OK. I'll be down in five, as soon as I've had a talk with Foaly. And, Juliet, don't mark them.'

'Understood.'

Holly smiled. Juliet was a piece of work. A chip off the Butler block. But she was a wild card. Even on stakeout she couldn't stop chattering for more than ten seconds. None of her brother's discipline. She was a happy teenager. A kid. She should not be in this line of business. Artemis had no business dragging her into his crazy schemes. But there was something about the Irish boy that made you forget your reservations. In the past sixteen months she had fought a troll for him, healed his entire family, dived into the Arctic Ocean and now she was preparing to disobey a direct order from Commander Root.

She opened a channel to LEP Operations.

'Foaly. Are you listening?

Nothing for several seconds, then the centaur's voice burst through the helmet's micro-speaker.

'Holly. Hold on. You're a bit fuzzy; I'm just going to fine-tune the wavelength. Talk to me. Say something.'

'Testing. One two. One two. Trolls cause terrible trouble in a tantrum.'

'OK. Gotcha. Crystal clear. How goes it in the Land of Mud?'

Holly gazed down at the city below her.

'No mud here. Just glass, steel and computers. You'd like it.'

'Oh no. Not me. Mud People are Mud People, no matter if they're wearing suits or loincloths. The only good thing about humans is the television. All we get on PPTV is reruns. I'm almost sorry the goblin generals' trial is over. Guilty on all counts, thanks to you. Sentencing is next month.'

Anxiety loosened its grip on Holly's stomach. 'Guilty. Thank heavens. Things can finally go back to normal.'

Foaly snickered. 'Normal? You're in the wrong job for normal. You can kiss normal goodbye if we don't get Artemis's gizmo back from Spiro.'

The centaur was right. Her life had not been *normal* since she'd been promoted to Recon from the vice squad. But did she really want a normal life? Wasn't that the reason she transferred from vice in the first place?

'So why the call?' asked Foaly. 'Feeling a bit homesick, are you?'

'No,' replied Holly. And it was true. She wasn't. The elf captain had barely thought of Haven since Artemis embroiled her in his latest intrigue. 'I need your advice.'

'Advice? Oh, really? That wouldn't be another way of asking for help now, would it? I believe Commander Root's words were "You got what you got." Rules are rules, Holly.'

Holly sighed. 'Yes, Foaly. Rules are rules. Julius knows best.'

'That's right. Julius knows best,' said Foaly, but he didn't sound convinced.

'You probably couldn't help anyway. Spiro's security is pretty advanced.'

Foaly snorted, and a centaur snorting is something to hear.

'Yeah, sure. What has he got? A couple of tin cans and a dog? Ooh scary.'

'I wish. There's stuff in this building that I've never seen before. Smart stuff.'

A small liquid-crystal screen flickered into life in the corner of Holly's visor. Foaly was broadcasting a visual from Police Plaza. Technically, not something he should be doing for an unofficial operation. The centaur was curious.

'I know what you're doing by the way,' said Foaly, wagging a finger.

'I have no idea what you mean,' said Holly innocently.

'*You probably couldn't help anyway. Spiro's security is pretty advanced*,' mimicked the centaur. 'You're trying to light a fire under my ego. I'm not stupid, Holly.'

'OK. Maybe I am. Do you want the straight truth?'

'Oh, you're going to tell me the truth now? Interesting tactic for the LEP.'

'The Spiro Needle is a fortress. There's no way in without you, even Artemis admits it. We're not looking for equipment, or extra fairy-power. Just advice over the airwaves, maybe a bit of camera work. Keep the lines open, that's all I'm asking.'

Foaly scratched his chin. 'No way in, eh? Even Artemis admits it.'

'"We can't do it without Foaly." His exact words.'

The centaur struggled to keep the smugness from his features.

'Have you got any video?'

Holly took a hand-held computer from her belt.

'Artemis shot some film inside the Needle. I'm mailing it to you now.'

'I need a blueprint of the building.'

Holly panned her visor left and right, so Foaly could see where she was.

'That's why I'm up here. To do an X-ray scan. It'll be in your mainframe in ten minutes.

Holly heard a bell chime in her speakers. It was a computer alert. Her mail had arrived in Police Plaza. Foaly opened the file.

'Key codes. OK. Cameras. No problem. Wait until I show you what I've developed for CCTV cameras. I'm fast-forwarding through the corridors. Dum de dum de dum. Ah, the vault. On the eighty-fifth. Pressure pads, antibiotic mats. Motion sensors. Temperature sensitive lasers. Thermal cameras. Voice-recognition, retina and gel-thumbprint scanners.' He paused. 'Impressive, for a Mud Man.'

'You're telling me,' agreed Holly. 'A bit more than two tin cans and a dog.'

'Fowl is right. Without me you're sunk.'

'So, will you help?'

Foaly had to milk the moment. 'I'm not promising anything, mind ...'

'Yes?'

'I'll keep a screen open for you. But if something comes up ...'

'I understand.'

'No guarantees.'

'No guarantees. I owe you a carton of carrots.'

'Two cartons. And a case of beetle juice.'

'Done.'

The centaur's face was flushed with the promise of a challenge.

'Will you miss him, Holly?' he asked suddenly.

Holly was caught off-guard by the question.

'Miss who?' she said, though she already knew.

'The Fowl boy, of course. If everything goes according to plan, we'll be wiped from his memory. No more wild plots or seat-of-the-pants adventures. It will be a quiet life.'

Holly made to avoid Foaly's gaze, although the helmet cam was point-of-view and the centaur could not see her.

'No,' she said. 'I will not miss him.'

But her eyes told the real story.

Holly circled the Needle several times at various altitudes, until the X-ray scanner had accumulated enough data for a 3D model. She mailed a copy of the file to Foaly in Police Plaza and returned to the van.

'I thought I told you not to mark them,' she said, bending over the fallen hit men.

Juliet shrugged. 'Hey. No big deal, fairy girl. I got carried away in the heat of battle. Just give him a shot of blue sparks and send him on his way.'

Holly traced a finger round the perfectly circular bruise on Chips's forehead.

'You should have seen me,' said Juliet. 'Bang, bang, and they were down. Never had a chance.'

Holly sent a solitary spark down her finger; it wiped away the bruise like a damp cloth cleaning a coffee ring.

'You could have used the Neutrino to stun them, you know.'

'The Neutrino? Where's the fun in that?'

Captain Short removed her helmet, glaring up at the teenage human.

'This is not supposed to be fun, Juliet. It's not a game. I thought you realized that, considering what happened to Butler.'

Juliet's grin disappeared. 'I know it's not a game, Captain. Maybe this is the way I deal with things.'

Holly held her gaze. 'Well then, maybe you're in the wrong line of work.'

'Or maybe you've been in this line of work too long,' argued Juliet. 'According to Butler, you used to be a bit of a wild card yourself.'

Mulch emerged from the bathroom. This time he had been applying a layer of sunblock. It was now the middle of the night, but the dwarf wasn't taking any chances. If this insertion went pear-shaped, as it probably would, then he could very well be on the run by morning.

'What's the problem, ladies? If you're fighting over

me, don't bother. I make it a point never to date outside my species.'

The tension deflated like a punctured balloon.

'Dream on, hairball,' said Holly.

'Nightmare, more like,' added Juliet. '*I* make it a point never to date anyone who lives in a dung heap.'

Mulch was unperturbed. 'You're both in denial. I have that effect on females.'

'I don't doubt it,' said Holly, grinning.

The LEP captain folded out a stowaway table and placed her helmet on top. She switched her helmet cam to Project, and opened the 3D plan of the Spiro Needle. It revolved in the air, a lattice of neon-green lines.

'OK, everyone. Here's the plan. Team One burns their way in through the wall of the eighty-fifth floor. Team Two goes in through the helipad door. Here.'

Holly marked the entrances by tapping the corresponding spot on the screen of her hand-held computer. An orange pulse appeared on the floating plan.

'Foaly has agreed to help, so he'll be with us over the airwaves. Juliet, you take this hand-held computer. You can use it to conference with us on the move. Just ignore the Gnommish symbols; we'll send you any files you need to view. Wear an earpiece though, to cut out the speakers. The last thing we need is computers beeping at the wrong moment. That little indent below the screen is a mike. Whisper-sensitive, so no need to shout.'

Juliet strapped the credit-card-sized computer on to her wrist.

'What are the teams, and what are their objectives?'

Holly stepped into the 3D image. Her body was surrounded by strobes of light.

'Team One goes after the security and switches the vault guards' oxygen canisters. Team Two goes after the box. Simple. We go in pairs. You and Mulch. Artemis and me.'

'Oh no,' said Juliet, shaking her head. 'I have to go with Artemis. He's my principal. My brother would stick to Artemis like glue, and so will I.'

Holly stepped out of the hologram. 'Won't work. You can't fly and you can't climb walls. There has to be one fairy per team. If you don't like it, take it up with Artemis next time you see him.'

Juliet scowled. It made sense. Of course it did. Artemis's plans always made sense. It was only too clear now why Artemis had not revealed the entire thing in Ireland. He knew she would object. It was bad enough being separated for the past six hours. But the most difficult phase of the mission lay ahead, and Artemis would not have a Butler at his shoulder.

Holly stepped back into the hologram. 'Team One, you and Mulch, climb the Needle and burn through on the eighty-fifth floor. From there, you place this video clip on a CCTV cable.'

Holly held up what looked like a twist of wire. 'Loaded fibre optic,' she explained. 'Allows for remote hijacking of any video system. With this in place, Foaly can send the signal from every camera in the building to our helmets. He can also send the humans any signal he wants them to see. You will also replace two oxygen cylinders with our own special mix.'

Juliet placed the video clip in her jacket pocket.

'I will enter from the roof,' continued Holly. 'From there, I proceed to Artemis's room. As soon as Team One gives us the all clear, we'll go after the C Cube.'

'You make it sound so easy,' said Juliet.

Mulch laughed. 'She always does that,' he said. 'And it never is.'

Team One, the Spiro Needle's Base

Juliet Butler had been trained in seven martial arts disciplines. She had learned to ignore pain and sleep deprivation. She could resist torture both physical and psychological. But nothing had prepared her for what she would have to endure to get into this building.

The Needle had no blind sides, with twenty-four-hour activity on each face, so they were forced to begin their ascent from the pavement. Juliet pulled the van round, double-parking it as close to the wall as she could.

They went out through the sunroof, draped in Holly's single sheet of camouflage foil. Juliet was clipped on to the Moonbelt on Mulch's waist.

She rapped on Mulch's helmet. 'You stink.'

Mulch's reply came through the cylindrical transmitter in Juliet's ear.

'To you, maybe, but to a dwarf female I am the essence of a healthy male. You're the one that stinks, Mud Girl. To me, you smell worse than a skunk in two-month-old socks.'

Holly stuck her head through the sunroof.

'Quiet!' she hissed. 'Both of you! We're on a tight schedule in case you'd forgotten. Juliet, your precious principal is stuck in a room up there waiting for me to show up. It's five minutes past four already. The guards are due to change in less than an hour, and I still have to finish mesmerizing these goons. We have a fifty-five-minute window here. Let's not waste it arguing.'

'Why can't you just fly us up to the ledge?'

'Basic military tactics. If we split up, then one team might make it. If we're together, then one goes down we all go down. Divide and conquer.'

Her words sobered Juliet. The fairy girl was right; she should have known that. It was happening again – she was losing concentration at a vital moment.

'OK. Let's go. I'll hold my breath.'

Mulch stuck both palms in his mouth, sucking any last vestiges of moisture from the pores.

$$ \text{⬡ ⊛ ⌷ • ⚲ • ◗ ⚲ • ◉ ⚳ • ⬡ • ◔ ⚲ • ⚲ •} $$

'Hold on,' he said, having removed his hands from his palate. 'Here we go.'

The dwarf flexed his powerful legs, leaping one and a half metres to the wall of the Spiro Needle. Juliet bobbed along behind, feeling for all the world as though she were underwater. The problem with riding a Moonbelt was that, as well as the weightlessness, you got the loss of coordination and sometimes the space nausea too. Moonbelts were designed for carrying inanimate objects, not live fairies, and certainly not human beings.

Mulch had not had a drink for several hours, causing his dwarf pores to open to the size of pinholes. They sucked noisily, latching on to the smooth external surface of the Spiro Needle. The dwarf avoided the tinted windows, sticking to the metal girders, because, even though the pair were draped in a sheet of camouflage foil, there were still enough limbs sticking out to be spotted. Cam foil did not render the wearer completely invisible. Thousands of micro-sensors, threaded through the material, analysed and reflected the surroundings, but one shower of rain could short out the whole thing.

Mulch climbed quickly, settling into a smooth rhythm. His double-jointed fingers and toes curled to grip the smallest groove. And where there were no grooves, the dwarf's pores adhered to the flat surface. His beard hair fanned out under the helmet's visor, probing the building's face.

Juliet had to ask. 'Your beard? That's a bit freaky. What's it doing? Searching for cracks?'

'Vibrations,' grunted Mulch. 'Sensors, currents, maintenance men.' Obviously, he wasn't going to devote any energy to full sentences. 'Motion sensor picks us up. We're finished. Foil or not.'

Juliet didn't blame her partner for saving his breath. They had a long way to go. Straight up.

As they cleared the buffer provided by the adjacent buildings the wind picked up. Juliet's feet were plucked from beneath her, and she fluttered from the dwarf's neck like a scarf. Rarely had she felt so helpless. Events were utterly beyond her control. Training counted for absolutely nothing in this situation. Her life was in Mulch's hands completely.

The floors slid by in a blur of glass and steel. The wind pulled at them with grabby fingers, threatening to spin the pair into the night.

'There's a lot of moisture up here from the wind,' gasped the dwarf. 'I can't hold on much longer.'

Juliet reached in, running a finger along the outer wall. It was slick with tiny beads of dew. Sparks were popping along the sheet of cam foil as the moisture-laden wind shorted out its micro-sensors. Patches of the foil failed altogether. The effect was of blocks of circuits apparently suspended in the night. The entire building was swaying too — maybe just enough to shake off a tired dwarf and his passenger.

Finally, the dwarf's fingers locked on to the ledge of the eighty-fifth floor. Mulch climbed on to the narrow outcrop, directing his visor into the building.

'This room is no good,' he said. 'My visor is picking up two motion detectors and a laser sensor. We need to move along.'

He scampered down the ledge, sure-footed as a mountain goat. This was his business, after all. Dwarfs did not fall off things. Not unless they were pushed. Juliet followed cautiously. Not even Madame Ko's Academy could have prepared her for this.

Finally Mulch arrived at a window that satisfied him.

'OK,' he said, his voice sounding strained in Juliet's earpiece. 'We got a sensor with a dead battery.'

His beard hair latched on to the windowpane. 'I don't feel any vibration, so nothing electrical running and no conversation. It seems safe.'

Mulch trickled a few drops of dwarf rock polish on to the toughened pane. It liquefied the glass immediately, leaving a puddle of turgid fluid on the carpet. With any luck the hole would remain undiscovered over the weekend.

'Ooh,' said Juliet. 'That stinks nearly as much as you do.'

Mulch did not bother returning the insult, preferring instead to tumble indoors to safety.

He checked the moonometer in his visor.

'Four twenty. Human time. We're behind schedule. Let's go.'

Juliet hopped through the hole in the window.

'Typical Mud Man,' said Mulch. 'Spiro spends millions on a security system, and it all falls apart because of one battery.'

Juliet drew an LEP Neutrino 2000. She flicked aside the safety cap and pressed the power button. The light changed from green to red.

'We're not in yet,' she said, making for the door.

'Wait!' hissed Mulch, grabbing her arm. 'The camera!'

Juliet froze. She'd forgotten the camera. They were barely a minute inside the building and she was already making mistakes. Concentrate, girl, concentrate.

Mulch aimed his visor at the recessed CCTV camera. The helmet's ion filter highlighted the camera's arc as a shimmering gold stream. There was no way past to the camera itself.

'There's no blind spot,' he said. 'And the camera cable is behind the box.'

'We'll just have to huddle close together behind the cam foil,' said Juliet, her lip curling at the idea.

Foaly's image popped up on the computer screen on her wrist. 'You could do that. But unfortunately cam foil doesn't work on-screen.'

'Why not?'

'Cameras have better eyes than humans. Did you ever

see a TV picture on television? The camera breaks down the pixels. If you go down that corridor behind cam foil, you're going to look like two people behind a projector screen.'

Juliet glared at the monitor. 'Anything else, Foaly? Maybe the floor is going to dissolve into a pool of acid?'

'Doubt it. Spiro is good, but he's not me.'

'Can't you loop the video feed, pony boy?' said Juliet into the computer's mike. 'Just send them a false signal for a minute?'

Foaly gnashed his horsey teeth. 'I am so unappreciated. No, I cannot set up a loop unless I am on-site, as I was during the Fowl siege. That is what the video clip is for. I'm afraid you're on your own up there.'

'I'll blast it then.'

'Negatori. A Neutrino blast would certainly knock out one camera, and possibly chain-react along the entire network. You may as well dance a jig for Arno Blunt.'

Juliet kicked the skirting board in frustration. She was falling at the first hurdle. Her brother would know what to do, but he was on the other side of the Atlantic. A mere six metres of corridor separated them from the camera, but it might as well have been a thousand metres of broken glass.

She noticed that Mulch was unbuttoning his bum-flap.

'Oh, great. Now the little man needs a potty break. This is hardly the time.'

$\theta\mathcal{R}\partial\cdot|\mathcal{R}\mathcal{L}\otimes\mathring{\ominus}\mathring{\gamma}\mathcal{L}\cdot\ominus\mathcal{L}\cdot\mathcal{R}\cdot\mathcal{U}\mathcal{R}\partial\mathcal{F}\cdot$

'I'm going to ignore your sarcasm,' said Mulch, lying flat on the floor, 'because I know what Spiro can do to people he doesn't like.'

Juliet knelt beside him. Not too close.

'I hope your next sentence is going to begin with "I have a plan."'

The dwarf appeared to be aiming his rear end.

'Actually ...'

'You're not serious.'

'Deadly. I have quite a considerable force at my disposal here.'

Juliet couldn't help smiling. The little guy was a dwarf after her own heart. Metaphorically. He was adapting to the situation, just as she would.

'All we have to do is swing the camera about twenty degrees on its stand and we have a clear run to the cable.'

'And you're going to do that with ... wind power?'

'Precisely.'

'What about the noise?'

Mulch winked. 'Silent, but deadly. I'm a professional. All you have to do is squeeze my little toe when I give you the word.'

In spite of arduous training in some of the world's toughest terrain, Juliet was not quite prepared to be involved in a wind offensive.

'Do I have to participate? It seems like a one-man operation to me.'

Mulch squinted at the target, adjusting his posterior accordingly.

'This is a precision burst. I need a gunner to pull the trigger so I can concentrate on aiming. Reflexology is a proven science with dwarfs. Every part of the foot is connected to a part of the body. And it just so happens that the left little toe is connected to my ...'

'OK,' said Juliet hurriedly. 'I get the picture.'

'Let's get on with it then.'

Juliet pulled Mulch's boot off. The socks were open-toed, and five hairy digits wiggled with a dexterity no human toes possessed.

'This is the only way?'

'Unless you have a better idea.'

Juliet gingerly grasped the toe, its black curly hairs obligingly parting to allow her access to the joint.

'Now?'

'Wait.' The dwarf licked his forefinger, testing the air. 'No wind.'

'Not yet,' muttered Juliet.

Mulch fine-tuned his aim. 'OK. Squeeze.'

Juliet held her breath, and squeezed. And in order to do the moment justice, it has to be described in slow motion.

Juliet felt her fingers close round the joint. The pressure sped up Mulch's leg in a series of jolts. The dwarf fought to keep his aim true, in spite of the spasms.

Pressure built in his abdomen and exploded through his bum-flap with a dull thump. The only thing Juliet could relate the experience to was crouching beside a mortar. A missile of compressed air shot across the room, heat blur surrounding it like waves of water.

'Too much top-spin,' groaned Mulch. 'I loaded it.'

The air ball spiralled towards the ceiling, shedding layers like an onion.

'Right,' urged Mulch. 'Right a bit.'

The next unlikely missile impacted against the wall a metre ahead of its target. Luckily, the ricochet clipped the camera box, sending it spinning like a plate on a stick. The intruders waited for it to settle with bated breath. The camera finally creaked to a halt after a dozen revolutions.

'Well?' asked Juliet.

Mulch sat up, checking the camera's ion stream through his visor.

'Lucky,' he breathed. 'Very lucky. We have a path straight through.' He slapped shut his smoking bum-flap. 'It's been a while since I launched a torpedo.'

Juliet took the video clip from her pocket, waving it in front of her wrist computer so Foaly could see it.

'So, I just wind this round any old cable? Is that it?'

'No, Mud Maid,' sighed Foaly, comfortable in his familiar role as unappreciated genius. 'That is a complex piece of nanotechnology, complete with microfilaments that act as receivers, broadcasters and clamps. Naturally it leeches its power from the Mud People's own system.'

'Naturally,' said Mulch, trying to keep his eyes open.

'You need to ensure that it is firmly clamped to one of the video cables. Luckily, its multi-sensor does not have to be in contact with all the wires, just one.'

'And which ones are the video wires?'

'Well … all of them.'

Juliet groaned. 'So I just wind it round any old cable?'

'I suppose so,' admitted the centaur. 'But wind it tightly. All the filaments have to penetrate.'

Juliet reached up, selected a wire at random and wound the clip round it.

'OK?'

There was a moment's pause while Foaly waited for reception. Below the surface, picture-in-picture screens began popping up on the centaur's plasma screen.

'Perfect. We have eyes and ears.'

'Let's go then,' said Juliet impatiently. 'Start the loop.'

Foaly wasted a minute delivering another lecture. 'This is much more than a loop, young lady. I am about to completely wipe moving patterns from the surveillance footage. In other words, the pictures they see in the surveillance booth will be exactly as they should be, except you won't be in them. Just be careful never to stand still or you'll become visible. Keep something moving, even if it's only your little finger.'

Juliet checked the digital clock on the computer face. 'Four thirty. We need to hurry.'

'OK. The security centre is one corridor over. We take the shortest route.'

Juliet projected the schematic into the air. 'Down this corridor here, two rights and there we are.'

Mulch strode past her to the wall.

'I said the shortest route, Mud Girl. Think laterally.'

The office was an executive suite, with a skyline view and floor-to-ceiling pine shelving. Mulch hauled back a section of the pine and knocked on the wall behind it.

'Plasterboard,' he said. 'No problem.'

Juliet closed the panel behind them. 'No debris, dwarf. Artemis said we weren't to leave any trace.'

'Don't worry. I'm not a messy eater.'

Mulch unhinged his jaw, expanding his oral cavity to basketball proportions. He opened his mouth to an incredible one hundred and seventy degrees, and took a whopping bite out of the wall. A ring of tombstone teeth soon reduced the wall to dust.

'A bi' dry,' he commented. 'Har' oo shwallow.'

Three bites later they were through. Mulch climbed into the next office without a crumb dropping from his lips. Juliet followed, pulling the pine shelving across to cover the hole.

The next office was not quite so salubrious, the dark cubby of a vice president. No city view, and plain metal shelving. Juliet rearranged the shelving to cover the newly excavated entrance. Mulch knelt at the door, his beard hair latching on to the wood.

'Some vibration outside. That's probably the compressor. Nothing irregular, so no conversation. I'd say we were safe.'

'You could just ask me,' said Foaly, in his helmet earpiece. 'I do have footage from every camera in the building. That's over two thousand, in case you're interested.'

'Thanks for the update. Well, are we clear?'

'Yes. Remarkably so. No one in the immediate vicinity, except a guard at the lobby desk.'

Juliet took two grey canisters from her backpack. 'OK. This is where I earn my keep. You stay here. This shouldn't take more than a minute.'

Juliet cracked open the door, creeping along the corridor on rubber-soled boots. Aeroplane-style lighting strips were inlaid in the carpet; otherwise, the only lighting came from exit boxes over the fire-escape doors.

The schematic on her wrist computer told her that she had twenty metres to go before reaching the security office. After that, she could only hope that the oxygen rack was unlocked. And why shouldn't it be? Oxygen canisters were hardly high-risk objects. At least she would have ample warning if any personnel happened to be doing their rounds.

Juliet crept, panther-like, down the corridor, her footfalls muffled by the carpet. On reaching the final corner she lay flat and inched her nose round the bend.

She could see the floor's security station. Just as Pex had revealed under the *mesmer*, the vault guard's oxygen canisters were slotted in a rack in front of the desk.

There was only one guard on duty, and he was busy watching basketball on a portable television. Juliet moved forward on her stomach until she was directly below the rack. The guard had his back to her, concentrating on the game.

'What the hell?' exclaimed the security man, who was roughly the size of a refrigerator. He had noticed something in a security monitor.

'Move!' hissed Foaly in Juliet's earpiece.

'What?'

'Move! You're showing up on the monitors.'

Juliet wiggled her toe. She had forgotten to keep moving. Butler would never have forgotten that.

Over her head, the guard employed the age-old method of rapid repair, slapping the monitor's plastic casing. The fuzzy figure disappeared.

'Interference,' he muttered. 'Stupid satellite TV.'

Juliet felt a bead of sweat run along the bridge of her nose. The younger Butler reached up slowly and slipped two substitute oxygen canisters into the rack. Although 'oxygen canisters' was a bit of a misnomer, because it wasn't oxygen in these canisters.

She checked her watch. It might already be too late.

TEAM TWO, ABOVE THE SPIRO NEEDLE

Holly hovered six metres above the Needle, waiting for the green light. She was not comfortable with this operation. There were too many variables. If this mission weren't so vital to the future of the fairy civilization, she would have refused to participate in it altogether.

Her mood did not improve as the night progressed. Team One was proving extremely unprofessional, bickering like a pair of adolescents. Although, to be fair to Juliet, she was barely beyond adolescence. Mulch, on the other hand, couldn't find his childhood with an encyclopaedia.

Captain Short followed their progress on her helmet visor, wincing at each new development. Finally, and against all the odds, Juliet managed to switch the canisters.

'Go,' said Mulch, doing his best to sound military. 'I say again, we have a go situation on the black op. code red thing.'

Holly shut off Mulch's communication in the middle of the dwarf's giggling fit. Foaly could open a screen in her visor if there was a crisis.

Below her the Spiro Needle pointed spacewards like the world's biggest rocket. Low fog gathered around its base, adding to the illusion. Holly set her wings to descend, dropping gently towards the helipad. She called up the video file of Artemis's entry to the Needle on her visor and slowed it down at the point where Spiro keyed in the access code for the rooftop door.

'Thank you, Spiro,' she said, grinning, as she punched in the code.

The door slid open pneumatically. Automatic lights flickered into life along the stairwell. There was a camera every six metres. No blind spots. This didn't matter to Holly, as human cameras could not detect a shielded fairy – unless they were of the type with an extremely high frame-per-second rate. And even then, the frames had to be viewed as stills to catch a glimpse of the fairy folk. Only one human had ever managed to do this. An Irish one, who was twelve years old at the time.

Holly floated down the stairwell, activating an Argon laser filter on her visor. This entire building could be crisscrossed with laser beams and she wouldn't know it until she set off an alarm. Even a shielded fairy had mass enough to stop a beam reaching its sensor, if only for a millisecond. The view before her turned a cloudy purple, but there were no beams. She was certain that wouldn't be the case when they came to the vault.

Holly continued her flight to the brushed-steel lift doors.

'Artemis is on eighty-four,' said Foaly. 'The vault is on eighty-five; Spiro's penthouse is on eighty-six, where we are now.'

'How are the walls?'

'According to the spectrometer, mostly plaster and wood in the partition walls. Except round key rooms, which are reinforced steel.'

'Let me guess: Artemis's room, the vault and Spiro's penthouse.'

'Dead on, Captain. But do not despair. I have plotted the shortest course. I am sending it to your helmet now.'

Holly waited a moment until a quill icon flashed in the corner of her visor, informing her that she had mail.

'Open mail,' she said into the helmet mike, enunciating clearly. A matrix of green lines superimposed themselves in front of her regular vision. Her trail was marked by a thick red line.

'Follow the laser, Holly. Foolproof. No offence.'

'None taken, for now. But if this doesn't work, I'll be so offended you won't believe it.'

The red laser led straight into the belly of the lift. Holly floated into the metal box and descended to the eighty-fifth floor. The guiding laser led her out of the lift and down the corridor.

She tried the door to an office on her left. Locked. Hardly surprising.

'I'm going to have to unshield to pick this lock. Are you sure my pattern is wiped from the video?'

'Of course,' said Foaly.

Holly could imagine the childish pout on his lips. She unshielded and took an Omnitool from her belt. The Omnitool's sensor would send an X-ray of the lock's workings to the chip and select the right bit. It even did the turning. Of course, the Omnitool only worked on keyhole locks, which, in spite of their unreliability, the Mud People still used.

In less than five seconds the door lay open before her.

'Five seconds,' said Holly. 'This thing needs a new battery.'

The red line in her visor ran to the office's centre, and then took a right-angle turn downwards, through the floor.

'Let me guess. Artemis is down there?'

'Yes. Asleep, judging by the pictures coming in from his iris-cam.'

'You said the cell was lined with reinforced steel.'

'True. But no motion sensors in the walls or roof. So all you have to do is burn through.'

Holly drew her Neutrino 2000. 'Oh, is that all?'

She chose a spot adjacent to a wall air conditioner and peeled back the carpet. Underneath, the floor was dull and metallic.

'No trace, remember?' said Foaly in her earpiece. 'That's vital.'

꙳⚙⚘⚛⚔⚘ · ⚙⚛⚙⚙⚙⚙ · ⚙⚘ · ⚔⚙⚙⚛

'I'll worry about that later,' said Holly, adjusting the air con to extract. 'For now, I need to get him out of there. We're on a schedule.'

Holly adjusted the Neutrino's output, concentrating the beam so it cut through the metal floor. Acrid smoke billowed from the molten gash, and was immediately siphoned off into the Chicago night by the air con.

'Artemis isn't the only one with brains around here,' grunted Holly, sweat streaming down her face in spite of the helmet's climate control.

'The air con stops the fire alarm going off. Very good.'

'Is he awake?' asked Holly, leaving the last centimetre of a half-metre square uncut.

'Wide-eyed and bushy-tailed, to use Centaurian imagery. A laser carving through the ceiling will do that to a person.'

'Good,' said Captain Short, cutting through the final section. The metal square twisted on a final strand of steel.

'Won't that make a lot of noise?' asked Foaly.

Holly watched the section fall.

'I doubt it,' she said.

CHAPTER 10: FĬNGERS AND THUMBS

 ARTEMĬS was meditating when the first laser-stroke cut through the ceiling. He rose from the lotus position, pulled his sweater back on and arranged some pillows on the floor. Moments later, a square of metal fell to the floor, its impact silenced by the cushions. Holly's face appeared in the hole.

Artemis pointed at the pillows. 'You anticipated me.'

The LEP captain nodded. 'Only thirteen, and already predictable.'

'I presume you used the air conditioner to vacuum the smoke?'

'Exactly. I think we're getting to know one another too well.'

Holly reeled a piton line from her belt, lowering it into the room.

'Make a loop at the bottom with the clamp and hop aboard. I'll reel you in.'

Artemis did as he was told and, in seconds, he was clambering through the hole.

'Do we have Mister Foaly on our side?' he asked.

Holly handed Artemis a small cylindrical earpiece. 'Ask him yourself.'

Artemis inserted the miracle of nanotechnology.

'Well, Foaly. Astound me.'

Below, in Haven City, the centaur rubbed his hands together. Artemis was the only one who actually understood his lectures.

'You're going to love this, Mud Boy. Not only have I wiped you from the video, not only did I erase the ceiling falling in, but I have created a simulated Artemis.'

Artemis was intrigued. 'A sim? Really? How exactly did you do that?'

'Simple really,' said Foaly modestly. 'I have hundreds of human movies on file. I borrowed Steve McQueen's solitary confinement scene from *The Great Escape* and altered his clothes.'

'What about the face?'

'I had some digital interrogation footage from your last visit to Haven. I put the two together and *voilà*. Our simulated Artemis can do whatever I tell him, whenever I say. At the moment, the sim is asleep, but in half an hour I may just instruct him to go to the bathroom.'

Holly reeled in her piton cord. 'The miracle of modern science. The LEP pours millions into your department, Foaly, and all you can do is send Mud Boys to the toilet.'

'You should be nice to me, Holly. I'm doing you a big favour. If Julius knew I was helping you, he'd be extremely angry.'

'Which is exactly why you are doing it.'

Holly moved quietly to the door, opening it a crack. The corridor was clear and silent, but for the drone of panning cameras and the hum of fluorescent lighting. One section of Holly's visor displayed miniature transparent feeds from Spiro's security cameras. There were six guards doing the rounds on the floor.

Holly closed the door.

'OK. Let's get going. We need to reach Spiro before the guards change.'

Artemis arranged the carpet over the hole in the floor. 'Have you located his apartment?'

'Directly above us. We need to get up there and scan his retina and thumb.'

An expression flashed across Artemis's face. Just for a second.

'The scans. Yes. The sooner the better.'

Holly had never seen that look on the human boy's features before. Was it guilt? Could it be?

'Is there something you're not telling me?' she demanded.

The expression vanished, to be replaced by the customary lack of emotion.

'No, Captain Short. Nothing. And do you really think that now is the time for an interrogation?'

Holly wagged a threatening finger. 'Artemis. If you mess with me now, in the middle of an operation, I won't forget it.'

'Don't worry,' said Artemis wryly. 'I will.'

Spiro's apartment was two floors directly above Artemis's cell. It made sense to reinforce the same block. Unfortunately, Jon Spiro did not like the idea of anyone spying on him, so there were no cameras in his section of the building.

'Typical,' muttered Foaly. 'Power-crazed megalomaniacs never like anyone to see their own dirty secrets.'

'I think someone's in denial,' said Holly, focusing a tight beam from her Neutrino at the ceiling.

A section of floating ceiling melted like ice in a kettle, revealing the steel above. Molten beads of metal ate into the carpet as the laser sliced through the flooring. When the hole was of sufficient diameter Holly shut down the beam and popped her helmet camera into the space.

Nothing appeared on the screen.

'Switching to infrared.'

A rack of suits sprang into focus. They might have been white.

'The wardrobe. We're in the wardrobe.'

'Perfect,' said Foaly. 'Put him to sleep.'

'He is asleep. It's ten to five in the morning.'

'Well, make sure he doesn't wake up then.'

Holly replaced the camera in its groove. She plucked a silver capsule from her belt and inserted it into the hole.

Foaly supplied the commentary for Artemis.

'The capsule is a Sleeper Deeper, in case you're wondering.'

'Gaseous?'

'No. Brainwaves.'

Artemis was intrigued. 'Go on.'

'Basically it scans for brainwave patterns, then replicates them. Anyone in the vicinity stays in the state they're in until the capsule dissolves.

'No trace?'

'None. And no after-effects. Whatever they're paying me, it isn't enough.'

Holly counted off a minute on her visor clock.

'OK. He's out, providing he wasn't awake when the Sleeper Deeper went in. Let's go.'

Spiro's bedroom was as white as his suits, except for the charred hole in the wardrobe. Holly and Artemis climbed through on to a white shag-pile carpet with

ᚠᚢᚩᚱ᛫ᚥᚯᚤ᛫ᚠᚱᚾᛁ᛫ᚩᚥᚢ᛫ᛒᚱᚾᛁ᛫

whitewood slide wardrobes. They stepped through the doors into a room that glowed in the dark. Futuristic furniture – white, of course. White spotlights and white drapes.

Holly took a moment to study a painting that dominated one wall.

'Oh, give me a break,' she said.

The picture was in oils. Completely white. There was a brass plaque beneath. It read 'Snow Ghost'.

Spiro lay in the centre of a huge futon, lost in the dunes of its silk sheets. Holly pulled back the covers, rolling him over on to his back. Even in sleep the man's face was malevolent, as though his dreams were every bit as despicable as his waking thoughts.

'Nice guy,' said Holly, using her thumb to raise Spiro's left eyelid. Her helmet camera scanned the eye, storing the information on chip. It would be a simple matter to project the file on to the vault's scanner and fool the security computer.

The thumb scan would not be so simple. Because the device was a gel scanner, the tiny sensors would be searching for the actual ridges and whorls of Spiro's thumb. A projection would not do. It had to be 3D. Artemis had come up with the idea of using a memory-latex bandage, standard issue in any LEP first-aid kit – and the same latex used to glue the mike to his throat. All they had to do was wrap Spiro's thumb in a bandage for a moment and they would have a mould of the digit. Holly spooled a bandage from her belt, tearing off a fifteen-centimetre strip.

'It won't work,' said Artemis.

Holly's heart sank. This was it. The thing that Artemis hadn't told her.

'What won't work?'

'The memory latex. It won't fool the gel scanner.'

Holly climbed off the futon. 'I don't have time for this, Artemis. *We* don't have time for it. The memory latex will make a perfect copy, right down to the last molecule.'

Artemis's eyes were downcast. 'A perfect model, true, but in reverse. Like a photo negative. Ridges where there should be grooves.'

'D'Arvit!' swore Holly. The Mud Boy was right. Of course he was. The scanner would read the latex as a completely different thumbprint. Her cheeks glowed red behind the visor.

'You knew this, Mud Boy. You knew it all along.'

Artemis didn't bother denying it.

'I'm amazed no one else spotted it.'

'So why lie?'

Artemis walked round to the far side of the bed, grasping Spiro's right hand.

'Because there is no way to fool the gel scanner. It has to see the real thumb.'

Holly snorted. 'What do you want me to do? Cut it off and take it with us?'

Artemis silence was response enough.

'What? You want me to cut off his thumb? Are you insane?'

Artemis waited patiently for the outburst to pass.

'Listen to me, Captain. It's only a temporary measure. The thumb can be reattached. True?'

Holly raised her palms. 'Just shut up, Artemis. Just close your mouth. And I thought you'd changed. The commander was right. There's no changing human nature.'

'Four minutes,' persisted Artemis. 'We have four minutes to crack the vault and get back. Spiro won't feel a thing.'

Four minutes was the textbook healing deadline. After that there were no guarantees that the thumb would take. The skin would bind, but the muscles and nerve endings could reject.

Holly felt as though her helmet were shrinking.

'Artemis, I'll stun you, so help me.'

'Think, Holly. I had no choice but to lie about my plan. Would you have agreed if I had told you earlier?'

'No. And I'm not agreeing now!'

Artemis's face glowed as pale as the walls. 'You have to, Captain. There is no other way.'

Holly waved Artemis aside as though he were a persistent fly and spoke into her helmet mike.

'Foaly, are you listening to this insanity?'

'It sounds insane, Holly, but if you don't get this technology back, we could lose a whole lot more than a thumb.'

'I can't believe it. Whose side are you on, Foaly? I don't even want to think about the legal ramifications of this.'

The centaur snickered. 'Legal ramifications? We're a tad beyond the court systems here, Captain. This is a secret operation. No records and no clearance. If this came out, we'd all be out of a job. A thumb here or there is not going to make any difference.'

Holly turned up the climate control in her helmet, directing a blast of cold air at her forehead.

'Are you sure we can make it, Artemis?'

Artemis ran a few mental calculations. 'Yes. I'm sure. And anyway, we have no option but to try.'

Holly crossed to the other side of the futon.

'I can't believe I'm even considering this.' She lifted Spiro's hand gently. He did not react, not so much as a sleep murmur. Behind his eyelids, Spiro's eyes jittered in REM sleep.

Holly drew her weapon. Of course, in theory, it was perfectly feasible to remove a digit and then magically reattach it. There would be no harm done, and quite possibly the injection of magic would clear up a few of the liver spots on Spiro's hand. But that wasn't the point. This was not how magic was supposed to be used. Artemis was manipulating the People to his own ends, once again.

'Fifteen-centimetre beam,' said Foaly in her ear. 'Very high frequency. We need a clean cut. And give him a shot of magic while you're doing it. It might buy you a couple of minutes.'

For some reason, Artemis was checking behind Spiro's ears.

'Hmm,' he said. 'Clever.'

'What?' hissed Holly. 'What now?'

Artemis stepped back. 'Nothing important. Continue.'

A red glow reflected from Holly's visor as a short, concentrated laser beam erupted from the nozzle of her Neutrino.

'One cut,' said Artemis. 'Clean.'

Holly glared at him. 'Don't, Mud Boy. Not a word. Especially not advice.'

Artemis backed off. Certain battles were won by retreating.

Using her left thumb and forefinger, Holly made a circle round Spiro's thumb. She sent a gentle pulse of magic into the human's hand. In seconds the skin tightened, lines disappeared and muscle tone returned.

'Filter,' she said into her mike. 'X-ray.'

The filter dropped and suddenly everything was transparent, including Spiro's hand. The bones and joints were clearly visible below the skin. They only needed the

⏛☌♒♒⚹ ⬡⚭⚹ ◌⫰◌♒⧫⬡⚹ ♒⚭☌⚹

print, so she would cut between the knuckles. It would be difficult enough reattaching under pressure without adding a complex joint into the equation.

Holly took a breath and held it. The Sleeper Deeper would act more effectively than any anaesthetic. Spiro would not flinch or feel the smallest jolt of discomfort. She made the cut. A smooth cut that sealed as it went. Not a drop of blood was spilt.

Artemis wrapped the thumb in a handkerchief from Spiro's closet.

'Nice work,' he said. 'Let's go. The clock is ticking.'

Artemis and Holly climbed back down through the wardrobe to the eighty-fifth. There was almost a mile and a half of corridor on this floor and six guards patrolling it in pairs at any one time. Their routes were specially planned so that one pair could always have an eyeball-sighting of the vault door. The vault corridor was a hundred metres long and took eighty seconds to travel. At the end of that eighty seconds, the next pair of guards stepped round the corner. Luckily, two of the guards were seeing things in a different light this particular morning.

Foaly gave them their cue.

'OK. Our boys are approaching their corner.'

'Are you sure it's them? These gorillas all look the same. Small heads, no necks.'

'I'm sure. Their targets are showing up bright and clear.'

Holly had painted Pex and Chips with a stamp generally used by customs and immigration for invisible visas. The stamps glowed orange when viewed through an infrared filter.

Holly pushed Artemis out the door in front of her. 'OK. Go. And no sarcastic comments.'

There was no need for the warning. Even Artemis Fowl was not inclined to be sarcastic at such a dangerous stage of the operation.

He ran down the corridor straight towards the two mammoth security guards. Their jackets protruded angularly beneath their armpits. Guns, no doubt. Big ones, with lots of bullets.

'Are you sure they're mesmerized?' he asked Holly, who was hovering overhead.

'Of course. Their minds are so blank it was like writing with chalk on a board. But I could stun them if you'd prefer.'

'No,' panted Artemis. 'No trace. There must be no trace.'

Pex and Chips were closer now, discussing the merits of various fictional characters.

'Captain Hook rocks,' said Pex. 'He would kick Barney's purple butt ten times out of ten.'

Chips sighed. 'You're missing the whole point of

Barney. It's a values thing. Butt-kicking is not the issue.'

They walked right past Artemis without seeing him. And why would they see him? Holly had mesmerized them not to notice anybody out of the ordinary on this floor, unless they were specifically pointed out to them.

The outer security booth lay before them. There were approximately forty seconds left before the next set of guards turned the corner. The unmesmerized set.

'Just over half a minute, Holly. You know what to do.'

Holly turned up the thermo coils in her suit so they were exactly at room temperature. This would fool the lattice of lasers that criss-crossed the vault's entrance. Next she set her wings to a gentle hover. Any more downdraughts could activate the pressure pad underfoot. She pulled herself forward, finding purchase along the wall where her helmet told her no sensors were hidden. The pressure pad trembled from the air displacement, but not enough to activate the sensor.

Artemis watched her progress impatiently.

'Hurry, Holly. Twenty seconds.'

Holly grunted something unprintable, dragging herself to within touching distance of the door.

'Video File Spiro 3,' she said, and her helmet computer ran the footage of Jon Spiro punching in the vault door code. She mimicked his actions and, inside the steel door, six reinforced pistons retracted, allowing the counterweighted door to swing wide on its hinges. All external alarms were automatically shut off. The secondary door stood firm, three red lights burning on its panel. Only three barriers left now. The gel pad, the retina scan and voice activation.

This kind of operation was too complicated for voice command. Foaly's computers had been known to misinterpret orders, even though the centaur insisted it was fairy error. Holly ripped back the Velcro strap covering the helmet command-pad on her wrist.

First, she projected a 3D image of Spiro's eyeball to a height of five foot six. The retina scanner sent out a revolving beam to read the virtual eyeball. Apparently satisfied, it disabled the first lock. A red light switched to green.

The next step was to call up the appropriate sound-wave file to trick the voice check. The equipment was very sophisticated, and could not be fooled by a recording. A human recording, that is. Foaly's digital mikes made copies that were indistinguishable from the real thing. Even stink worms, whose entire bodies were covered with ears, could be attracted by a worm-mating hiss from Foaly's recording equipment. He was currently in negotiation with a bug-collection agency for the patent.

Holly played the file through her helmet speakers. 'Jon Spiro. I am the boss, so open up quick.'

Alarm number two disengaged. Another green light.

'Excuse me, Captain,' said Artemis, an undercurrent of apprehension creeping into his voice. 'We're almost out of time.'

He unwrapped the thumb and stepped past Holly, on to the red floor plate. Artemis pressed the thumb into the scanner. Green gel oozed into the severed digit's whorls. The alarm display flashed green. It had worked. Of course it had. The thumb was genuine, after all.

But nothing else happened. The door did not open.

Holly punched Artemis in the shoulder.

'Well? Are we in?'

'Apparently not. The punching is not helping my concentration, by the way.'

Artemis glared at the console. What had he missed? Think, boy, think. Put those famed brain cells to work. He leaned closer to the secondary door, shifting his weight from his back leg. Beneath him, the red plate squeaked.

'Of course!' exclaimed Artemis. He grabbed Holly, hugging her close.

'It's not just a red marker,' he explained hurriedly. 'It's weight-sensitive.'

Artemis was right. Their combined mass was close enough to Spiro's own to hoodwink the scales. Obviously a mechanical device, a computer would never have been fooled. The secondary door slid into its groove below their feet.

Artemis handed Holly the thumb.

'Go,' he said. 'Spiro's time is running out. I'm right behind you.'

Holly took the thumb. 'And if you're not?'

'Then we go to Plan B.'

Holly nodded slowly. 'Let's hope we don't have to.'

'Let's hope.'

Artemis strode into the vault. He ignored the fortune in jewels and bearer bonds, heading straight for the Cube's perspex prison. There were two bullish security guards blocking the way. Both men had oxygen masks strapped over their faces and were unnaturally still.

'Excuse me, gentlemen. Would either of you mind if I borrowed Mister Spiro's Cube?'

Neither man responded. Not so much as a flicker of an eyebrow. This was undoubtedly because of the paralytic gas in their oxygen tanks, concocted from the venom of a nest of Peruvian spiders. The gas was similar in chemical make-up to a salve used by South-American natives as an anaesthetic.

Artemis keyed in the code, which Foaly was reciting in his ear, and the four sides of the perspex box descended into the column on silent motors, leaving the C Cube unprotected. He reached out a hand for the box ...

SPIRO'S BEDROOM

Holly climbed through the wardrobe into Spiro's bedroom. The industrialist lay in the same position she had left him, his breathing regular and normal. The stopwatch on Holly's visor read 4:57 a.m. and counting. Just in time.

Holly unwrapped the thumb gingerly, aligning it with the rest of the digit. Spiro's hand felt cold and unhealthy to her touch. She used the magnification filter in her visor to zoom in on the severed thumb. As close as she could figure, the two halves were lined up.

'Heal,' she said, and the magical sparks erupted from the tips of her fingers, sinking into the two halves of Spiro's thumb. Threads of blue light stitched the dermis and epidermis together, fresh skin breaking through the old to conceal the cut. The thumb began to vibrate and bubble. Steam vented from the pores forming a mist around Spiro's hand. His arm shook violently, the shock travelling across his bony chest. Spiro's back arched until Holly thought it would snap, then the industrialist collapsed back on to the bed. Throughout the entire process, his heart never skipped a beat.

A few stray sparks skipped along Spiro's body like stones on a pond, targeting the areas behind both ears, exactly where Artemis had been looking earlier. Curious. Holly pulled back one ear to reveal a crescent-shaped scar, rapidly being erased by the magic. There was a matching scar behind the other ear.

Holly used her visor to zoom in on one of the scars.

'Foaly. What do you make of these?'

'Surgery,' replied the centaur. 'Maybe our friend Spiro got himself a facelift. Or maybe …'

'Or maybe it's not Spiro,' completed Holly, switching to Artemis's channel. 'Artemis. It's not Spiro. It's a double. Do you hear me? Respond, Artemis.'

Artemis didn't reply. Maybe because he wouldn't; maybe because he couldn't.

THE VAULT

Artemis reached out a hand for the box, and a false wall hissed back pneumatically. Behind it stood Jon Spiro and Arno Blunt. Spiro's smile was so wide he could have swallowed a slice of watermelon.

He clapped his hands, jewellery jangling. 'Bravo, Master Fowl. Some of us didn't think you'd make it this far.'

Blunt took a hundred-dollar bill from his wallet and handed it to Spiro.

'Thank you very much, Arno. I hope this teaches you not to bet against the house.'

264

Artemis nodded thoughtfully. 'In the bedroom. That was a double.'

'Yes. Costa, my cousin. We got the same shaped head. One or two cuts and we could be peas in a pod.'

'So you set the gel scanner to accept his print.'

'For one night only. I wanted to see how far you'd get. You're an amazing kid, Arty. No one ever made it into the vault before, and you'd be amazed how many professionals have tried. There are obviously a few glitches in my system, something the security people will have to look at. How did you get in here anyway? You don't appear to have Costa with you.'

'Trade secret.'

Spiro stepped down from a low platform. 'No matter. We'll review the tapes. There are bound to be a couple of cameras you couldn't rig. One thing is for sure; you didn't do it without help. Check him for an earpiece, Arno.'

It took Blunt less than five seconds to find the earpiece. He plucked it out triumphantly, crushing the tiny cylinder beneath his boot.

Spiro sighed. 'I have no doubt, Arno, that that little electronic wonder was worth more than you will make in a lifetime. I don't know why I keep you around. I really don't.'

Blunt grimaced. This set of teeth was perspex, half-filled with blue oil. A macabre wave machine.

'Sorry, Mister Spiro.'

᠄⏅⏃⏃᠄᠄ᛜᛟ᠄᠄ᛜᛜ᠄᠄ᛜᛟᛜᛜᛟ᠄

'You will be sorrier still, my dentally challenged friend,' said Artemis, 'because Butler is coming.'

Blunt took an involuntary step backwards.

'Don't think that mumbo jumbo is scaring me. Butler is dead. I saw him go down.'

'Go down, perhaps. But did you see him die? If I remember the sequence of events correctly, after you shot Butler, he shot you.'

Blunt touched the sutures on his temple. 'A lucky shot.'

'Lucky? Butler is a proud marksman. I wouldn't say that to his face.'

Spiro laughed delightedly. 'The kid is messing with your mind, Arno. Thirteen years old and he's playing you like a grand piano in Carnegie Hall. Get yourself a spine, man; you're supposed to be a professional.'

Blunt tried to pull himself together, but the ghost of Butler haunted his features.

Spiro plucked the C Cube from its cushion. 'This is fun, Arty. All this tough talk and repartee, but it doesn't mean anything. I win again; you've been outflanked. This has all been a game to me. Amusement. Your little operation has been most educational, if pathetic. But you gotta realize that it's over now. You're on your own, and I don't have time for any more games!'

Artemis sighed, the picture of defeat. 'All of this has been a lesson, hasn't it? Just to show me who's boss.'

'Exactly. It takes some people a while to learn. I find the smarter the enemy, the bigger the ego. You had to realize that you were no match for me before you would do what I asked.' Spiro placed a bony hand on the Irish boy's shoulder. Artemis could feel the weight of his jewellery. 'Now listen carefully, kid. I want you to unlock this Cube. No more blarney. I never met a computer nerd yet who didn't leave himself a back door. You open this baby up now, or I'm gonna stop being amused, and, believe me, you don't want that.'

Artemis took the red Cube in both hands, staring at its flat screen. This was the delicate phase of his plan. Spiro had to believe that once again he had outmanoeuvred Artemis Fowl.

'Do it, Arty. Do it now.'

Artemis ran a hand across his dry lips.

'Very well. I need a minute.'

Spiro patted his shoulder. 'I'm a generous man. Take two.' He nodded at Blunt. 'Stay close, Arno. I don't want our little friend setting any more booby traps.'

Artemis sat at the stainless-steel table, exposing the Cube's inner workings. He quickly manipulated a complicated bunch of fibre optics, removing one strand altogether. The LEP blocker. After less than a minute he resealed the Cube.

Spiro's eyes were wide with anticipation, and dreams of unlimited wealth danced in his brain.

⊠▭ · ⌘☺♆⊗ · ◎♋♌♒♋ · ∪♋♪

'Good news, Arty. I want good news only.'

Artemis was more subdued now, as if the reality of his situation had finally eaten through his cockiness.

'I rebooted it. It's working. Except ...'

Spiro waved his hands. Bracelets jingled like cat bells. 'Except! This better be an itty bitty except kinda thing.'

'It's nothing. Hardly worth mentioning. I had to revert to version 1.0; version 1.2 was coded strictly to my voice patterns. 1.0 is less secure, if a bit more temperamental.'

'Temperamental. You're a box, not my grandmother, Cube.'

'I am not a box!' said Foaly, the Cube's new voice, thanks to the removed blocker. 'I am a marvel of artificial intelligence. I live therefore I learn.'

'See what I mean?' said Artemis weakly. The centaur was going to blow it. Spiro's suspicions must not be aroused at this stage.

Spiro glared at the Cube, as though it were an underling.

'Are you gonna give me attitude, mister?'

The Cube did not reply.

'You have to address it by name,' explained Artemis. 'Otherwise it would answer every question within hearing distance of its sensors.'

'And what is its name?'

Juliet often used the term 'duh'. Artemis would not

use such colloquialisms himself, but it would be apt at this particular moment.

'Its name is Cube.'

'OK, Cube. Are you going to give me attitude?'

'I will give you whatever is in my processor's capacity to give.'

Spiro rubbed his palms with childish glee, jewellery flashing like ripples in a sunset sea.

'OK, let's try this baby out. Cube, can you tell me — are there any satellites monitoring the building?'

Foaly was silent for a moment. Artemis could imagine him calling up his Sat-track information on a screen.

'Just one at the moment, though, judging from the ion trails, this building has been hit with more rays than the *Millennium Falcon*.'

Spiro shot Artemis a glance.

'His personality chip is faulty,' explained the boy. 'That's why I discontinued him, it. We can fix that at any time.'

Spiro nodded. He didn't want his very own technological genie growing the personality of a gorilla.

'What about that group, the LEP, Cube?' he asked. 'They were monitoring me in London. Are they watching?'

'The LEP? That's a Lebanese satellite TV network,' said Foaly, following Artemis's instructions. 'Game shows mostly. Their footprint doesn't reach this far.'

'OK, forget about them, Cube. I need to know that satellite's serial number.'

Foaly consulted a screen.

'Ah … Let me see. US, registered to the federal government. Number ST1147P.'

Spiro clenched both fists. 'Yes! Correct. I happen to already have that information myself. Cube, you have passed my test.'

The billionaire danced around the laboratory, reduced to childish displays by his greed.

'I'm telling you, Arty, this has taken years off me! I feel like putting on a tuxedo and going to the prom.'

'Indeed.'

'I don't know where to start. Should I make my own money? Or should I rip off somebody else's?'

Artemis forced a smile. 'The world is your oyster.'

Spiro patted the Cube gently. 'Exactly. That's exactly what it is. And I'm going to take every pearl it has to offer.'

Pex and Chips arrived at the vault door, guns drawn.

'Mister Spiro!' stammered Pex. 'Is this some kind of drill?'

Spiro laughed. 'Oh, look. Here comes the cavalry. An eternity too late. No, this is not a drill. And I would dearly love to know how little Artemis here got past you two!'

The hired muscle stared at Artemis as though he

had just appeared from nowhere. Which, for their mesmerized brains, he had.

'We don't know, Mister Spiro. We never saw him. Do you want us to take him outside for a little accident?'

Spiro laughed, a short nasty bark. 'I gotta new word for you two dumb-bells. *Expendable.* You are and he isn't, just yet. Get it? So just stand there and look dangerous, otherwise I may replace you with two shaved gorillas.'

Spiro gazed into the Cube's screen, as though there were nobody else in the room. 'I reckon I've got twenty years left in me. After that the world can go to hell as far as I'm concerned. I don't have any family, no heirs. There's no need to build for the future. I'm going to suck this planet dry, and with this Cube I can do whatever I want to whoever I want.'

'I know the first thing I'd do,' said Pex. His eyes seemed surprised that the words were coming out of his mouth.

Spiro froze. He wasn't used to being interrupted in mid-rant.

'What would you do, dumb-bell?' he said. 'Buy yourself a booth at Merv's Rib 'n' Roast?'

'No,' said Pex. 'I'd stick it to those Phonetix guys. They've been rubbing Spiro Industries' nose in it for years.'

It was an electric moment. Not only because Pex had

actually had an idea, but because it was actually a good one.

The notion lit a thoughtful spark in Spiro's eyes.

'Phonetix. My biggest competitors. I hate those guys. Nothing would give me greater satisfaction than to destroy that bunch of second-rate phone freaks. But how?'

Now it was Chips' turn. 'I hear they're working on a new top-secret communicator. Super-life battery, or something.'

Spiro did a double take. First Pex, now Chips? Next thing you knew they'd be learning to read. Nevertheless ...

'Cube,' said Spiro, 'I want you to access the Phonetix database. Copy the schematics for all their projects in development.'

'No can do, boss man. Phonetix is operating on a closed system. No Internet connection whatsoever in its R & D department. I have to be on-site.'

Spiro's euphoria disappeared. He rounded on Artemis.

'What is he talking about?'

Artemis coughed, clearing his throat. 'The Cube cannot scan a closed system unless the omni-sensor is actually touching the computer or, at least, close by. Phonetix is so paranoid about hackers that the research and development lab is completely contained, buried under several floors of solid rock. They don't even have e-mail. I know because I've tried to hack it myself a few times.'

'But the Cube scanned the satellite, didn't it?'

'The satellite is broadcasting. And if it's broadcasting, the Cube can trace it.'

Spiro toyed with the links of his ID chain. 'So, I'd have to go to Phonetix.'

'I wouldn't recommend it,' said Artemis. 'It's a lot to risk for the sake of a personal vendetta.'

Blunt stepped forward. 'Let me go, Mister Spiro. I'll get those plans.'

Spiro chewed on a handful of vitamin supplements from a dispenser on his belt.

'It's a nice idea, Arno. Good work. But I am reluctant to hand control of the Cube over to anyone else. Who knows what temptation they might yield to? Cube, can you disable the Phonetix alarm system?'

'Can a dwarf blow a hole in his pants?'

'What was that?'

'Eh … Nothing. Technical term. You wouldn't understand it. I have already disabled the Phonetix system.'

'What about the guards, Cube? Can you disable them?'

'No problemo. I could remote-activate the internal security measure.'

'Which is?'

'Tanks of vapour inside the air vents. Sleeping gas. Illegal, by the way, according to Chicago State Law. But clever, no after-effects, untraceable. The intruder comes to in lock-up two hours later.'

Spiro cackled. 'Those paranoid Phonetix boys. Go ahead, Cube, knock 'em out.'

'Night night,' said Foaly, with a glee that seemed all too real.

'Good. Now, Cube, all that stands between us and the Phonetix blueprints is an encrypted computer.'

'Don't make me laugh. They haven't invented a unit of time short enough to measure how long it will take me to crack the Phonetix hard disk.'

Spiro clipped the Cube on to his belt. 'You know something? I'm starting to like this guy.'

Artemis made one last sincere-sounding attempt to contain the situation. 'Mister Spiro, I really don't think that this is a good idea.'

'Of course you don't,' laughed Jon Spiro, jangling towards the door. 'That's why I'm bringing you along.'

Phonetix Research & Development Laboratories, Chicago's Industrial Sector

Spiro selected a Lincoln Town Car from his extensive garage. It was a nineties model, with fake registration. He often used it as a getaway vehicle. It was old enough to be unremarkable, and even if the police did get a shot of the plates, it wouldn't lead them anywhere.

Blunt parked opposite the Phonetix R & D lab's main

entrance. A security guard was visible at his desk behind the glass revolving door. Arno pulled a pair of fold-up binoculars from the glove compartment. He focused on the guard.

'Sleeping like a baby,' he announced.

Spiro clapped him on the shoulder.

'Good. We have less than two hours. Can we do it?'

'If this Cube is as good as it says it is, then we can be in and out in fifteen minutes.'

'It's a machine,' said Artemis coldly. 'Not one of your steroid-munching associates.'

Blunt glanced over his shoulder. Artemis sat in the back seat, squashed between Pex and Chips.

'You're very brave all of a sudden.'

Artemis shrugged. 'What have I got to lose? After all, things can hardly get worse.'

There was a normal door beside the revolving one. The Cube remote-activated the buzzer, admitting the band of intruders to the lobby. No alarms sounded, and no platoon of security guards came rushing to detain them.

Spiro strode down the corridor, emboldened by his new-found technological friend and the thought of finally putting Phonetix out of business. The security lift put up no more resistance to the Cube than a picket fence would to a tank, and soon Spiro and Co. were riding the eight floors down to the sunken laboratory.

'We're going underground,' chortled Pex. 'Down where the dinosaur bones are. Did you know that after a million billion years dinosaur dung turns into diamonds?'

Usually a comment like that would have been a shootable offence, but Spiro was in a good mood.

'No, I didn't know that, Pex. Maybe I should pay your wages in dung.'

Pex decided that it would be better for his finances if he just kept his mouth shut from then on.

The lab itself was protected by a thumbprint scanner. Not even gel. It was a simple matter for the Cube to scan the fingerprint on the plate then project it back on to the sensor. There wasn't even a key-code back-up.

'Easy,' crowed Spiro. 'I should have done this years ago.'

'A little credit would be nice,' said Foaly, unable to hide his pique. 'After all, I did get us in here and disable the guards.'

Spiro held the box before him. 'Not crushing you into scrap metal, Cube, is my way of saying thank you.'

'You're welcome,' grumbled Foaly.

Arno Blunt checked the security monitor bank. Throughout the facility, guards lay unconscious, one with half a rye sandwich stuffed in his mouth.

'I gotta admit it, Mister Spiro. This is beautiful. Phonetix is even gonna have to foot the bill for the sleeping gas.'

Spiro glanced towards the ceiling. Several camera lights winked red in the shadows.

'Cube, are we gonna have to raid the video room on our way out?'

'It ain't gonna happen,' said Foaly, the method actor. 'I wiped your patterns from the video.'

Artemis was suspended by the armpits between Pex and Chips.

'Traitor,' he muttered. 'I gave you life, Cube. I am your creator.'

'Yeah, well, maybe you made me too much like you, Fowl. *aurum potestas est*. Gold is power. I'm just doing what you taught me.'

Spiro patted the Cube fondly. 'I love this guy. He's like the brother I never had.'

'I thought you had a brother?' said Chips, puzzled, which was not unusual for him.

'OK,' said Spiro. 'He's like a brother I actually like.'

The Phonetix server was located in the centre of the lab. A monolithic hard drive, with python-like cables rippling out to various workstations.

Spiro unclipped his new best friend from his belt.

'Where do you need to be, Cube?'

'Just pop me down on the lid of the server, and my omni-sensor will do the rest.'

Spiro complied and, in seconds, schematics were flickering across the C Cube's tiny screen.

'I have them,' crowed Spiro, his hands two fists of triumph. 'That's the last snide e-mail with stock prices I get from these guys.'

'Download complete,' said Foaly smugly. 'We have every Phonetix project for the next decade.'

Spiro cradled the Cube against his chest.

'Beautiful. I can launch our version of the Phonetix phone before they do, make myself a few extra million before I release the Cube.'

Arno's attention was focused on the security monitors.

'Eh, Mister Spiro. I think we have a situation here.'

'A situation?' growled Spiro. 'What does that mean? You're not a soldier any more, Blunt. Speak English.'

The New Zealander tapped a screen as if that would change what he was seeing.

'I mean, we have a problem. A big problem.'

Spiro grabbed Artemis by the shoulders.

'What have you done, Fowl? Is this some kind of …?'

The accusation died before it could be completed. Spiro had noticed something.

'Your eyes. What's wrong with your eyes? They don't match.'

Artemis treated him to his best vampire smile.

'All the better to see you with, Spiro.'

In the Phonetix lobby, the sleeping security guard suddenly regained her senses. It was Juliet. She peeped

278

out from under the brim of a borrowed cap to make sure Spiro had not left anyone in the corridor.

Following Artemis's capture in Spiro's vault, Holly had flown them both to Phonetix to initiate Plan B.

Of course, there had been no sleeping gas. For that matter there had only been two guards. One was taking a restroom break and the other was doing the rounds of the upper floors. Still, Spiro wasn't to know that. He was busy watching Foaly's family of sim security snoring all over the building, thanks to a video clip on the Phonetix system.

Juliet lifted the desk phone and dialled three numbers.

9 … 1 … 1

Spiro reached two fingers delicately into Artemis's eye, plucking out the iris-cam. He studied it closely, noting the microcircuitry on the concave side.

'This is electronic,' he whispered. 'Amazing. What is it?'

Artemis blinked a tear from his eye. 'It's nothing. It was never here. Just as I was never here.'

Spiro's face twisted in sheer hatred. 'You were here all right, Fowl, and you'll never leave here.'

Blunt tapped his employer on the shoulder. An act of unforgivable familiarity.

'Boss, Mister Spiro. You really need to see this.'

*

Juliet stripped off her Phonetix Security jacket. Underneath she wore a Chicago PD SWAT uniform. Things could get hairy in the R & D Lab, and it was her job to make sure that Artemis did not get hurt. She hid behind a pillar in the lobby and waited for the sirens.

Spiro stared at the lab's security monitors. The pictures had changed. There were no more guards slumbering around the facility. Instead, the screens played a tape of Spiro and his cronies breaking into Phonetix. With one crucial difference: there was no trace of Artemis on the screen.

'What's happening, Cube?' spluttered Spiro. 'You said that we'd all be wiped from the tapes.'

'I lied. It must be the criminal personality I'm developing.'

Spiro smashed the Cube against the floor. It remained intact.

'Tough polymer,' said Artemis, picking up the microcomputer. 'Almost unbreakable.'

'Unlike you,' retorted Spiro.

Artemis looked like a doll between Pex and Chips. 'Don't you understand yet? You're all on tape. The Cube was working for me.'

'Big deal. So we're on tape. All I have to do is pay the security booth a visit and take the recordings.'

'It's not going to be that simple.'

Spiro still believed that there was a way out.

'And why not? Who's gonna stop me? Little old you?'

Artemis pointed to the screens. 'No. Little old them.'

The Chicago PD brought everything they had, and a few things they had to borrow. Phonetix was the city's biggest single employer, not to mention one of the top five subscribers to the Police Benevolent Fund. When the 911 call came in the duty sergeant put out a citywide summons.

In less than five minutes there were twenty uniforms and a full SWAT team beating on the Phonetix doors. Two choppers hovered overhead and eight snipers lined the roofs of the adjacent buildings. No one was leaving the area, unless they were invisible.

The Phonetix security guard had returned from his rounds and just noticed the intruders on the monitors. Shortly after that he noticed a group of Chicago PD uniforms tapping the door with their gun barrels.

He buzzed them in. 'I was just about to call you guys,' he said. 'There's a buncha intruders in the vault. They musta tunnelled in or somethin', 'cause they didn't come past me.'

The security guard on a restroom break was even more surprised. He was just finishing off the sports section of the *Herald Tribune* when two very serious-looking men in body armour burst into the cubicle.

𐀀𐀁𐀂·𐀃𐀄𐀅𐀆𐀇𐀈·𐀉𐀊𐀋𐀌𐀍𐀎𐀏·𐀐·

'ID?' growled one, who apparently did not have the time for full sentences.

The security guard held up his laminated card with a shaking hand.

'Stay put, sir,' advised the other police officer. He didn't have to say it twice.

Juliet slipped out from behind the pillar, joining the ranks of the SWAT team. She pointed her gun and roared with the best of them, and was instantly assimilated into the group. Their assault was cut short by a tiny problem. There was only one access-point to the lab. The lift shaft.

Two officers prised open the lift door with crowbars.

'Here's our dilemma,' said one. 'We cut the power, then we can't get the lift up here. If we call the lift up here first, then we tip off our intruders.'

Juliet shouldered herself to the front of the group.

'Excuse me, sir. Let me go down on the cables. I blow the doors and you cut the power.'

The commander did not even consider it. 'No. Too dangerous. The intruders would have plenty of time to put a hundred rounds into the lift. Who are you anyway?'

Juliet took a small gripper from her belt. She clipped it on to the lift cable and hopped into the shaft.

'I'm new,' she said, disappearing into the blackness.

*

In the laboratory, Spiro and Co. were hypnotized by the monitors. Foaly had allowed the screens to show what was actually happening on the upper levels.

'SWAT,' said Blunt. 'Helicopters. Heavy armament. How did this happen?'

Spiro smacked his own forehead repeatedly.

'A set-up. This entire thing. A set-up. I suppose Mo Digence was working for you too?'

'Yes. Pex and Chips too, even if they didn't know it. You would never have come here if I'd suggested it.'

'But how? How did you do this? It's not possible.'

Artemis glanced at the monitors. 'Obviously it is. I knew you would be waiting for me in the Spiro Needle vault. After that, all I had to do was use your own hatred of Phonetix to lure you here, out of your environment.'

'If I go down, so do you.'

'Incorrect. I was never here. The tapes will prove it.'

'But you *are* here!' roared Spiro, his nerves shot. His whole body vibrated and spittle sprayed from his lips in a wide arc. 'Your dead body will prove it. Give me the gun, Arno. I'm going to shoot him.'

Blunt could not hide his disappointment, but he did as he was told. Spiro pointed the weapon with shaky hands. Pex and Chips stepped rapidly to one side. The boss was not known for his marksmanship.

'You have taken everything from me,' he shouted. 'Everything.'

Artemis was strangely calm. 'You don't understand, Jon. It's like I told you. I am not here.' He paused for breath. 'And one more thing. About my name – Artemis – you were right. In London, it is generally a female name, after the Greek goddess of archery. But every now and then a male comes along with such a talent for hunting that he earns the right to use the name. I am that male. Artemis the hunter. I hunted you.'

And just like that, he disappeared.

Holly had been hovering above Spiro and Co. all the way from the Spiro Needle to the Phonetix building. She had got permission to enter the facility minutes earlier when Juliet had called to enquire about the public tours.

Juliet had put on her best cutesy voice for the security guide.

'Hey, mister, is it OK if I bring my invisible friend?'

'Sure it is, honey,' replied the guide. 'Bring your security blanket too, if it makes you happy.'

They were in.

Holly hovered at ceiling level, following Artemis's progress below. The Mud Boy's plan was fraught with risk. If Spiro decided to shoot him in the Needle, then it was all over.

But no, just as Artemis predicted, Spiro had opted to gloat for as long as possible, basking in the glow of his own demented genius. But, of course, it wasn't his own genius. It was Artemis's. The boy had orchestrated this whole operation from beginning to end. It had even been his idea to mesmerize Pex and Chips. It was crucial that they plant the idea to invade Phonetix.

Holly was ready when the lift door opened. She had her weapon charged and targets selected. But she couldn't go. Wait for the signal.

Artemis dragged it out. Melodramatic to the end. And then, just when Holly was about to disregard her orders and start blasting, he spoke.

'I am that male. Artemis the hunter. I hunted you.'

Artemis the hunter. The signal.

Holly squeezed the manual throttle on her wing rig and descended, stopping short a metre from the ground. She clipped Artemis on to a retractable cord on her Moonbelt, then dropped a sheet of cam foil in front of him. To everybody in the room, it would seem as though the boy had disappeared.

'Up we go,' she said, though Artemis could not hear her, and opened the throttle wide. In under a second they were nestled safely among the cables and ducts that ran along the ceiling.

Below them, Jon Spiro lost his mind.

Spiro blinked. The boy had gone! Just gone! It couldn't be. He was Jon Spiro! Nobody outsmarted Jon Spiro!

He turned to Pex and Chips, gesticulating wildly with the gun.

'Where is he?'

'Huh?' said the bodyguards, in perfect unison. Unrehearsed.

'Where is Artemis Fowl? What did you do with him?'

'Nothing, Mister Spiro. We were just standing here playing the shoulder game.'

'Fowl said you were working for him. So hand him over.'

Pex's brain was churning. This was an operation akin to a food blender mixing concrete.

'Careful, Mister Spiro, guns are dangerous. Especially the end with the hole.'

'This isn't over, Artemis Fowl,' Spiro roared at the ceiling. 'I will find you. I will never give up. You've got Jon Spiro's word on it. My word!'

He began to fire random shots, blowing holes in monitors, vents and conduits. One even came within a metre of Artemis.

Pex and Chips were not quite sure what was going on, but decided that it might be a good idea to join in the fun. They pulled out their weapons and began shooting up the lab.

Blunt did not get involved. He considered his employment contract terminated. There was no way out of this for Spiro – it was every man for himself. He crossed to the wall's metal panelling and began to

⚛🜨🝋🜍🝒 · 🜺🜍 · 🜔🝒🜊🜊🝑 🜏 · ⊕🜊🜊🝒 ➤ ·

dismantle it with a power screwdriver. A section dropped from its casing, behind it a five-centimetre cable space, then solid concrete. They were trapped.

Behind him, the lift door dinged.

Juliet was crouched in the lift shaft.

'We're clear,' said Holly in her earpiece. 'But Spiro is shooting up the lab.'

Juliet frowned. Her principal was in danger. 'Knock them out with the Neutrino.'

'I can't. If Spiro is unconscious when the police arrive, he could claim a frame-up.'

'OK. I'm going in.'

'Negative. Wait for SWAT.'

'No. You take out the weapons. I'll handle the rest.'

Mulch had given Juliet a bottle of dwarf rock polish. She poured a little puddle on the lift roof and it dissolved like fat on a pan. Juliet hopped into the carriage, crouching low in case Blunt decided to put a few rounds into the lift.

'On three.'

'Juliet.'

'I'm going on three.'

'OK.'

Juliet reached up to the door-open button. 'One.'

Holly drew her Neutrino, locking all four targets into her visor's targeting system.

'Two.' She unshielded for accuracy, the vibration would throw her aim right off. For a few seconds she would have to hide behind the foil with Artemis.

'Three.'

Juliet pressed the button.

Holly squeezed off four shots.

Artemis had less than a minute to make his move. Less than a minute while Holly targeted and disarmed Spiro and Co. The circumstances were hardly ideal – screaming, gunfire and general mayhem. But then again, what better time to implement the final step in this stage of the plan? A very vital step.

The second Holly unshielded to fire, Artemis scrolled out a perspex keyboard from the C Cube's base and began to type. In seconds, he had hacked into Spiro's bank accounts – all thirty-seven of them, in institutions from the Isle of Man to the Caymans. The various account numbers locked into place. He had access to each secret fund.

The Cube quickly ran a tot on the total funds: 2.8 billion US dollars, not counting the contents of various safety deposit boxes, which could not be touched over the Net. 2.8 billion dollars. Plenty to restore the Fowl's status as one of the top five richest Irish families.

Just as he was about to complete the transaction Artemis remembered his father's words. His father, returned to him by the fairy folk ...

'... *And what about you, Arty? Will you make the journey with me? When the moment comes will you take your chance to be a hero?*...'

Did he really need billions of dollars?

Of course I need it. *aurum potestas est*. Gold is power.

Really? Will you take your chance to be a hero? To make a difference?

Because he could not groan aloud, Artemis rolled his eyes and gritted his teeth. Well, if he was going to be a hero, he would be a well paid one. He quickly deducted a ten per cent finder's fee from the 2.8 billion, then sent the rest to Amnesty International. He made the transaction irreversible, in case he weakened later on.

Artemis wasn't finished yet. There was one more good deed to be attended to. The success of this venture depended on Foaly being too busy watching the show to notice Artemis hacking into his system.

He brought up the LEP site and set the code breaker working on a password. It took ten valuable seconds per character, but he was soon flying around LEP micro-sites. Artemis found what he needed on Perp Profiles. Mulch Diggums's complete arrest record. From there, it was a simple matter to follow the electron trail back to the original search warrant for Mulch's dwelling. Artemis changed the date on the warrant to read the day *after* Mulch's arrest. This meant that all subsequent arrests and convictions were null and void. A good lawyer would have him out of prison in a heartbeat.

'I have not finished with you yet, Mulch Diggums,' he whispered, logging out and clipping the Cube on Holly's belt.

Juliet came through the door so fast her limbs were a blur. The jade ring trailed behind her like a fishing lure on the end of a line.

Butler would never take chances like this, she knew. He would have some perfectly practical, safe plan – which was why he had his blue diamond tattoo and she didn't. Well, maybe she didn't want a tattoo. Maybe she wanted a life of her own.

She quickly assessed the situation. Holly's aim was true. The two gorillas were rubbing their scorched hands and Spiro was stamping his feet like a spoiled child. Only Blunt was on the floor, going for his gun.

Even though the bodyguard was on his hands and knees, he was still almost at her eye level.

'Aren't you going to give me a chance to get up?' he asked.

'No,' said Juliet, whipping the jade ring around like the stone that felled Goliath. It impacted on the bridge of Blunt's nose, cracking it and effectively blinding him for a couple of minutes. Plenty of time for the Chicago Police to get down the shaft.

Blunt was now out of the game. Juliet had expected to feel some satisfaction, but all she felt was sadness. There was no joy in violence.

Pex and Chips felt they should do something. Perhaps disabling the girl would earn them a bonus from Mister Spiro? They circled Juliet, fists raised.

Juliet wagged a finger at them. 'Sorry, boys. You have to go to sleep.'

The bodyguards ignored her, tightening the radius of their circle.

'I said go to sleep.'

Still no response.

'You have to use exactly the words that I mesmerized them to respond to,' said Holly in her ear.

Juliet sighed. 'If I must. OK, gentlemen; Barney says go to sleep.'

Pex and Chips were snoring before they hit the ground.

That just left Spiro, and he was too busy gibbering to be any threat. He was still gibbering when the SWAT team put the cuffs on him.

'I'll talk to you back at base,' said the SWAT captain sternly to Juliet. 'You're a danger to your comrades and yourself.'

'Yessir,' said Juliet contritely. 'I don't know what came over me, sir.'

She glanced upwards. A slight heat haze seemed to be drifting towards the lift shaft. The principal was safe.

*

Holly holstered her weapon, buzzing up her shield.

'Time to go,' she said, the volume on her PA turned to minimum.

Holly wrapped the cam foil tightly round Artemis, making certain no limbs were peeking out. It was imperative they leave while the lift was empty. Once forensics and the press got there, even a slight shimmer in the air might be caught on film.

As they flew across the room, Spiro was being led from the lab. He had finally managed to calm down.

'This is a set-up,' he proclaimed in his best innocent voice. 'My lawyers are gonna rip you guys apart.'

Artemis could not resist speaking as they floated past his ear.

'Farewell, Jon,' he whispered. 'Never mess with a boy genius.'

Spiro howled at the ceiling like a demented wolf.

Mulch was waiting across the street from the Phonetix lab, revving the van like a Grand Prix driver. He sat behind the wheel on an orange crate, with a short plank taped to his foot. The other end of the plank was taped to the accelerator.

Juliet studied the system nervously. 'Shouldn't you untie that foot in case you need to use the brakes?'

'Brakes?' laughed Mulch. 'Why would I use the brakes? I'm not doing my driving test here.'

In the back of the van, Artemis and Holly simultaneously reached for their seat belts.

⊍Ⴑ◊⬠•ᲚᲠᎰᎩ➞•ᲚᏰᎠᎨᎯᎩᲜ•ᎧᏅ⊕•ᎧᏰᏰ🦀

CHAPTER II: THE INVISIBLE MAN

FOWL MANOR

THEY reached Ireland without major incident, though Mulch did attempt to escape Holly's custody fifteen times – including once on the Lear jet, where he was discovered in the bathroom with a parachute and a bottle of dwarf rock polish. Holly did not let him out of her sight after that.

Butler was waiting for them at Fowl Manor's front door.

'Welcome back. Glad to see everyone's alive. Now I need to go.'

Artemis put a hand on his arm.

'Old friend. You're in no condition to go anywhere.'

Butler was determined. 'One last mission, Artemis. I have no choice. Anyway, I've been doing Pilates. I feel much more limber.'

'Blunt?'

'Yes.'

'But he's in prison,' protested Juliet.

Butler shook his head. 'Not any more.'

Artemis could see that his bodyguard was not about to be turned from his path.

'At least take Holly. She can be of some help.'

Butler winked at the elf. 'I was counting on it.'

The Chicago police had put Arno Blunt in a van, with a couple of officers. Two would be sufficient, they reasoned, as the perp was handcuffed and manacled. They revised this opinion when the van was discovered six miles south of Chicago, with the officers manacled and no sign of the suspect. To quote Sergeant Iggy Lebowski's report: *'The guy ripped those handcuffs apart as though they were links in a paperchain. He came at us like a steam train. We never had a chance.'*

But Arno Blunt did not escape clean. His pride had taken a severe beating in the Spiro Needle. He knew that word of his humiliation would soon spread through the bodyguard network. As Pork Belly LaRue later put it on the Soldiers for Hire web site: *'Arno done got hisself outsmarted by some snot-nosed kid.'* Blunt was painfully aware that he would have to suffer chortles every time he walked into a room full of tough guys – unless he avenged the insult paid to him by Artemis Fowl.

⊕⊘⋃⊛⊘⊃⧖⊘⊟⌾·⊘⊟⧚⋃⊛⌾⧖·⊰⊟⧖·

The bodyguard knew that he had minutes before Spiro gave up his address to the Chicago PD, so he packed a few spare sets of teeth and took the shuttle to O'Hare International Airport.

Blunt was delighted to find that the authorities had not yet frozen his Spiro corporate credit card, and used it to purchase a first class British Airways Concorde ticket to London Heathrow. From there he would enter Ireland on the Rosslare ferry. Just another one of five hundred tourists visiting the land of the leprechaun.

It wasn't a terribly complicated plan, and it would have worked if it hadn't been for one thing: the passport official at Heathrow just happened to be Sid Commons, the ex-Green Beret who had served with Butler on bodyguard duty in Monte Carlo. The second Blunt opened his mouth alarm bells went off in Commons' head. The gentleman before him fitted the description Butler had faxed over perfectly. Right down to the strange teeth. Blue oil and water, if you don't mind. Commons pressed a button under his desk and, in seconds, a squad of security men relieved Blunt of his passport and took him into custody.

The chief security official took out his mobile phone as soon as the detainee was under lock and key. He dialled an international number. It rang twice.

'The Fowl residence.'

'Butler? It's Sid Commons, in Heathrow. A man came through here you might be interested in. Funny teeth, neck tattoos, New Zealand accent. Detective Inspector Justin Barre faxed out the description from Scotland Yard a few days ago; he said you might be able to ID him.'

'Do you still have him?' asked the manservant.

'Yes. He's in one of our holding cells. They're running a check right now.'

'How long will that take?'

'A couple of hours, max. But if he's the professional you say he is, a computer check won't turn up anything. We need a confession to turn him over to Scotland Yard.'

'I will meet you in the Arrivals hall under the departure board in thirty minutes,' said Butler, severing the connection.

Sid Commons stared at his mobile phone. How could Butler possibly get there in thirty minutes from Ireland? It wasn't important. All Sid knew was that Butler had saved his life a dozen times in Monte Carlo all those years ago, and now the debt was about to be repaid.

Thirty-two minutes later, Butler showed up in the Arrivals hall.

Sid Commons studied him as they shook hands.

'You seem different. Older.'

'The battles are catching up with me,' said Butler, a palm across his heaving chest. 'Time to retire, I think.'

'Is there any point asking how you got here?'

𝕬𝕾𝕽𝕵𝕺𝕽 · 𝕾𝕬𝕽 · 𝖀𝕬𝕭𝕺𝕵𝕬𝕾 ·

Butler straightened his tie. 'Not really. You're better off not knowing.'

'I see.'

'Where's our man?'

Commons led the way towards the rear of the building, past hordes of tourists and card-bearing taxi drivers.

'Through here. You're not armed, are you? I know we're friends, but I can't allow firearms in here.'

Butler spread his jacket wide. 'Trust me. I know the rules.'

They took a security lift up two floors, and followed a dimly lit corridor for what seemed like miles.

'Here we are,' said Sid eventually, pointing at a glass rectangle. 'In there.'

The glass was actually a two-way mirror. Butler could see Arno Blunt seated at a small table, drumming his fingers impatiently on the Formica surface.

'Is that him? Is that the man who shot you in Knightsbridge?'

Butler nodded. It was him all right. The same indolent expression. The same hands that had pulled the trigger.

'A positive ID is something, but it's still your word against his and, to be honest, you don't look too shot.'

Butler laid a hand on his friend's shoulder. 'I don't suppose –'

Commons didn't even let him finish. 'No. You can not

go in there. Absolutely not. I'd be out of a job, for sure; and anyway, even if you did prise a confession out of him, it would never hold up in court.'

Butler nodded. 'I understand. Do you mind if I stay? I want to see how this turns out.'

Commons agreed eagerly, relieved that Butler hadn't pressured him.

'No problem. Stick around as long as you like. But I have to get you a visitor's badge.' He strode down the corridor, then turned.

'Don't go in there, Butler. If you do, we lose him forever. And anyway, there are cameras all over this place.'

Butler smiled reassuringly. Something he didn't do very often.

'Don't worry, Sid. You won't see me in that room.'

Commons sighed. 'Good. Great. It's just sometimes when you get that look in your eye …'

'I'm a different man now. More mature.'

Commons laughed. 'That'll be the day.'

He rounded the corner, his chuckles lingering in the air. He was no sooner gone than Holly unshielded by Butler's leg.

'Cameras?' hissed the bodyguard from the corner of his mouth.

'I checked the ion beams. I'm clear right here.' She pulled a sheet of camouflage foil from her backpack, laying it on the floor. She then twisted a video clip around a cable tacked to the cell's outer wall.

'OK,' she said, listening to Foaly's voice in her ear. 'We're in. Foaly has wiped our patterns from the video. We are camera and mike-proof now. Do you know what to do?'

Butler nodded. They had been through this before, but Holly had a soldier's need to double-check.

'I'm going to shield again. Give me a second to move, then put the foil on and do your thing. I give you two minutes, tops, before your friend returns. After that you're on your own.'

'Understood.'

'Good luck,' said Holly, shimmering out of the visible spectrum.

Butler waited a beat, then took two steps to the left. He picked up the foil and draped it over his head and shoulders. To the casual passerby, he was now invisible. But if anyone paused on his or her way down the corridor, something of the manservant's bulk was bound to be poking out from under the foil. Best to move quickly. He slid the latch on the cell door across and stepped inside.

Arno Blunt was not unduly worried. This was a bum rap. How long could you be held for having novelty false teeth, for heaven's sake? Not much longer, that was for sure. Maybe he would sue the British government for trauma, and retire home to New Zealand.

The door swung open thirty centimetres, then closed again. Blunt sighed. It was an old interrogator's trick. Let the prisoner sweat for a few hours, then open the door to make him think help was on the way. When no one entered the prisoner would be plunged into even deeper despair. Ever closer to breaking point.

'Arno Blunt,' sighed a voice from nowhere.

Blunt stopped drumming his fingers and sat up straight.

'What is this?' he sneered. 'Are there speakers in here? That's lame, guys. Really lame.'

'I've come for you,' said the voice. 'I've come to even the score.'

Arno Blunt knew that voice. He'd been dreaming about it since Chicago, ever since the Irish kid had warned him Butler would return. OK, it was ridiculous; there were no such things as ghosts. But there was something about Artemis Fowl's stare that made you believe everything he told you.

'Butler? Is that you?'

'Ah,' said the voice. 'You remember me.'

Arno took a deep, shuddering breath. Composing himself.

'I don't know what's going on here, but I'm not falling for it. What? I'm supposed to cry like a baby now, because

you found somebody who sounds like one of my ...
Somebody I knew?'

'This is no trick, Arno. I'm right here.'

'Sure. If you're right there, why can't I see you?'

'Are you sure you can't see me, Arno? Look closely.'

Blunt's stare hopped wildly around the room. There
was no one else in there. No one. He was certain of it. But
there was a patch of air in the corner of the room that
seemed to be bending light, like a floating mirror.

'Ah, you've spotted me.'

'I've spotted nothing,' said Blunt shakily. 'All I see is a
heat blur. Maybe from a vent or something.'

'Oh, really?' said Butler, throwing off the cam foil. To
Blunt it seemed as though he had stepped from the air.
The bodyguard stood abruptly, catapulting his chair
against the wall.

'Oh, God! What are you?'

Butler bent his knees slightly. Ready for action. He was
older now, true. And slower. But the fairy magic had
bolstered his reaction time, and he had so much more
experience than Blunt. Juliet would have liked to handle
this job for him, but there were some things you had to
finish personally.

'I am your guide, Arno. I've come to take you home.
There are a lot of people waiting to see you.'

'H-h-home?' stammered Blunt. 'What do you mean
home?'

Butler took a step forward. 'You know what I mean, Arno. Home. The place you've always been headed. The place you've sent so many others. Including me.'

Blunt pointed a shaky finger. 'You stay away from me. I killed you once, I can do it again.'

Butler laughed. It was not a pleasant sound. 'That's where you're wrong, Arno. I can't be killed again. Anyway, death is no big deal, not compared to what comes after.'

'What comes after ...'

'There is a hell, Arno,' said Butler. 'I've seen it and, believe me, so will you.'

Blunt was utterly convinced; after all, Butler had appeared from nowhere.

'I didn't know,' he sobbed. 'I didn't believe it. I never would have shot you, Butler. I was just following Spiro's orders. You heard him give the order. I was just the metal man; that's all I've ever been.'

Butler laid a hand on his shoulder. 'I believe you, Arno. You were just following orders.'

'That's right.'

'But that's not enough. You need to clear your conscience. If you don't, I have to take you with me.'

Blunt's eyes were red with tears. 'How?' he pleaded. 'How do I do that?'

'Confess your sins to the authorities. Leave nothing out, or I will be back.'

Blunt nodded eagerly. Prison was better than the alternative.

'Remember, I will be watching. This is your one chance to save yourself. If you don't take it, I will be back.'

Blunt's teeth popped from his open mouth, rolling across the floor.

'Don' worry. I'll confesh. I promish.'

Butler lifted the cam foil, concealing himself completely.

'See that you do, or there'll be hell to pay.'

Butler stepped into the corridor, stuffing the foil inside his jacket. Seconds later, Sid Commons reappeared with a security badge.

He caught sight of Arno Blunt standing stunned in his cell.

'What did you do, Butler?' he said.

'Hey, it wasn't me. Check your tapes. He just went crazy, talking to thin air. Yelling how he wanted to confess.'

'He wants to confess? Just like that?'

'I know how it sounds, but that's what happened. If I were you, I'd give Justin Barre a call over at Scotland Yard. I have a feeling that Blunt's statement could clear up a lot of outstanding cases.'

Commons squinted at him suspiciously. 'Why do I have a feeling that you know more than you're telling?'

'Search me,' said Butler. 'But feelings aren't evidence,

and your own surveillance tapes will prove that I never set foot in that room.'

'Are you sure that's what they'll show?'

Butler glanced at the patch of air shimmering above Sid Commons's shoulder.

'I am positive,' he said.

FOWL MANOR

THE return trip from Heathrow took over an hour, thanks to some particularly strong turbulence and an easterly wind over the Welsh hills. When Holly and Butler finally touched down in the grounds of Fowl Manor the LEP was busy humping their mind-wiping gear up the avenue, under cover of night.

Butler unclipped himself from the Moonbelt, leaning against the trunk of a silver birch.

'You OK?' asked Holly.

'Fine,' replied the bodyguard, massaging his chest. 'It's this Kevlar tissue. Handy if you get shot with a small calibre, but it's playing havoc with my breathing.'

Holly sheathed her mechanical wings. 'It's the quiet life for you from now on.'

Butler noticed an LEP pilot attempting to park his

shuttle in the double garage, nudging the Bentley's bumper.

'Quiet life?' he muttered, heading for the garage. 'I wish.'

Once Butler had finished terrorizing the pixie pilot he made for the study. Artemis and Juliet were waiting for him. Juliet hugged her brother so tightly that the air was squeezed from his lungs.

'I'm OK, little sister. The fairies have fixed it so that I will live to well over a hundred. I'll still be around to keep an eye on you.'

Artemis was all business. 'How did you fare, Butler?'

Butler opened a wall safe behind an air-conditioning vent.

'Pretty well. I got everything on the list.'

'What about the custom job?'

Butler laid out six small vials on the baize-covered desk.

'My man in Limerick followed your instructions to the letter. In all his years in the trade, he's never done anything like this. They're in a special solution to stop corrosion. The layers are so fine that once they come into contact with the air they begin to oxidize right away, so I suggest we don't insert them until the last possible moment.'

'Excellent. In all probability, I am the only one who will

need these, but, just in case, we should all put them in.'

Butler held the gold coin up by its leather thong. 'I copied your diary and fairy files on to a laser minidisc, then brushed on a layer of gold leaf. It won't stand up to close examination, I'm afraid, but molten gold would have destroyed the information on the disc.'

Artemis tied the thong round his neck. 'It will have to do. Did you plant the false trails?'

'Yes. I sent an e-mail that has yet to be picked up, and I hired a few megabytes on an Internet storage site. I also took the liberty of burying a time capsule in the maze.'

Artemis nodded. 'Good. I hadn't thought of that.'

Butler accepted the compliment, but he didn't believe it. Artemis thought of everything.

Juliet spoke for the first time. 'You know, Artemis. Maybe it would be better to let these memories go. Give the fairies some peace of mind.'

'These memories are part of who I am,' responded Artemis.

He examined the vials on the table, selecting two.

'Now, everybody, it's time to put these in. I'm sure the People are eager to wipe our minds.'

Foaly's technical crew set up shop in the conference room, laying out a complex assembly of electrodes and fibre-optic cable. Each cable was connected to a plasma screen that converted brainwaves to actual binary information. In layman's terms, Foaly would be able to read the humans' memories like a book and edit out what shouldn't be there. Possibly the most incredible part of the entire procedure was that the human brain itself would supply alternative memories to fill the blank spots.

'We could do the mind wipes with a field kit,' explained Foaly, once the patients were assembled. 'But field kits are just for blanket wipes. It would erase everything that's happened over the past sixteen months. That could have serious implications for your emotional development, not to mention your IQ. So, better we use the lab kit and simply erase the memories that pertain to the People. Obviously, we will have to erase the days you spent in fairy company completely. We can't take any chances there.'

Artemis, Butler and Juliet were seated round the table. Technical gnomes swabbed their temples with disinfectant.

'I've thought of something,' said Butler.

'Don't tell me,' interrupted the centaur. 'The age thing, right?'

Butler nodded. 'A lot of people know me as a forty-year-old man. You can't wipe them all.'

'Way ahead of you, Butler. We're going to give your face a laser peel while you're unconscious. Get rid of some of that dead skin. We even brought a cosmetic surgeon to give your forehead a Dewer injection to smooth out the wrinkles.'

'Dewer?'

'Fat,' explained the centaur. 'We take it from one area, and inject it into another.'

Butler was not enthused by the idea. 'This fat. It doesn't come from my behind, does it?'

Foaly shuffled uncomfortably. 'Well, it doesn't come from *your* behind.'

'Explain.'

'Research has shown that of all the fairy races, dwarfs have the greatest longevity. There's a miner in Poll Dyne who is allegedly over two thousand years old. Haven't you ever heard the expression "smooth as a dwarf's bottom"?'

Butler slapped away a technician who was attempting to attach an electrode patch to his head.

'Are you telling me that fat from a dwarf's backside is going to be injected into my head?'

Foaly shrugged. 'The price of youth. There are pixies on the west bank paying a fortune for Dewer treatments.'

Butler spoke through gritted teeth. 'I am not a pixie.'

'We've also brought some gel to colour any hair you may decide to grow in the future, and some pigment dye to cover the cell corruption on your chest,' continued the centaur hurriedly. 'By the time you wake up, your exterior will look young again, even if your interior is old.'

'Clever,' said Artemis. 'I expected as much.'

Holly entered with Mulch in tow. The dwarf was wearing cuffs and looking extremely sorry for himself.

'Is this really necessary,' he whined, 'after all we've been through?'

'My badge is on the line,' retorted Holly. 'The commander said to come back with you, or not at all.'

'What do I have to do? I donated the fat, didn't I?'

Butler rolled his eyes. 'Please, no.'

Juliet giggled. 'Don't worry, Dom. You won't remember a thing about it.'

'Knock me out,' said Butler. 'Quickly.'

'Don't mention it,' grumbled Mulch, attempting to rub his behind.

Holly uncuffed the dwarf, but stayed within grabbing distance.

'He wanted to say goodbye, so here we are.' She nudged Mulch with her shoulder. 'So, say goodbye.'

Juliet winked. 'Bye, Smelly.'

'So long, Stinker.'

'Don't go chewing through any concrete walls.'

'I don't find that kind of thing funny,' said Mulch, with a pained expression.

'Who knows. Maybe we'll see each other again.'

Mulch nodded at the technicians, busy firing up their hard drives.

'If we do, thanks to these people, it'll be the first time.'

Butler knelt to the dwarf's level.

'You look after yourself, little friend. Stay clear of goblins.'

Mulch shuddered. 'You don't have to tell me that.'

Commander Root's face appeared on a roll-down screen erected by an LEP officer.

'Maybe you two would like to get married?' he barked. 'I don't know what all the emotion is about. In ten minutes you people won't even remember this convict's name!'

'We have the commander online,' said a technician, a tad unnecessarily.

Mulch stared at the button camera mounted on the screen. 'Julius, please. Do you realize that all of these humans owe me their lives? This is an emotional moment for them.'

Root's rosy complexion was exaggerated by poor reception.

'I couldn't care less about your touchy feely moment. I'm here to make sure this wipe goes smoothly. If I know our friend Fowl, he's got a few tricks up his sleeve.'

'Really, Commander,' said Artemis. 'Such suspicion is wounding.'

But the Irish teenager couldn't suppress a grin. Everybody knew that he would have hidden items to spark residual memories; it was up to the LEP to find them. Their final contest.

Artemis stood and approached Mulch Diggums.

'Mulch. Of all the fairy People, I will miss your services the most. We could have had such a future together.'

Mulch looked a touch teary. 'True. With your brains and my special talents.'

'Not to mention your mutual lack of morals,' interjected Holly.

'No bank on the planet would have been safe,' completed the dwarf. 'A missed opportunity.'

Artemis tried his best to look sincere. It was vital for the next step in the plan.

'Mulch, I know you risked your life betraying the Antonelli family, so I'd like to give you something.'

Mulch's imagination churned with visions of trust funds and offshore accounts.

'There's no need. Really. Although it was incredibly brave, and I was in mortal danger.'

'Exactly,' said Artemis, untying the gold medallion from round his neck. 'I know this isn't much, but it means a lot to me. I was going to keep it, but I realized that in a few minutes it will mean absolutely nothing. I would like you to have it; I think Holly would too. A little memento of our adventures.'

'Gee,' said Mulch, hefting the medallion. 'Half an ounce of gold. Great. You really broke the bank there, Artemis.'

Artemis gripped the dwarf's hand. 'It's not always about money, Mulch.'

Root was craning his neck, trying to see more. 'What's that? What has he given to the convict?'

Holly snatched the medallion, holding it up for the camera.

'Just a gold coin, Commander. I gave it to Artemis myself.'

Foaly glanced at the small medal. 'Actually this kills two stink worms with one skewer. The medallion could have triggered some residual memories. Highly unlikely, but possible.'

'And the other stink worm?'

'Mulch gets something to look at in prison.'

Root mulled it over for several moments.

'OK. He can keep it. Now get that convict into the shuttle and let's get on with this. I've got a Council meeting in ten minutes.'

Holly led Mulch out, and Artemis realized that he really was sorry to see the dwarf go. But more than that, he was sorry that the memory of their friendship could be gone forever.

The technicians descended like flies on a carcass. In seconds every human in the room had electrodes attached to temples and wrists. Each set of electrodes ran through a neural transformer and on to a plasma screen. Memories flickered on the screens.

Foaly studied the images. 'Way too early,' he announced. 'Calibrate them to sixteen months ago. Actually, make that about three years. I don't want Artemis planning his initial kidnap all over again.'

'Bravo, Foaly,' said Artemis bitterly. 'I was hoping you might miss that.'

The centaur winked. 'That's not all I didn't miss.'

On the pull-down screen, Root's pixelated mouth stretched into a smile.

'Tell him, Foaly. I can't wait to see the human's face.'

Foaly consulted a file on his hand-held computer.

'We checked your e-mail and guess what?'

'Do tell.'

'We found a fairy file, just waiting to be delivered. We also ran a search on the Internet in general. And lo and behold, someone with your e-mail address had rented some storage megabytes. More fairy files.'

Artemis was unrepentant. 'I had to try. I'm sure you understand.'

'Nothing else you want to tell us about?'

Artemis opened his eyes wide, the epitome of innocence. 'Nothing. You're too clever for me.'

Foaly took a laserdisc from a toolbox, sliding it into the drive of a networked computer on the table. 'Well, just in case, I'm going to detonate a data charge in your computer system. The virus will leave your files unharmed, unless they pertain to the People. Not only

315

that but the virus will monitor your system for a further six months, just in case you have outwitted us somehow.'

'And you're telling me all this because I won't remember it anyway.'

Foaly did a little four-step, clapping his hands together. 'Exactly.'

Holly pushed through the door, dragging a metallic capsule behind her.

'Look what they found buried in the grounds.' She flipped the lid, pouring the capsule's contents on the Tunisian rug. Several computer disks and hard copies of Artemis's diary fanned across the carpet.

Foaly examined a disk. 'Something else you forgot to mention?'

Artemis was not quite so cocky now. His lifelines to the past were being cut one by one.

'It slipped my mind.'

'That's it, I suppose. There's nothing else.'

Artemis returned to his chair, folding his arms. 'And if I say yes, you'll believe me, I suppose.'

Root laughed so hard that it seemed the screen was shaking.

'Oh, yes, Artemis. We trust you completely. How could we not after all you've put the People through? If you don't mind, we'd like to ask you a few questions under the *mesmer,* and this time you won't be wearing sunglasses.'

Sixteen months previously, Artemis had successfully deflected Holly's hypnotic gaze with mirrored sunglasses. It was the first time he had outwitted the fairies. It was not to be the last.

'Well then, let's get on with it.'

'Captain Short,' barked Root. 'You know what to do.'

Holly removed her helmet, massaging the tips of her ears to get the circulation going.

'I'm going to mesmerize you and ask a few questions. It's not the first time you've been under, so you know that the procedure is not painful. I advise you to relax; if you try to resist, it could cause memory loss or even brain damage.'

Artemis held up his palm. 'Wait a moment. Am I right in thinking that when I wake up again this will all be over?'

Holly smiled. 'Yes, Artemis. This is goodbye, for the last time.'

Artemis's face was composed, in spite of the emotions churning inside him.

'Well then, I have a few things to say.'

Root was curious, in spite of himself. 'One minute, Fowl. Then nighty night.'

'Very well. Firstly, thank you. I have my family and friends around me thanks to the People. I wish I didn't have to forget that.'

Holly laid a hand on his shoulder. 'It's better this way, Artemis. Believe me.'

'And secondly, I want you all to think back to the first time you met me. Remember that night?'

Holly shuddered. She remembered the cold individual who had attacked her at a magical hot spot in southern Ireland. Commander Root would never forget escaping an exploding tanker by the skin of his wings, and Foaly's first glimpse of Artemis had been a recording of the negotiations for Holly's release. He had been a despicable creature.

'If you take away the memories and influences of the People,' continued Artemis, 'I might become that person again. Is that what you really want?'

It was a chilling thought. Were the People responsible for Artemis's transformation? And were they to be responsible for changing him back?

Holly turned to the screen. 'Is it possible? Artemis has come a long way. Do we have the right to destroy all that progress?'

'He's right,' added Foaly. 'I never thought I would say this, but I kinda like the new model.'

Root opened another computer window on the screen. 'The Psych Brotherhood did this probability report for us. They say the chances of a reversion are slim. Fowl will still have strong positive influences from his family and the Butlers.'

'The Psych Brotherhood?' objected Holly. 'Argon and

his cronies? And when exactly did we start trusting those witch doctors?'

Root opened his mouth to yell, but thought better of it. Not something that happened every day.

'Holly,' he said, almost gently. 'The future of our culture is at stake here. The bottom line is that Artemis's future is not our problem.'

Holly's mouth was a grim slash. 'If that's true, then we're as bad as the Mud People.'

The commander decided to revert to his usual mode of communication.

'Listen to me, Captain,' he roared. 'Being in command means making tough decisions. Not being in command means shutting up and doing what you're told. Now mesmerize those humans before we lose the link.'

'Yes, sir. Whatever you say, sir.'

Holly stood directly in front of Artemis, careful to make eye contact.

'Goodbye, Holly. I won't see you again, though I'm sure you will see me.'

'Just relax, Artemis. Deep breaths.'

When Holly spoke again, her voice was layered with bass and alto. The hypnotic layers of the *mesmer*.

'That was some job we did on Spiro, eh?'

Artemis smiled sleepily. 'Yes. The last adventure. No more hurting people.'

'How do you come up with these plans?'

Artemis's lids drooped. 'Natural ability, I suppose. Handed down by generations of Fowls.'

'I bet you would do anything to hang on to your fairy memories?'

'Almost anything.'

'So what *did* you do?'

Artemis smiled. 'I played a few little tricks.'

'What kind of tricks?' pressed Holly.

'It's a secret. I can't tell you.'

Holly added a few more layers to her voice.

'Tell me, Artemis. It will be our secret.'

A vein pulsed in Artemis's temple. 'You won't tell? You won't tell the fairies?'

Holly glanced guiltily at the screen. Root gestured at her to continue.

'I won't tell. It will be just between us.'

'Butler hid a capsule in the maze.'

'And?'

'I sent myself an e-mail. But I expect Foaly to find that. It's to throw him off-guard.'

'Very clever. Is there anything you don't expect him to find?'

Artemis smiled craftily. 'I hid a file on an Internet storage site. Foaly's data charge won't affect it. The providers will mail me a reminder in six months. When I retrieve the data it should trigger residual memories and possibly total recall.'

'Anything else?'

'No. The storage site is our last hope. If the centaur finds that, then the fairy world is lost forever.'

Root's image crackled on the screen. 'OK. The uplink is breaking up. Knock them out and wipe them. Tape the whole process. I won't believe Artemis is out of the game until I see the footage.'

'Commander. Maybe I should ask the others a few questions.'

'Negative, Captain. Fowl said it himself. The storage site was their last hope. Hook them up and run the program.'

The commander's image disappeared in waves of static.

'Yes, sir.' Holly turned to the technical crew. 'You heard the fairy. Let's go. Sun up is in a couple of hours. I want us below ground before that.'

The techies checked that the electrodes had strong contacts, then unwrapped three sets of sleep goggles.

'I'll do that,' said Holly, taking the masks.

She hooked the elastic over Juliet's ponytail.

'You know something?' she said. 'Personal protection is a cold business. You have too much heart for it.'

Juliet nodded slowly. 'I'll try to hold on to that thought.'

Holly settled the eyepieces gently.

'I'll keep an eye on you.'

Juliet smiled. 'See you in my dreams.'

Holly pressed a small button on the sleep mask, and a combination of hypno-lights in the eyepieces and sedative administered through the seals knocked Juliet out in less than five seconds.

Butler was next. The technical crew had added a length of elastic to the mask's strap so that it could encircle his shaven crown.

'Make sure Foaly doesn't go crazy with that mind wiper,' said the bodyguard. 'I don't want to wake up with four decades of nothing in my head.'

'Don't worry,' said Holly reassuringly. 'Foaly generally knows what he's doing.'

'Good. Remember, if the People ever do need help, I'm available.'

Holly pressed the button.

'I'll remember that,' she whispered.

Artemis was last in the line. In his mesmerized state he seemed almost peaceful. For once, there were no thought lines wrinkling his brow and, if you didn't know him, he could almost be a normal thirteen-year-old human.

Holly turned to Foaly. 'Are you sure about this?'

The centaur shrugged. 'What choice do we have? Orders are orders.'

Holly placed the mask over Artemis's eyes and pushed the button. Seconds later, the teenager slumped in his chair. Immediately, lines of Gnommish text began to flash across the screen behind him. In the days of Frond, Gnommish had been written in spirals. But reading in spirals gave most fairies a migraine.

'Commence deleting,' ordered Foaly. 'But keep a copy. Some time when I have a few weeks off I'm going to find out what makes this guy tick.'

Holly watched Artemis's life being written in green symbols on the screen.

'This doesn't feel right,' she commented. 'If he found us once, he could find us again. Especially if he becomes the monster he used to be.'

Foaly tapped commands into an ergonomic keyboard. 'Maybe. But next time we'll be ready.'

Holly sighed. 'It's a pity, because now we were almost friends.'

The centaur snorted. 'Sure. Like you can be friends with a viper.'

Holly suddenly shut her helmet visor, hiding her eyes.

'You're right, of course. We could never have been friends. It was circumstance that pushed us together, nothing more.'

Foaly patted her shoulder. 'That's the girl. Keep your ears up. Where are you going?'

'Tara,' replied Holly. 'I'm going to fly. I need the fresh air.'

'You don't have clearance for a flight,' objected Foaly. 'Root will have your badge.'

'For what?' said Holly, firing up her wings. 'I'm not supposed to be here, remember?'

And she was gone, flying in a lazy loop through the entrance hall. She cleared the main door with centimetres to spare, climbing quickly into the night sky. For a second, her slim frame was backlit by the full moon, and then she disappeared, vibrating out of the visible spectrum.

Foaly watched her go. Emotional creatures, elves. In some respects they made the worst Recon operatives. All decisions were taken by the heart. But Root would never fire Holly, because policing was what she was born to do. And anyway, who else would save the People if Artemis Fowl ever found them again?

Mulch sat in the shuttle's holding booth feeling extremely sorry for himself. He tried to sit on the bench without actually touching it with his tender behind. Not an easy task.

Things did not look good, it had to be said. Even after all he'd done for the LEP they were going to lock him up for at least a decade. Just for stealing a few measly bars of gold. And it didn't seem likely that he'd get an opportunity to escape. He was surrounded by steel and laser bars, and would remain so until the shuttle docked in Haven. After that it was a quick jaunt to Police Plaza, a summary hearing and off to a secure facility until his beard turned grey. Which it would, if he

324

was forced to spend more than five years out of the tunnels.

But there was hope. A tiny glimmer. Mulch forced himself to wait until all the technical staff had cleared their equipment from the shuttle. Then he casually opened his right hand, rubbing his temples with thumb and forefinger. What he was actually doing was reading the tiny note concealed in his palm – the one slipped to him by Artemis Fowl when they shook hands.

I have not finished with you yet, Mulch Diggums –

the note read.

On your return, tell your lawyer to check the date on the original search warrant for your cave. When you are released keep your nose clean for a couple of years. Then bring the medallion to me. Together we will be unstoppable.

Your friend and benefactor,
Artemis Fowl the Second

Mulch crumpled the note. He made a cylinder of his fingers and sucked the paper into his mouth. His dwarf molars quickly destroyed the evidence.

Mulch breathed deeply through his nose. It wasn't time to pop the Skaylian Rock Worm Wine cork just yet. A review of his case could take months, possibly years. But there was hope.

The dwarf wrapped his fingers round Artemis's medallion. Together they would be unstoppable.

EPILOGUE

I have decided to keep a diary. In fact, I am surprised that the idea has never occurred to me before. An intellect such as mine should be documented so that future generations of Fowls can take advantage of my brilliant ideas.

Of course, I must be careful with such a document. As valuable as it would be to my descendants, it would be more valuable to the law enforcement agents who are forever trying to gather evidence against me.

It is even more important that I keep this journal a secret from my father. He is not himself since his escape from Russia. He has become obsessed with nobility and heroism. Abstract concepts at best. As far as I know, nobility and heroism are not accepted by any of the world's major banks. The family's fortune is in my hands, and I will preserve it in the way I always have, through ingenious plots. Most of these plots will be illegal. The best always are. Real profit lies in the shadowy areas beyond the law.

I have decided, however, out of respect for my parents' values, to change my criteria for victim selection. It would seem better for the world's ecology if several global corporations went bankrupt, and so I have resolved to help them on their way. Not victimless crimes, but ones where few tears will be shed for the injured parties. This does not mean that I have become a weak, latter-day Robin Hood. Far from it. I intend to reap substantial benefits from my crimes.

My father is not the only one to have changed. Butler has grown old almost overnight. His appearance is the same as ever, but he has slowed down considerably, no matter how he tries to hide it. But I will not replace him. He has been a loyal employee, and his expertise in matters of intelligence will be invaluable. Perhaps Juliet will accompany me when actual protection is needed, though she now claims that a life in personal protection is not for her. Next week she travels to the United States to try out for a wrestling team. Apparently she has chosen 'Jade Princess' as her stage name. I can only hope that she fails the audition. Though I doubt it. She is a Butler, after all.

Of course, I have some ongoing ventures that I can work on without the aid of a bodyguard. In recent years I have developed software to divert funds from various bank accounts to my own. This software will have to be upgraded to stay ahead of the computer crime squads. Version 2.0 should be online within six months. Then there is my talent for art forgery. In the past I have favoured the Impressionists, but now, for some reason, I am drawn to more fantastical subject matter, such as the fairy creatures depicted by Pascal Hervé in his Magical World series. But these projects must be suspended temporarily, for today I discovered that I am the victim of a conspiracy.

The day began strangely. When I awoke I experienced an instant of weakness. For a single moment before I opened my eyes, I felt content, my drive to accumulate wealth forgotten. This has never happened before. Perhaps the mood was left over from some magical dream, or perhaps my father's new-found positive attitude is contagious. Whatever the cause, I must be careful to avoid such lapses in the future. With my father in his current frame of mind, this is no time to lose my resolve. I must remain as driven as always. Crime is the way forward for the Fowls. Aurum potestas est.

Minutes later, a greater mystery presented itself. As I washed my face at the basin, a tiny object fell from one of my eyes. Close examination in the lab revealed it to be a semi-corroded, tinted contact lens. Not only that, but a mirrored layer had been added behind the tinted lens. Ingenious. Undoubtedly the work of a master craftsman. But to what purpose? It is strange, but even though I have no knowledge of this lens, or how it came to be in my eye, I feel the answer is somewhere in my own brain. Hidden in the shadows.

Imagine my surprise when Juliet and Butler discovered mirrored lenses in their own eyes. These lenses are so clever they could have been my own invention, so obviously this unknown adversary must not be underestimated.

I will track the culprit down, make no mistake. No clue will be left uninvestigated. Butler has a contact in Limerick, an expert in the field of lenses and scopes. He may recognize our intruder's handiwork. Butler is on his way there, as I write.

And so, a new chapter begins in the life of Artemis Fowl the Second. In a matter of days my father returns with his new-found conscience. I will shortly be shipped off to boarding school, where I will have access to a pathetic computer centre and an even more pathetic laboratory. My bodyguard seems to be too old for physical tasks and there is an unknown adversary planting strange objects on my very person.

Overwhelming difficulties, you may think. An ordinary person would draw the shutters and hide from the world. But I am no ordinary person. I am Artemis Fowl, the latest in the Fowl crime dynasty, and I will not be turned from my path. I will find whoever planted those lenses and they will pay for their presumption. And once I am rid of this nuisance, my plans will proceed unhindered. I shall unleash a crime wave the like of which has never been seen. The world will remember the name of Artemis Fowl.

JUST WHEN YOU THOUGHT IT WAS SAFE
TO VENTURE UNDERGROUND . . .
ARTEMIS FOWL IS BACK.

ARTEMIS FOWL

AND THE OPAL DECEPTION

The fairy People need him.

Oh dear.

Read on for a preview of the chaos to come . . .

The access tunnel smelled like a blast furnace. Ancient swirls of melted ore hung from the roof and the ground underfoot was cracked and treacherous. Each footfall punctured a crust of soot, leaving a trail of deep footprints. There was another set of footprints – leading to the shadowy figure huddled on the ground, a short distance from the chute itself.

'There,' said Root.

'Got him,' said Holly, resting the bullseye of her laser sight on the figure's trunk.

'Keep him covered,' ordered the commander. 'I'm going down.'

Root advanced along the tunnel, keeping well out of Holly's line of fire. If Scalene did make a move, Holly would need a clear shot. But the general, if it were him, squatted immobile, his spine curled along the tunnel wall. His frame was covered by a full-length hooded cape.

The commander turned on his helmet PA so he could be heard above the howl of core wind.

'You there. Stand facing the wall. Place your hands on your head.'

The figure did not move. Holly had not expected it to. Root stepped closer, always cautious, knees bent, ready to dive to one side. He poked the figure's shoulder with his Neutrino 3000.

'On your feet, Scalene.'

The poke was sufficient to knock the figure sideways. The goblin keeled over, landing face up on the tunnel floor. Soot flakes fluttered around him like disturbed bats. The hood flopped to one side, revealing the figure's face, most importantly the eyes.

'It's him,' said Root. 'He's been mesmerized.'

The general's slitted eyes were bloodshot and vacant. This was a serious development, as it confirmed that somebody else had planned the escape, and Holly and Root had walked into a trap.

'I recommend we leave,' said Holly. 'Immediately.'

'No,' said Root, leaning over the goblin. 'Now that we're here, we might as well take Scalene back with us.'

He placed his free hand on the goblin's collar, preparing to haul him to his feet. Later, Holly would record in her report that it was at this precise moment that things began to go terribly wrong. What had been a routine — albeit strange — assignment suddenly became an altogether more sinister affair.

'Do not touch me, elf,' said a voice. A hissing, goblin voice. Scalene's voice. But how could that be? The general's lips had not moved.

Root reared back, then steadied himself. 'What's going on here?'

Holly's soldier's sense was buzzing at the base of her neck. 'Whatever it is, we won't like it. We should go, Commander, right now.'

Root's features were thoughtful. 'That voice came from his chest.'

'Maybe he had surgery,' said Holly. 'Let's get out of here.'

The commander reached down, flipping Scalene's cape aside. There was a metal box strapped to the general's chest. The box was thirty centimetres square, with a small screen in the centre. There was a shadowy face on the screen, and it was talking.

'Ah, Julius,' it said in Scalene's voice. 'I knew you'd come. Commander Root's famous ego would not allow him to stay out of the action. An obvious trap, and you walked straight into it.'

The voice was definitely Scalene's, but there was something about the phrasing, the cadence. It was too sophisticated for a goblin. Sophisticated, and strangely familiar.

'Have you figured it out yet, Captain Short?' said the voice. A voice that was changing. Slipping into a higher register. The tones were no longer male, not even goblin. *That's a female talking*, thought Holly. *A female that I know*.

A face appeared on the screen. A beautiful and malicious face, its eyes bright with hate. Opal Koboi's face. The rest of the head was swathed in bandages, but the features were only too visible.

Holly began to speak rapidly into her helmet mike.

'Foaly, we have a situation here. Opal Koboi is loose. I repeat, Koboi is loose. This whole thing is a trap. Cordon off the area, five-hundred-metre perimeter, and bring in the medical warlocks. Someone is about to get hurt.'

The face on the screen laughed, tiny pixie teeth glinting like pearls.

'Talk all you want, Captain Short. Foaly can't hear you. My device has blocked your transmissions as easily as I blocked your seeker-sleeper and the substance scan that I assume you ran. Your little centaur friend can see you, though. I left him his precious lenses.'

Holly immediately zoomed in on Opal's pixelated face. If Foaly got a shot of the pixie, he would figure out the rest.

Again Koboi laughed. Opal was genuinely enjoying herself.

'Oh, very good, Captain. You were always a smart one. Relatively speaking, of course. Show Foaly my face and he will initiate an alert. Sorry, to disappoint you, Holly, but this entire device is constructed from stealth ore and is practically invisible to the artificial eye. All Foaly will see is a slight shimmer of interference.'

Stealth ore had been developed for space vehicles. It absorbed every form of wave or signal known to fairy or man and so was virtually invisible to everything but the naked eye. It was also incredibly expensive to manufacture. Even the small amount necessary to cover Koboi's device would have cost a warehouse full of gold.

Root straightened quickly. 'The odds are against us here, Captain. Let's move out.'

Holly didn't bother with relief. Opal Koboi wouldn't make things that easy. There was no way they were just walking out of here. If Foaly could hijack the terminal's computers, then so could Koboi.

Opal's laugh stretched to an almost hysterical screech.

'Move out? How very tactical of you, Commander. You really need to expand your vocabulary. Whatever next? Duck and cover?'

Holly peeled back a Velcro patch on her sleeve, revealing a Gnommish keyboard. She quickly accessed her helmet's LEP criminal database, opening Opal Koboi's file in her visor.

'Opal Koboi,' said Corporal Frond's voice. The LEP always used Lili Frond for voice-overs and recruitment videos. She was glamorous and elegant, with flowing blonde tresses and inch-long manicured nails that were absolutely no use in the field. 'LEP enemy number one. Currently under guard in the J. Argon Clinic. Opal Koboi is a certified genius, scoring over three hundred on the standardized IQ test. She is also a suspected megalomaniac, with an obsessive personality. Studies indicate that Koboi may be a pathological liar and suffer from mild schizophrenia. For more detailed information please consult the LEP central library on the second floor of Police Plaza.'

Holly closed the file. An obsessive genius and a pathological liar. Just what they needed. The information didn't help a lot; what it told her she pretty much already knew. Opal was loose, she wanted to kill them and she was smart enough to figure out how to do it.

Opal was still enjoying her triumph.

'You don't know how long I have waited for this moment,' the pixie said, then paused. 'Actually, you *do* know. After all, you were the ones who wrecked my plan. And now I have you both.'

Holly was puzzled. Opal may have had serious mental issues, but that could not be confused with stupidity. Why would she prattle on? Was she trying to distract them?

The same thought occurred to Root. 'Holly! The doors!'

Holly whirled round, to see the blast doors sliding across, their engines masked by core wind. If those doors closed, they would be completely cut off from the LEP, and at the mercy of Opal Koboi.

Holly targeted the magnetic rollers along the doors' upper rim, sinking blast after blast from her neutrino into their mechanisms. The doors jerked in their housings but did not stop. Two of the rollers blew out, but the massive portals' momentum carried them together. They connected with an ominous bong.

'Alone at last,' said Opal, sounding for all the world like an innocent college fairy on her first date.

Root pointed his weapon at the device belted round Scalene's middle, as if he could somehow hurt Koboi.

'What do you want?' he demanded.

'You know what I want,' replied Opal. 'The question is, how am I going to get it? What form of revenge would be the most satisfying? Naturally, you will both end up dead, but that's not enough. I want you to suffer as I did, discredited and despised. One of you at least — the other will have to be sacrificed. I don't really care which.'

Root retreated to the blast doors, motioning for Holly to follow.

'Options?' he whispered, his back to Koboi's device. Holly raised her visor, wiping a bead of sweat from her brow. The helmets were air conditioned, but sometimes sweating had nothing to do with temperature.

'We have to get out of here,' she said. 'The chute is the only way.'

Root nodded. 'Agreed. We fly up far enough to clear Koboi's blocker signal, then alert Major Kelp.'

'What about Scalene? He's mesmerized to the gills, he can't look after himself. If we do escape, Opal is not going to leave him around as evidence.'

It was basic criminal logic. Your typical 'take over the world' types were not averse to knocking off a few of their own if it meant a clean getaway.

Root actually growled. 'It really tugs my beard to put us in harm's way over a goblin, but that's the job. We take Scalene with us. I want you to sink a few charges into that box round his waist, and when the buzzing stops I throw him over my shoulder and we're off up E37.'

'Understood,' said Holly, lowering the setting on her weapon to minimum. Some of the charge would be transferred to Scalene, but it wouldn't do much more than dry up his eyeballs for a couple of minutes.

'Ignore the pixie. Whatever she says, keep your mind on the job.'

'Yes, sir.'

Root took several deep breaths. Somehow it calmed Holly to see the commander as nervous as she was. 'OK. Go.'

The two elves turned and strode rapidly towards the unconscious goblin.

'Have we come up with a little plan?' said Koboi mockingly from the small screen. 'Something ingenious, I hope. Something I haven't thought of?'

Grim-faced, Holly tried to shut out the words, but they wormed their way into her thoughts. Something ingenious? Hardly. It was simply the only option open to them. Something Koboi hadn't thought of? Doubtful. Opal could conceivably have been planning this for almost a year. Were they just about to do exactly what she wanted?

'Sir . . .' began Holly, but Root was already in position beside Scalene.

Holly fired six charges at the small screen. All six impacted on Koboi's pixelated features. Opal's image disappeared in a storm of static. Sparks squeezed between the metal seams and acrid smoke leaked through the speaker grid.

Root hesitated for a moment, allowing any charge to disperse, then he grabbed Scalene firmly by the shoulders.

Nothing happened.

I was wrong, thought Holly, releasing a breath she did not realize she'd been holding. *I was wrong, thank the gods Opal has no plan.* But it wasn't true, and Holly didn't really believe it.

The box around Scalene's midriff was secured by a set of octo-bonds, eight telescoping cables often used by the LEP to restrain dangerous criminals. They could be locked and unlocked remotely and, once cinched, could not be removed without the remote or an angle grinder. As soon as Root leaned over, the octo-bonds released and whiplashed around the commander's torso, freeing Scalene and drawing the metal box tight to Root's own chest.

Koboi's face appeared on the reverse side of the box.

The smokescreen had been just that: a smokescreen.

'Commander Root,' she said, almost breathless with malice, 'it looks like you're the sacrifice.'

'D'Arvit!' swore Root, beating the metal box with the butt of his pistol. The cords tightened until Root's breath came in agonized spurts. Holly heard more than one rib crack. The commander fought the urge to sink to his feet. Magical blue sparks played around his torso, automatically healing the broken bones.

Holly rushed forward to help, but before she could reach her superior officer an urgent beeping began to emanate from the device's speaker. The closer she got, the louder the beep.

'Stay back,' grunted Root. 'Stay back. It's a trigger.'

Holly stopped in her soot tracks, punching the air in frustration. But the commander was probably right. She had heard of proximity triggers before. Dwarfs used them in the mines. They would set a charge in the tunnels, activate a proximity trigger and then set it off from a safe distance, using a stone.

Opal's face reappeared on the screen.

'Listen to your Julius, Captain Short,' advised the pixie. 'This is a moment for caution. Your commander is quite right – the tone you hear is indeed a proximity trigger. If you come too close, he will be vaporized by the explosive gel packed into the metal box.'

'Stop lecturing and tell us what you want,' snarled Root.

'Now, now, Commander, patience. Your worries will be over soon enough. In fact they are already over, so why don't you just wait quietly while your final seconds tick away.'

Holly circled the commander, keeping the beep constant, until her back was to the chute.

'There's a way out of this, Commander,' she said. 'I just need to think. I need a minute to sort things out.'

'Let me help you to *sort things out*,' said Koboi mockingly, her childlike features ugly with malice. 'Your LEP comrades are currently trying to laser their way in here, but of course they will never make it in time. And you can bet that my old school chum, Foaly, is glued to his video screen. So what does he see? He sees his good friend Holly Short apparently holding a gun on her commander. Now why would she want to do that?'

'Foaly will figure it out,' said Root. 'He beat you before.'

Opal tightened the octo-bonds remotely, forcing the commander to his knees. 'Maybe he would figure it out, at that. If he had time. But unfortunately for you, time is almost up.'

On Root's chest, a digital readout flickered into life. There were two numbers on the readout. A six and a zero.

Sixty seconds.

'One minute to live, Commander. How does that feel?'

The numbers began ticking down.

The ticking and the beeping and Opal's snide sniggers drilled into Holly's brain.

'Shut it down, Koboi. Shut it down, or I swear I'll . . .'

Opal's laughter was unrestrained. It echoed through the access tunnel like the attack screech of a harpie,

'You will what? Exactly? Die beside your commander?'

More cracks. More ribs broken. The blue sparks of magic circled Root's torso like stars caught in a whirlwind.

'Go now,' he grunted. 'Holly, I am ordering you to leave.'

'With respect, Commander. No. This isn't over yet.'

'Forty-eight,' said Opal, in a happy, sing-song voice. 'Forty-seven.'

'Holly! Go!'

'I'd listen if I were you,' said Koboi. 'There are other lives at stake. Root is already dead – why not save someone who can be saved?'

Holly moaned. Another element in an already overloaded equation.

'Who can I save? Who's in danger?'

'Oh, no one important. Just a couple of Mud Men.'

Of course, thought Holly, *Artemis and Butler. Two others who had put a stop to Koboi's plan.*

'What have you done, Opal?' said Holly, shouting above the proximity trigger and core wind.

Koboi's lip drooped, mimicking a guilty child.

'I'm afraid I may have put your human friends in danger. At this very moment they are stealing a package from the International Bank in Munich. A little package I prepared for them. If Master Fowl is as clever as he is supposed to be, he won't open the package until he reaches the Kronski Hotel and can check for booby traps. Then a bio-bomb will be activated, and "Bye bye, obnoxious humans". You can stay here and explain all this. I'm sure it won't take more than a few hours to sort it out with Internal Affairs. Or you can try to rescue your friends.'

Holly's head reeled. The commander, Artemi, Butler. All about to die. How could she save them all? There was no way to win.

'I will hunt you down, Koboi. For you, there won't be a safe inch on the planet.'

'Such venom. What if I gave you a way out? One chance to win.'

Root was on his knees now, blood leaking from the corner of his mouth. The blue sparks were gone, he was out of magic.

'It's a trap,' he gasped, every syllable making him wince. 'Don't be fooled again.'

'Thirty,' said Koboi. 'Twenty-nine.'

Holly felt her forehead throb against the helmet pads. 'OK. OK, Koboi. Tell me quickly. How do I save the commander?'

Opal took a deep theatrical breath. 'On the device. There's a sweet spot. Two-centimetre diameter. The red dot below the screen. If you hit that spot from outside the trigger area, then you overload the circuit. If you miss, even by a hair, you set off the explosive gel. It's a sporting chance — more than you gave me, Holly Short.'

Holly gritted her teeth. 'You're lying. Why would you give me a chance?'

'Don't take the shot,' said Root, strangely calm. 'Just get out of range. Go and save Artemis. That's the last order I'll ever give you, Captain. Don't you dare ignore it.'

Holly felt as though her senses were being filtered through a metre of water. Everything was blurred and slowed down.

'I don't have any choice, Julius.'

Root frowned. 'Don't call me Julius! You always do that just before you disobey me. Save Artemis, Holly. Save him.'

Holly closed one eye, aiming her pistol. The laser

sights were no good for this kind of accuracy. She would have to do it manually.

'I'll save Artemis next,' she said.

She took a deep breath, held it, and squeezed the trigger. Holly hit the red spot. She was certain of it. The charge sank into the device, spreading across the metal face like a tiny bush fire.

'I hit it,' she shouted at Opal's image. 'I hit the spot.'

Koboi shrugged. 'I don't know. I thought you were a fraction low. Hard luck. I mean that sincerely.'

'No!' screamed Holly.

The countdown on Root's chest ticked faster than before, flickering through the numbers. There were only moments left now.

The commander struggled to his feet, raising the visor on his helmet. His eyes were steady and fearless. He smiled gently at Holly. A smile that laid no blame. For once there wasn't even a touch of feverish temper in his cheeks.

'Be well,' he said, and then an orange flame blossomed in the centre of his chest.

The explosion sucked the air from the tunnel, feeding on the oxygen. Multicoloured flames roiled like the plumage of battling birds. Holly was shunted backwards by a wall of shock waves, the force impacting on every surface inch facing the commander. Microfilaments blew in her suit as they were overloaded with heat and force. The camera cylinder on her helmet popped right out of its groove, spinning into E37.

Holly herself was borne bodily into the chute, spinning like a twig in a cyclone. Sonix sponges in her earpieces sealed automatically as the sound of the explosion caught up with the blast. The commander had disappeared inside a ball of flame. He was gone, there was no doubt about it. Even magic could not help him now. Some things are beyond fixing.

The contents of the access tunnel, including Root and Scalene, disintegrated into a cloud of shrapnel and dust, particles ricocheting off the tunnel walls. The cloud surged down the path of least resistance, which was, of course, directly after Holly. She barely had time to activate her wings and climb a few metres before flying shrapnel drilled a hole in the chute wall below her.

Holly hovered in the vast tunnel, the sound of her own breathing filling her helmet. The commander was dead. It was unbelievable. Just like that, at the whim of a vengeful pixie. Had there been a sweet spot on the device? Or had she actually missed the target? She would probably never know. But to the LEP observers it would seem as though she had shot her own commander.

Holly glanced downwards. Below her, fragments from the explosion were spiralling towards the Earth's core. As they neared the revolving magma sphere, the heat ignited each one, utterly cremating all that was left of Julius Root. For the briefest moment the particles twinkled, gold and bronze, like a million stars falling to earth.

Holly hung there for several minutes, trying to absorb what had happened. She couldn't. It was too awful. Instead, she froze the pain and guilt, preserving it for later. Right now she had an order to follow. And she would follow it, even if it were the last thing she ever did, because it had been the last order Julius Root would ever give.

Holly increased the power to her wings, rising through the massive charred chute. There were Mud Men to be saved.

THE PEOPLE –
A SPOTTER'S GUIDE

There are many different types of fairy and, with each one, it's important to know what you are dealing with. This is just some of the information collected by Artemis Fowl during his adventures. It is confidential and must *not* fall into the wrong hands. The future of the People depends on it.

ELVES

Distinguishing features: About one metre tall. Pointy ears. Brown skin. Red hair.
Character: Intelligent. Strong sense of right and wrong. Very loyal. Sarcastic sense of humour, although that might just be a particular female LEP officer.
Loves: Flying, either in a craft or with wings.
Situations to avoid: They really don't like it if you kidnap them and take their gold.

DWARFS

Distinguishing features: Short, round and hairy. Large tombstone teeth – good for grinding . . . well, anything really. Unhingable jaws enabling them to excavate tunnels. Sensitive beard hair. Skin capable of acting like suction cups when dehydrated. Smelly.
Character: Sensitive. Intelligent. Criminal tendencies.
Loves: Gold and precious gems. Tunnelling. The dark.
Situations to avoid: Being in a confined space with them when they have been tunnelling and have a build-up of trapped air. If they reach for the bum flap on their trousers, get out of there . . .

TROLLS

Distinguishing features: Huge – as big as an elephant. Light-sensitive eyes. Hate noise. Hairy with dreadlocks. Retractable claws. Teeth! – lots and lots of teeth. Tusks like a wild boar (a really wild boar). Green tongue. Exceptionally strong. Weak point at the base of the skull.
Character: Very, very stupid – the troll has a tiny brain. Mean and bad-tempered.
Loves: Eating – anything. A couple of cows would make a light snack.
Situations to avoid: Are you joking? If you even think a troll is near, run like the wind.

Goblins

Distinguishing features:
Scaly. Lidless eyes – they lick their eyeballs to keep them moist. Able to throw fireballs. They go on all fours when speed is important. Forked tongue. Less than a metre tall. Slimy, fire-proof skin.
Character: Not clever, but cunning. Argumentative. Ambitious. Power-hungry.
Loves: Fire. A good argument. Power.
Situations to avoid: Don't get in the way if they're throwing a fireball.

Sprites

Distinguishing features:
About one metre tall. Pointy ears. Green skin. Wings.
Character: Average intelligence. Generally happy-go-lucky attitude.
Loves: Flying – more than anything else under or above the Earth.
Situations to avoid: Watch out for low-flying sprites – they don't always look where they're going.

Centaurs

Distinguishing features:
Half-man, half-pony. Hairy – obviously! Hooves can get very dry.
Character: Extremely intelligent. Vain. Paranoid. Kind. Computer geeks.
Loves: Showing off. Inventing.
Situations to avoid: They aren't very dangerous physically, but they will sulk if you criticize their latest invention, mess with their hard drive or borrow their hoof moisturizer.

Pixies

Distinguishing features:
About one metre tall. Pointy ears. Apart from their ears and their height, pixies look almost human.
Character: Extremely intelligent. No morals. Cunning. Ambitious. Greedy.
Loves: Power and money. Chocolate.
Situations to avoid: Never get on the wrong side of a pixie, especially one as clever and ruthless as Opal Koboi, unless you are as brilliant as Artemis Fowl, of course.

FOWL FILE

BUTLER

Weapons Expertise
92
— high level of proficiency in all small arms; military grade marksmanship

Unarmed Combat Skills
93
— youngest graduate from Madam Ko's Personal Protection Academy

Stamina
88
— pain and fatigue threshold surpasses human levels

Stealth
79
— remarkable, given his size. Believed to have been trained by ninjas

Loyalty
85
— unquestionable. By his Master's side from the day he was born

BRIEF ENCOUNTERS
WITH...
BUTLER

Butler intimidates me, to be honest. There's something about him. It's hard to put your finger on. Actually, it's not hard at all. The man is huge. Massive. Talking to him is like getting into the ring with one of those professional wrestlers. And then there's the head perched on top of those mountainous shoulders. That head is the shape and colour of a very large coconut, complete with rough bits. You've heard the saying that a person's face looks lived in? Well, Butler's face looks lived on. The man has more lumps and bumps than a country lane. I said it to him once. If you're so good, I said, how come you get hit so much? So he looked at me with his piercing pebble eyes, and he said, 'I may get hit, but Master Artemis does not.'

Nothing in his words could be interpreted as a threat. But I decided then and there never to even pat Artemis on the back, in case Butler over-reacted.

Eoin Colfer

ARTEMIS FOWL

THE GRAPHIC NOVEL

Of course, it had started with the Internet.
But then it always does.

Alien abductions. UFO sightings.
Leylines. Ancient stone circles.

And the People.
It always came back to the People.

Trawling through gigs of data, he had compiled a database from the thousands of references to fairies he'd found from countries all over the world.

Each human civilization had its own term for the People. But there was no doubt that the reports referred to the same hidden race.

Many stories whispered of a special book carried by each fairy.

It was their bible containing the history of their race. It also contained their laws, their rules... and their weaknesses.

Any human who came into possession of such a book would have an entirely new species to exploit.

Of course, this book was said to be written in Gnommish, so even if someone could steal a copy, it would be of absolutely no use to any human.

RELIVE THE ADVENTURE, THE MAGIC,
THE MIND-BLOWING TECHNOLOGY,
THE BEGINNING.
AS YOU'VE NEVER SEEN IT BEFORE.

ARTEMIS FOWL

THE GRAPHIC NOVEL

Your story starts here . . .

Do you **love books** and
discovering new stories?
Then **www.puffin.co.uk**
is the place for you . . .

• Thrilling adventures, fantastic fiction
and laugh-out-loud fun

• Brilliant videos featuring your favourite authors
and characters

• Exciting competitions, news, activities,
the Puffin blog and SO MUCH more . . .

www.puffin.co.uk